blood
orange

Also by Drusilla Campbell

The Edge of the Sky
Wildwood

blood orange

Drusilla Campbell

KENSINGTON PUBLISHING CORP.
http://www.kensingtonbooks.com

KENSINGTON BOOKS are published by

Kensington Publishing Corp.
119 West 40th Street
New York, NY 10018

All Kensington Titles, Imprints, and Distributed Lines are available at special quantity discounts for bulk purchases for sales promotions, premiums, fund-raising, and educational or institutional use.

Special book excerpts or customized printings can also be created to fit specific needs. For details, write or phone the office of the Kensington Special Sales Manager: Kensington Publishing Corp., 119 West 40th Street, New York, NY 10018, attn: Special Sales Department, Phone: 1-800-221-2647.

Kensington and the K logo Reg. U.S. Pat. & TM Off.

ISBN-13: 978-0-7582-5394-1
ISBN-10: 0-7582-5394-X

First Trade Paperback Printing: July 2005
First Mass Market Printing: June 2010

10 9 8 7 6 5 4 3 2 1

Printed in the United States of America

For Margaret Ellen

Prologue

In the back of my garden a blood orange tree struggles for life. Its effort to be fruitful against the odds touches my heart. Valiant and struggling . . . maybe that's me I'm describing: Dana Cabot struggling to be better. But there is nothing valiant in me. I have proved myself a liar and coward too many times to have illusions.

Does this explain why I take the time to fertilize and prune and mulch my little tree when everything else in the garden must hobble along as best it can? Having failed myself and others, I want and need to prove I can do better.

In its protected corner my gawky blood orange grows slowly. In a year or two, if all goes well, it may bear fruit. Perhaps then we will all have healed. I long for that day, for summertime, a girl's voice, and the raspberry sweetness of the blood red fruit.

Chapter 1

Dana Cabot stood in the doorway to the undercroft holding a pastry box full of twenty-six dollars' worth of still-warm croissants. How typically Episcopalian to use the medieval word *undercroft* to designate what was essentially a basement consisting of one large room and five smaller ones connected by a narrow hallway. The walls of the undercroft were covered with Sunday school bulletin boards and pictures of Jesus as infant, boy, and man. And photos of Bailey Cabot.

HAVE YOU SEEN THIS LITTLE GIRL?
Seven-year-old Bailey Cabot was abducted from her home on May 29, 2004. At the time she wore a pink and lime green dotted Swiss dress. Bailey's hair is light brown, her eyes are brown, and she's four feet, one inch tall.

Red and green sticky circles dotted the maps of southern California and western Arizona that were stuck to the walls with strips of masking tape. Green meant the county had been leafleted; red indicated a Bailey task force had been started in one or more church congregations. Lutherans and Presbyterians, Methodists and Unitarians had all become involved. Yellow circles showed that thousands of ID photos of Bailey had been distributed all over California, Arizona, and Nevada. On a map of the United States blue circles indicated an e-mail campaign underway from San Diego to Vermont.

A three-page article had appeared in *People* magazine: "HAVE YOU SEEN BAILEY CABOT?"

There could be no one left in the United States who had not heard that Bailey Cabot had been stolen from behind her own front door. *If it were propaganda,* Dana thought, *we'd have won the war by now.*

Instead of circles on the maps, Dana wished the committee had used stars like those Bailey showed off on the work she brought home from Phillips Academy. The stars were a code that had been explained to the parents in a special letter mailed from the principal's office: a single star meant good effort, and all the children got that, no matter what; two meant progress; three were cause for a celebration. No one celebrated circles; circles went nowhere, and only emphasized the futility and frustration of the search for Bailey that had started in one place, gone all around the world, and ended up right back where it started, with a big zero. Circles meant nothing; circles were holes to fall into. Dana wanted constellations like the Big Dipper, Orion, and the reliable North Star pointing the way to Bailey.

Dana's hands began to shake. Beth Gordon strode across the room and took the box from her.

"These are going to be appreciated."

Dana looked at the empty room and wondered by whom.

How could she not have foreseen what had to happen eventually, that the women and men who had come forth immediately and with such optimism would eventually grow tired of spending their days in a gloomy basement pretending their cause was not a hole in the ground. She did not blame the others for giving up. She herself wanted to give up sometimes.

Even her husband, David, when he talked about Bailey, had begun to get a discouraged sideways look around his eyes. As much as she wanted to talk about this with him, she could not make herself ask the question. *Will we ever find her?* All their years together they had been each other's support and encouragement. When David's professional football career was over, she told him he would ace the California bar and be another kind of star. Her Ph.D. efforts dragged on and on, but he told her she was brilliant anyway. And when doctors said there was something wrong with Bailey's mind, they had held each other up. It was the way their marriage had worked until Bailey vanished. For comfort and support they were no good to each other now.

For a few weeks she had attended a support group for the families of children who had disappeared. As if agony could be slotted into an appointment book, the group had met every Tuesday night at seven in a church basement virtually indistinguishable from the undercroft. On a table to one side of the circled chairs, coffee and tea and some kind of cake or cookies were set out. Dana remembered the hum of the air conditioner and the almost constant sound of bodies shifting on the uncomfortable metal chairs. Heavy sighs, the rustle of clothing and scuffle of shoes on the linoleum floor. No one was at ease in that room. No one wanted to be there. Mothers and fathers, boyfriends, grandparents, everyone either overweight or way too thin, the jittery eyes Morse coding the need for a smoke: they all had stories. Their children had vanished from highway rest stops, shopping malls, on the way to school. Ordinary children, not one of them spectacular in any way. Little boys in OshKosh B'Gosh overalls with tape on the temples of their small eyeglasses. Girls in school uniforms or cutoffs, their hair in ponytails or curly or cut short and straight with bangs that hung down over their eyebrows. Dana saw there was an epidemic, a virus of vanishment running through the cities and suburbs of America, with hardly a family left uninfected. "Support group" was a misnomer. The sad faces and stories only deepened Dana's misery and fed the rage she struggled to suppress.

She was not a quitter. Her emotions never got the better of her good sense. She was stubborn and dogged once she set her mind on something. These were traits that had served her well and brought her far from her beginnings. But sometimes she wished she had been made differently.

Beth's teenage grandson, Jason, came through the door from the parish kitchen. A fidgety, beanpole boy in baggy pants and a baseball cap worn backward, he stopped when he saw Dana. From across the room she could see the color rise in his cheeks.

"Oh. Mrs. Cabot. Hi."

He saw the croissants.

"Help yourself," Dana said.

Beth gestured for him to open a folding chair for Dana. Beth was a tall, stately woman somewhere in age between sixty and eighty, with broad, straight shoulders and the posture of a cadet. Before May, Dana had known her only as a familiar face at the eight o'clock Eucharist. Since Bailey's disappearance she had learned of Beth's troubled family history. A son gone bad, a grandson named Jason whom she doted on despite his problems with authority. When Bailey was taken, the shyly adoring Jason had been the first to offer Dana his help, and then Beth and the churchwomen had come forth bearing food—the calming, soporific casseroles, the tortilla bakes and shepherd's pies. While David and Dana were still stuporous with shock, Jason and the women of St. Thomas's Episcopal Church had organized the Bailey Fund and raised a phone tree with branches all over the vast diocese of San Diego, stretching into Orange County, Los Angeles, and Arizona. They held a banquet and raised thousands of dollars to cover the cost of materials and printing, though, of course, by now expenses had gone far beyond that. Beth told Dana not to worry about money. The ECW was managing the finances. And a good thing, too. Dana had not looked at a bank statement in three months. She and David were deeply in debt, but it did not matter. There was only room for Bailey in her mind.

Bailey: a seven-year-old with her mother's brown eyes and her daddy's heart-shaped mouth and dimpled chin. She had not quite mastered skipping and could not tell time. She had been teaching herself to whistle. She was so pretty and her smile so extraordinarily sunny and dimpled, it was not immediately obvious that there was something wrong. At first Dana and David had not wanted to believe it, and after a dozen trips to doctors of all varieties up and down the coast, they knew no more than what they had guessed themselves. There had been a genetic glitch, and nothing could be done about the slow learning, the obsessive behavior and unpredictable moods. Bailey was not autistic or OCD, the experts said. She was mentally slow and easily frustrated. There might be a mood disorder, but they would not know until she was older.

Beth gestured to the empty room. "It's one of those days when everyone has an appointment they made months ago. They'll be coming in later. Do you know I have to arrange to see my dermatologist six months in advance, he's that busy?"

She's embarrassed. Because no one is here.

Jason said, "Me and my friend, we're gonna post these here at all the interstate rest stops." He held up a new flyer printed on bright yellow paper with Bailey's school photo in the center. Three front teeth out, but she grinned from ear to ear with no idea of how funny she looked. By now that empty space would be filled in.

Stop.

Beth said, "Jason likes road trips. He's going to drive up I-5 and then down 101."

"What about your job?" Dana asked the boy.

"The copy shop don't care." He scuffed his feet into the worn linoleum and added, looking at the floor, "They done all the printing for half price."

Beth patted Dana's arm. "In their way, they're part of this, too. We all are. This time next week there'll be new pictures of Bailey from here to the Oregon border."

Dana imagined a mountain of paper litter, thousands of trees slaughtered in the name of Bailey Cabot. What happened to these flyers when they'd been read—presuming that anyone looked at them anymore, that people were not sick of the subject of missing children. Who could blame them? Why would anyone want to think about lost children unless life forced the subject upon them? She bit into a chocolate croissant that was dust on her tongue and sawdust in her throat. Sugar thickened on her taste buds, and she realized she had not eaten since lunch the day before. She put her hand over her mouth and swallowed hard.

Beth sat beside her. "Tomorrow there'll be half a dozen people down here typing and making calls and all that good stuff. Don't you worry."

"Do I seem ungrateful?" Dana asked. Misery had

made her transparent to others, but to herself she was mystery and dark corners. "I am grateful, though. Truly. Without everything you've done, Beth . . ."

"If the shoe were on the other foot, wouldn't you be helping me? Of course you would."

Dana could not think how to respond. She could not remember the kind of person she had been before May twenty-ninth. Those days were on the other side of time, in a universe where the only problems were money, snagging time for herself, and making sure the details of life ran smoothly.

"What can I do?" she asked the older woman.

Beth stood up and looked around, hands on hips, her broad shoulders straight as a T square. She and the women like her held the church on their shoulders. "If we make pom-pom streamers for car antennas, the churchwomen will distribute them along with photos." Walking across the room to a cupboard, she dragged out a box full of rolls of three-quarter-inch satin ribbon in lime and pink. "These came in as a donation day before yesterday. Lime and pink were her favorite colors, right? You told me that?"

Dana nodded. She blinked, and her eyelids ached.

"By next Sunday afternoon there'll be thousands of these on car antennas from here to L.A. If I have to tie this ribbon around their throats, no one's going to forget Bailey. I promise you that." Beth seemed to read Dana's mind. "I know they look trivial, kind of silly in a way, but they're not. Our biggest challenge is to keep the public thinking about Bailey, watching for her."

The first few weeks Dana had not been able to sleep but refused the sleeping pills the doctor prescribed, fearing that if she started taking them she would sink into oblivion. One night she dreamed of Bailey at the glass, Bailey knocking at the window crying "Mommy" and Dana too deeply asleep to notice. When Dana was five and her mother left her with her grandmother, she had for weeks slept sitting up and wearing shoes, terrified she might not hear the lugging idle of her mother's old Chrysler New Yorker if it pulled up to the curb.

Beth was saying, "The worst thing that can happen, is if we let people forget—"

"Forget?"

"I don't mean that you'd forget, Dana. Not you, not anyone who ever knew . . ." Beth stopped, looking stranded.

These days no one talked to Dana as if she were a normal person. They treated her like fragile goods, broken by a breath. And she had lost the gift of conversation. She imagined hostility and irritation all around her; her feelings were easily hurt, and she took offense even when she knew none was intended.

The door to the hall opened, and Lexy Neuhaus, the priest at St. Tom's and Dana's best friend, stepped into the room.

"Dana, I thought I'd find you here. I saw your car parked under the telephone line getting pooped on big time."

Dana lifted her shoulders and let them drop. She hadn't washed her car in three months.

"Can I steal her for a little while, Beth?"

"Go right ahead. I'm fine here. Jason and I have plenty to do."

Lexy looked at the blue box from Bella Luna. "Do I see chocolate croissants?" She turned her head away, moaning. "Sometimes I think the whole course of history might have changed if Satan had offered Jesus a chocolate croissant."

Chapter 2

Lexy held the door open, and Dana passed through, ahead of the priest but aware of the businesslike click of her high heels on the cement stairs as they both stepped into the bright September heat. Without speaking they walked across the tree-shaded parking lot separating the church from the remodeled single-story house of no distinction that held the church offices. Their feet crunched on the litter of curled oak leaves. Though the September days were still hot in San Diego, the nighttime temperatures had begun to drop into the sixties; and in front of the office the leaves on a pair of large liquidambar trees were changing from bright green to orange and glossy red. The shrubs and flowers had spent too many long, warm days madly manufacturing chlorophyll. In the planters lining the path the marigolds, zinnias, and pink cosmos nodded on their leggy stems and looked fevered, on the verge of breakdown, as exhausted as Dana.

In the heat Dana's white polo shirt stuck to her back, and she felt dumpy beside Lexy, who always managed to look stylish in priestly garb and collar and ankle-breaking high heels. Like many at St. Tom's, Dana had been confused and vaguely put out when the search committee called a redheaded former model, a divorced woman and recovering alcoholic, to replace St. Tom's retiring priest. Some parishioners had drifted off to churches with more conventional clergy. Those who remained praised the wisdom of the search committee and fell in love with Lexy's humor and plain speaking, the goodness she carried within her.

Before Bailey disappeared, Dana and Lexy had made progress in overcoming the inhibitions imposed by Lexy's clerical collar. The first time they met for coffee at Bella Luna, Lexy had told her, "Hardly anyone speaks to me like a real human being anymore, and even my brothers have stopped giving me a bad time. They don't know how much I long to be silly." She was not a Bible-quoting priest. "I refuse to act like I'm holy. I'm as big a sinner as anyone."

Gradually, Dana and Lexy had worked through their histories to what Dana thought of as the "deep stuff": God and family and feelings, and though there was much she believed she would never talk about to Lexy or anyone, their friendship had been a revelation of freedom to Dana.

But Bailey's disappearance had set a wall of awkwardness between them. Lexy was God's representative at St. Tom's, and Dana was angry with God.

Lexy's office occupied what had once been the master bedroom of the bungalow. Across from a large corner window open to the street, a wall of bookcases was packed tight with books that Dana had at first assumed were seminary texts. Looking closer she saw Buddhist titles as well as psychology, biology, and physics, Sufi poetry, the enneagram, and even astrology.

"I don't mean to be rude, Lexy, but can we cut to the

chase here?" Dana perched on the edge of a worn leather couch. "I've got a lot to do today."

Lying had always come easily.

Lexy sat behind her desk. "I've been missing you."

Dana had not been in church the past two Sundays. If it weren't for the Bailey Committee, she would have stopped attending altogether.

"I always like to watch you during my sermons. Your face is so responsive."

"I'm not even sure what that means." What she did understand was that Lexy wanted to control this conversation and move at her own pace. Short of walking out, Dana was stuck. She slipped down off the arm of the couch and onto a cracked, overstuffed cushion. She used to love this couch and the long talks with Lexy, both of them stretched out, their heads propped on the padded arms at either end. Lexy and David were the only people Dana had ever completely trusted.

Lexy said, "The first time I remember seeing you, you were wearing a green sweater—it must have been around Christmastime. . . . That would be right. It was the first Sunday of Advent, and I'd only been at St. Tom's for a couple of weeks. Very insecure."

Dana did not believe a woman six feet tall ever felt insecure.

"I talked about 'keeping' Advent, and you just sat there shaking your head." Lexy's laugh was deep-throated and hearty. She was the fifth child of six and the only girl. Dana imagined her learning to laugh with her brothers. "I thought about stopping right there and asking if you wanted to preach for me. Or we could do one of those point-counterpoint things like on TV."

"You seemed so out of touch. How was I supposed to keep Bailey content with an Advent calendar and a wreath? The day after Thanksgiving she started nagging for a tree." Dana strangled on the words.

"You took me on right after the service. You can be tough, Dana." Lexy removed her plain gold earrings, hoops the size of quarters, and laid them on the blotter in front of her. She massaged her earlobes. "Like right now, what you want to do is punch me out."

Dana smiled.

"Am I right?"

"Do you blame me?"

"You're mad at God and that makes you mad at me. Yeah, I blame you. It's not fair to me." She played with the earrings. "I'm more than a priest, Dana. I'm your friend."

Dana focused on the earrings—circles—and refused to be drawn in.

"I don't think it matters to God that you don't believe right now. I mean He'd probably rather you did, but under the circumstances . . ." Lexy tipped back. Over the years the back of her office chair had rubbed a raw swipe on the woodwork behind her desk. "Dana, humans are the ones who want our faith to hold steady under all conditions. And I don't think it's about God most of the time. I think we want a steady faith because it makes our lives more pleasant. It's a control thing. Doubt equals discomfort in most people's lives. Belief means security and every question has an answer, the more simplistic and concrete the better."

"You're saying God doesn't care one way or the other?" Dana fiddled with the frayed cording around the leather cushion. "That's supposed to make me feel better?"

"I'm saying if you lose faith for a while when your daughter's abducted, God understands."

"That's big of Him."

"None of this means we aren't still friends, Dana."

But don't count on me for a Christmas present this year. Dana was becoming as bad-tempered as her grandmother, Imogene.

Imogene had rained on every parade Dana ever took part in, squatted on every float she ever built, and slept through every song she ever marched to. To get out of Imogene's house Dana had learned to shape reality by focusing on her goals and depending on only herself. Emotions like anger and disappointment undermined her determination, so she taught herself not to feel them, to bury them deep. Since Bailey's disappearance this had become harder to do.

Lexy said, "What if He's a She? Do you hate her, too?"

"A female god wouldn't let children be hurt."

"It's the big question, isn't it?" Lexy examined her red acrylic nails. "If God is good, how can He, She, or It let such awful things happen in the world?" She grinned, looking beautiful. "Maybe you'd be happier as a fundamentalist, Dana. They always have answers for situations like this."

"And all you have is questions. Don't you even have an opinion, Lexy, a theory?"

"Sure I do, but you're not going to like it."

Dana smiled. "When has that ever stopped you?"

"Maybe some lessons are so hard, the only teacher is pain."

Dana rolled her eyes. "I was hoping for something more original."

"The truth is just the truth, Dana. It doesn't have to be original or startling. It just is."

"That sounds like an excuse for not having any answer at all."

The skin over Lexy's high cheekbones turned a bright pink.

"Shit." Dana laid her head against the back of the couch and closed her eyes. "I'm sorry. I know I'm being a jerk. I'm not . . . myself."

"Sure you are." Lexy's eyes were neon green. "You're probably more yourself right now than you've ever been. Grieving, bitching, and angry: this is Dana Cabot without the high-gloss enamel." Lexy held up her nails. "Under this plastic or whatever it is, you should see my nails. Pitiful. But they're me. This other stuff is just cover-up. I accept that."

Dana's brain was too battered to come up with a response. *Remember me when I was funny and resilient and determined—not taking razor swipes at the people who love me,* she thought.

In the office the only sound was the low whir of the air-conditioning. Dana pressed her fingertips against her eyelids. How hard would she have to push to blind herself? On the other side of the door a phone rang. She looked at Lexy and saw stars.

"What did you want to speak to me about?"

Lexy put her earrings back on. "A hitch in the facilities. Nothing serious, but we have to move the Bailey office. We're in a constant space crunch around here, you know that. Too many people need that big room in the undercroft. So I'm going to put you guys in the room at the back of the offices." She pointed behind Dana. "It's not huge, but you can leave everything out. Lock the door and come back, no one'll disturb your stuff."

Dana thought of taking down the smiling Bailey posters, the maps and blowups of flyers, of rolling them up, of carrying the computers across the parking lot, of running yards and yards of new extension cords. Though no one would say so out loud, the move looked like a demotion. What had been an active cause would seem less so in a small back room. She wanted to kick Lexy's desk. She wanted to kick Lexy.

"I have a selfish reason for doing this, Dana." Lexy waited, and finally Dana looked at her. "I miss seeing you. I don't have many friends, not real friends, and I thought . . ."

"I can't be anyone's friend."

Not even her husband's. David and Dana slept in a bed that felt at once cramped and too vastly wide. They ate silent meals at the dining room table and occasionally, when David was not working late, watched television together with the room completely dark so they could not see each other's faces.

"I know you mean well, but there's no way you or anyone else can understand." Even the people in the support group: their love and loss had seemed inferior to Dana's. "I think about her all day, and at night I dream about her. I can't get away from her. In my mind I see her in the most horrible situations and I can't turn off the pictures. It's like I'm being tortured, my eyelids are pinned back and I have to watch the awful . . ."

Sometimes she hoped Bailey was dead. Better dead than suffering as in those imagined scenes.

"Oh, Dana. Poor Dana."

She did not want Lexy's sympathy, nor her empathy, and definitely not her Christian charity. Nor did she want others to share her feelings. Not even David. She was just as happy he had found distraction in the Filmore case and left her in sole possession of the black and bottomless grief and guilt. If she could not have her daughter back, she would have these.

"I have to go." Dana stepped toward the door quickly to avoid Lexy's hug. Her hand on the knob, she said, "Beth knew about the move out of the undercroft?"

Lexy nodded.

"And she didn't want to tell me, right?" Dana stared at the toes of her tennis shoes. "It's not that I don't appreciate . . . I don't mean to be so hard to get along with. I just . . . am."

Lexy stood beside her. Dana smelled the green-grass and citrus fragrance she wore.

"Listen to me, Dana."

"No."

"The only way through this—"

Dana shook her head. The last thing she wanted to hear now was a religious cliché.

"I'm your best friend," Lexy said. "You're mine."

"If that's true, then you'll leave me alone." Dana's eyes burned. She clenched her jaw and turned for the door. With her hand on the knob she added, "I can't be anyone's friend."

Chapter 3

Four months earlier

Every afternoon at two-thirty Dana Cabot's cell phone rang. Five days a week the driver of the Phillips Academy minibus said more or less the same thing: "I'm at the corner of Goldfinch and Washington. Two minutes, Mrs. Cabot."

The staff at Phillips Academy said Bailey needed structure if she was to learn to manage life. And after three years, the routines, the very basic classes, and the constant positive reinforcement had paid off. Bailey was learning her letters, knew the names and values of coins, and recognized the numbers on an old-fashioned clock face—although eleven was likely to be called *one-one* and twelve, *one-two*. Since December she had become amusingly pedantic on the subject of community services. Police, firefighters: she knew what all of them did and shared her knowledge with everyone, including the housekeeper-and-babysitter, Guadalupe, who spoke no English at all. At Christmas she had insisted on baking cookies for the drivers of the recycling and garbage trucks who called out hello to her when they made their Thursday pickups.

Dana sat on the bottom stair and put on her shoes

and socks. Moby Doby walked up to her, his nails clicking on the hardwood, licked her hand, and sat, eyeing her expectantly.

"Are you learning to read time, too?"

Keeping Bailey's schedule today meant Dana had rushed home from her job at Arts and Letters, leaving Rochelle with three customers—one an art historian with an interest in Early Renaissance Italian art, which happened to be Dana's field. Or would be, once she finished her thesis. Were it not for Bailey, she would be sitting in Bella Luna drinking a double capp, discussing the influence of Giotto.

She believed she was not cut out for a life of self-sacrifice. Almost any woman would be a better mother than she for a child like Bailey.

She did not socialize with mothers from Phillips Academy. She told herself she did not want to hear them complain. Secretly she feared conversations with those women would reveal that they never complained at all, that only she resented her child's demands.

Dana blamed Bailey's disability on her side of the chromosome equation. In the North Park neighborhood where she grew up, kids had called her grandmother "loony" because she'd dressed like a bag lady and yelled at them and shook her fist if they walked or rode their bikes across her pitiful square of front lawn. As for her mother, on any test for mental health she would definitely score on the peculiar side of the bell curve. She had abandoned Dana, her only child, before Dana was five years old.

When Bailey's medical and psychological reports came in, David Cabot had sprung into defense mode before anyone could accuse him of contributing to her problems. Not only did he personally possess all the requisite DNA for scholarship, ordered thinking, and rationality, but every single person in his family was smart and accomplished. David's brother and sister held advanced degrees, and he had been an honor student and a star athlete, accepted by *Law Review,* and Order of the Coif. His father had been a judge, albeit a certifiable sexist, racist, and workaholic. His mother wrote poetry and chaired committees and sang in the community choir. She spoke four languages, and Dana had never seen her when she wasn't stoned on Valium.

The phone rang.

"Hi, Mrs. Cabot. We're at the stoplight, Washington and Goldfinch. See you in two."

San Diego's chilly spring fog had burned off, leaving behind a misty blue sky; a cool breeze disturbed the pipe chimes in the olive tree in the front yard. Dana wished she had worn a sweater.

She slapped Moby's bony hindquarters. "Let's run, kiddo." He took off at a lope, Dana following.

Before Bailey was born Dana had run several half-marathons, but since then she rarely had the time for more than a mile or two. Often she ran at night or at dawn through the Mission Hills neighborhood. As if she were visiting an aquarium, she looked in the windows of the houses she passed. She wasn't sure what she was looking for. Validation perhaps. Some indication that her childhood had not been *wacko* as David claimed. In the kitchens and living rooms of strangers' homes she wanted to see another little girl eating a macaroni-and-ketchup sandwich, another grandmother asleep in front of the television with a yellow cat around her shoulders like a fur collar.

On the far side of the park the cherry red Phillips Academy minibus idled at curbside. Dana waved to the driver, and the pneumatic doors wheezed open. Bailey bounded out and hurled herself at her mother, grabbing her around the hips and almost toppling her.

"I played football, Mommy."

At the end of the day, Bailey was always a beautiful mess. One butterfly barrette gone, hair wild and tangled, the buckle on one of her beloved shocking pink, strappy plastic sandals hanging by a stitch.

Resentment and ambivalence and dreams of Giotto vanished, incinerated by a love so fiercely protective it rocked Dana. "What happened to your shoe?"

"I was like Daddy." Moby trotted beside Bailey closely enough so her hand skimmed the back of his neck.

"I didn't know they let you play football at Phillips."

"I ran, and then I fell down." Bailey stopped and pulled up the leg of her size-six cargo pants, revealing a knee covered with pink and yellow bandages and layers of gauze. Looking up at her mother, dark eyes alight with gold flecks in the park's dappled sunlight, she said, "I'm brave, Mommy. Like Daddy."

Dana whisked her up into her arms and spun around, then made a controlled tumble onto the grass with herself on top, buzz-blowing into Bailey's neck while the little girl squealed joyfully and Moby barked and pranced on his toes. Before the squeals turned to tears—the change could occur in a millisecond—Dana let Bailey go.

At the same moment a white van turned onto Miranda Street and paused in front of their house.

Bailey began shouting, "S'cream man, s'cream man."

Several things happened at the same time.

Dana saw that the rear bumper of the van had a sticker on it.

There was a crash of glass and a squeal of brakes.

Moby barked furiously and dashed in front of the van.

Dana heard Moby's sharp *kye-eye* cry; the van swerved and sped off; and Bailey began to scream.

Chapter 4

At about the same time, in an interview room in San Diego's downtown jail, David Cabot studied his client across a Formica-topped table and through the bars separating them.

It was a crappy place to be on a beautiful May afternoon.

The prosecutor had argued that a man with Frank Filmore's financial resources and international connections constituted a bail risk, so this Ph.D. chemist was spending the months before his trial downtown in the county lockup, wearing a two-piece cotton uniform that made him look more like an emergency-room nurse in scrubs than a man accused of a capital crime. David's associate, Gracie Perez, sat beside him in the small room, asking the questions—essentially the same questions they'd been asking since taking on the case. No fact or gap or contradiction in Filmore's story could be overlooked. It was the same way in football. All it took was a hole in the line and the other guy was in for the TD.

To David most of life could be compared to football. Gracie, the whole office, and half the San Diego bar laughed at his metaphors, but for him football comparisons were a useful way of sorting life out; and if some people thought he was a half-smart jock, he didn't care. In the courtroom they discovered how wrong they were.

To the right of Gracie and David, near the door of the cramped and windowless room, Allison, a paralegal, was taking down questions and answers on a steno pad. An audio recorder would be easier, but David had yet to meet a defendant willing to be taped.

David listened to Filmore talk and assumed that three quarters of what he heard was either a bald lie or a cheap wig. Guilty or innocent, rich or destitute, you put a guy in jail and he forgot how to tell the truth. And the longer you gave him to think about his answers, the more he'd make it up and bullshit. The unjustly accused lied because they were afraid; the guilty lied because they thought they were smarter than the system. They were also afraid, but they'd never admit it. David didn't want to get too jaundiced in his view of the men and women he defended, but he doubted Filmore was the one in a million actually telling the truth. Although he had sworn he wouldn't let the law make him a cynic, there were days—like today and yesterday and probably tomorrow—when he could feel the negativity creeping up on him like mold.

It had been a long day, and his neck and shoulders were tight. He glanced at his watch. God willing, in an hour he'd be at the club playing racquetball with his law partner, Marcus Klinger. Then a sauna and a massage. He had a regular weekly appointment with a therapist whose thumbs knew how to find the knot at the nape of his neck. She didn't talk. She wouldn't ask him how he could stand to be in the same room with a man like Frank Filmore.

He imagined his father laughing and shaking his fat

index finger in his face. *Scum of the earth, boy. Watch it don't rub off.* Claybourne Cabot had been a hanging West Virginia judge whose best friends were the coal-mine owners in the southern part of the state. When he got drunk, which was once a week on Sunday starting right after church and going on until he passed out, he would tell anyone in earshot that the government could save a heap of cash if it would dispense with courts and lawyers for ninety percent of the people arrested. "Put 'em down the mines and forget the sons of bitches," he'd say. One of his coal-mine cronies would drawl in response, "Whatdya wanna do, C.C.? Ruin us?" Claybourne Cabot laughed so gustily, people thought he had a sense of humor. "Serve you right, you brass-balled pirates."

It galled David to recognize that when it came down to the bones of it, he practiced law much as his father had adjudicated. Judge Cabot had assumed if you were in court you'd done something bad now or in a previous life, so he might as well punish you hard. Guilt and innocence had been irrelevancies to the judge. They weren't important to David, either, although in the early days of a defense the question of guilt or innocence popped up in his mind like an irritating ad on a computer screen. Especially in a capital case like this one, with Frank Filmore's life on the block. At the preliminary hearing the prosecutor, Les Peluso, was going to argue for murder with special circumstances, leaving open the possibility of the death penalty. Peluso wanted to be mayor of San Diego, and as far as he, the press, and public were concerned, Filmore's trial was only a formality on his way to that position.

Right now David was less interested in Filmore's answers to Gracie's questions than he was in his client's mannerisms and body language, the way his right eyebrow twitched and he rubbed at it with the knuckle of his index finger. David learned a lot about people when he tuned out the words and just watched the body.

On television child killers were invariably homely, with pocky skin and small, mean eyes. Filmore was fit and handsome in a slick, saturnine way. A "hottie," according to Allison, who believed him innocent, framed by cops trying to cover up sloppy police work. She was twenty-two, and this was her first case. Her reaction to Filmore's appearance would be important information for David when it came time to choose a jury. Who would find him most appealing? Young women without children, or thirty-something guys resentful of authority and short on empathy?

David's stomach growled. After tennis and a massage, what he wanted was a three-inch filet so rare it moaned when he cut into it. But he couldn't charge another expensive dinner. Dana wrote the checks, and she knew how much interest they were paying on their Master-Card and Visa accounts, all seven of them. One of these days, David thought, he was going to be able to throw down cash for a hundred-dollar steak dinner. Frank Filmore was going to do it for him.

Gracie asked Filmore to account for his activities on the day three-year-old Lolly Calhoun was snatched from her backyard. He answered calmly, with a slightly clipped accent.

David interrupted, leaning forward. "You English, Frank? South African, maybe?"

"People ask me that." Filmore had a good smile and even white teeth with a chip out of a front incisor. Allison said it was the kind of imperfection that gave his face appeal. "Born and raised in California."

The movie-star smile was all wrong on a man facing

a possible death penalty. And jurors did not like defendants with phony accents.

David, Gracie, and Les Peluso had been study partners in law school, and there had been a time when they were either young or foolish enough to confide their ambitions to one another. Peluso wanted to be mayor. David wanted the big-ticket cases where drama and stakes were high. Gracie the same. He wondered as he watched Filmore answer Gracie's questions if it was really ethical to see a client as a means to a career goal, as a way out of debt and on to Court TV.

Gracie disliked Filmore as much as he did, but she hid her feelings behind a cool authority. She listened to him, her gaze locked on his, her expression impassive and clinical. In all things legal she was implacably self-contained. *And just as ambitious as me,* David thought. He liked that about her.

The mystery of Gracie tantalized him. She was his best friend, the person apart from Dana whom he trusted most. But friendship and respect didn't stop him from wondering about her body and what she would be like in bed. Last year she had worn a backless dress to Cabot and Klinger's Christmas party, and for a couple of weeks afterward David could not look at her without thinking of her gorgeous honey brown back, the shapely and muscular swale of her spine. He wanted to put his hand on the small of it to know if it felt as warm as it looked. He had caught a glimpse of a tattoo and fantasized about it, imagining something African, winged and tribal extending down the curve of her hip.

Gracie asked Filmore, "Why didn't you go to work that day?"

"I told you, my wife didn't feel well."

"Do you always stay home if your wife's sick?"

"When I can." Circles of sweat ringed the sleeves of Filmore's cotton shirt, but he flashed the smile and beaming teeth. "Wouldn't you?"

"The problem is," Gracie said to Filmore, "your wife didn't tell anyone at work she was sick."

"She's not a complainer; and, besides, we made a deal we wouldn't tell anyone about the baby until after the first trimester. We were sort of superstitious—you can understand. If we said anything too soon and it didn't work out . . ." He massaged his thick knuckles. "We'd been trying a long time. Years. We'd begun to lose hope, and then Marsha came up pregnant." He looked at Gracie and flashed the smile again. "It just seemed too good to be true."

None of this was new, though Filmore's answers were getting more detailed and emotionally nuanced. For now that was okay.

Gracie said, "According to her coworkers she seemed perfectly well."

"And she was. She ate a few crackers. That's all it took to settle her stomach. Sandra had a harder time." A flicker of confusion jerked across Filmore's face. "I suppose poor Sandra Calhoun's still pregnant. Is she?"

Gracie didn't miss a beat. "Go on with your story, Frank."

"Oh. Well, in the morning—we were all early risers—Marsha and Sandra Calhoun liked to hang over the fence, drink a cup of coffee." Again he grinned disarmingly. "They were never too sick for coffee."

"You said it was a secret, this pregnancy."

"Under the circumstances, two women, neighbors and both pregnant, Marsha had to tell Sandra. They'd compare how crummy they felt, and then they went on with their lives. At least Marsha did. I worked at home that day, I have that kind of job."

"Did anybody see you at home that afternoon?"

Filmore pursed his lips. "I've told you, I don't like outside help in the home."

A privacy nut with a twitchy eyebrow.

"What about the mail or UPS?" Gracie asked.

"I talked to my wife during the day. On the phone. I made some business calls. Does that help?"

David hoped phone company records would back this up, but even if they did, it would not prove much. Frank Filmore had plenty of time between calls to dart into the backyard of the house next door, snatch Lolly, and deposit her in the trunk of his 2002 Lexus sedan. Les Peluso would be sure to mention this. The good news for the defense was the police had found no evidence of her body anywhere in either the Lexus or the BMW Marsha Filmore had driven to work that day. But they hadn't stopped looking. They expected a flake of skin or drop of blood to turn up eventually. They would dismantle the cars down to the atomic level if they had to.

Gracie said, "According to the police report Sandra Calhoun called 911 a bit after nine, but before that she knocked on your front door to see if Lolly was with you. Why did she do that?"

"How should I know? We were neighbors. And Lolly was a sweet kid. I liked her when she wasn't whining."

"You didn't answer the door."

"Well, no, I didn't."

"Why was that?"

He lifted his hands, showing his smooth pale palms. "My office is on the other side of the house, Ms. Perez. I had the door closed, and I listen to music with a headset when I'm working. Helps me focus."

"Cops knocked on the door, too."

"I'm sorry," he said. "I really am. If I had heard them . . ."

"Do you love your wife?" Gracie asked.

"Of course I love her. And I'd never do anything to hurt her, to spoil what we have. She knows that." Filmore's large dark eyes filled with tears. "She knows I never—"

"Then in the late afternoon you went out," David said. "Where'd you go?"

"Well, again, I've said this before, I try to run several times a week. My time was good in the San Diego Marathon last year."

Big fucking deal.

"Where did you run that day?"

"Catalina Avenue, down the grade to the place where they train the dolphins, and then back up."

"You live in University City and you drove all the way to Point Loma?"

"Obviously you're not a runner or you'd know that variety keeps the training fresh."

Filmore loved the sound of his own voice. He definitely could not be trusted on the stand.

"Anyone see you?"

"If you mean that I talked to, no. No one."

Outside, a siren wailed up First Street headed for Harbor View Hospital. In the wake of its passing, David heard the clang of the trolley one block up. Four people in the tiny interview room, four sets of lungs inhaling the air-conditioned oxygen, exhaling lunchtime garlic and coffee: no wonder David had a headache. Filmore appeared not to mind the crowd. He probably thought he deserved Jesus Christ and the Twelve Apostles at his table after writing a check for one hundred thousand dollars payable to Cabot and Klinger. Their biggest retainer to date.

Not for the first time, it occurred to David that for a man who loved to be out of doors and who enjoyed the camaraderie of sport, he'd chosen a strange, confined, and confining profession. Maybe he should have been a coach. That's what his uncle wanted for him. Instead he was going to spend the next thirty years in jails and courtrooms defending the Constitution. Which nobody seemed to care about anymore.

Gracie might hate Filmore or feel nothing at all; you'd never know from her cool velvet voice, almost a monotone but with a hint of challenge, like she dared Filmore to give her a hard time. She asked, "What happened after your run?"

"I've said this before." He looked over at Allison. "Don't you read her notes?"

"Tell us again," David said.

"I knew it was the night my wife was going to her book club . . ."

But that night Marsha Filmore had stayed home, had gone next door to give moral support and comfort to Lolly Calhoun's mother and father.

"So I just pulled on my sweats and drove up to Carlsbad to see *Lord of the Rings*. It was so good, I stayed to see it twice."

It was a lame alibi. Without proof no jury would buy it.

"Why'd you go to Carlsbad?"

"I wanted to stop at the outlet stores, but when I got there I didn't have my credit card so I just went to the movie."

The alibi wasn't lame, it was paraplegic.

At the theater no one remembered his good-looking face, and he hadn't kept the ticket stub. David wrote a note to send Allison out to the theater with photos. A pretty blonde with blue eyes and plenty on top, she might be able to coax something out of one of the guys there.

Three-year-old Lolly had been chloroformed and strangled. The evidence against Filmore was flimsy. A few fingerprints that could have been left at any time over the last few months and a crummy alibi. Surprising, really, that the government thought it had enough to convict.

Lolly had been tied in a plastic bag and tossed down the side of a hill near Lakeside. By the time a rider found her body, coyotes had torn the bag open.

David drank from his water bottle, hoping to wash away the bile burning his throat. He thought of Bailey, of the life bursting out of her. He could not think of her as retarded or emotionally disturbed; he never used these terms to describe her. She was Bailey, and he loved her, and if anyone ever laid a hand on her he would commit murder.

He had to figure out a way to keep Bailey out of his thoughts or he'd lose the objectivity he needed to defend his client.

Frank Filmore was saying something, declaring something. Gracie looked at David and raised her perfect eyebrows. His attention snapped back.

"I did not do this . . . this awful, this horrendous thing. You must believe—You believe me, don't you, David? I'm innocent."

David heard his father's voice saying only an idiot lawyer believed his client.

"It really doesn't matter if I believe you or not, Frank, and it's not my job to prove your innocence."

"I have a lovely wife; we're expecting a baby. Why would I do such a thing? And Lolly, I loved Lolly, I used to watch her swimming in her little pool—"

"I don't want to hear this."

"But how can you prove I'm innocent if you don't—"

David rubbed the back of his neck. "It's not my job to prove you're innocent. What Gracie and I do is, we make the prosecutor prove you're *guilty*. We see that justice is done. That's all we do."

Frank Filmore looked offended. "You're saying you don't believe me?"

"I'm saying what I believe is irrelevant. You can be telling the truth or lying like crazy, what we have to do is make the prosecutor prove his case one hundred percent. It's like in football."

Allison laughed, then quickly covered her mouth.

"The ref's job is to make sure the teams play fair, win fair. That's all a defense attorney's supposed to do, make sure the prosecutor follows the rules."

Gracie said, "David used to play ball, Frank."

"I hope you won. I hope you won all the time."

A guard knocked on the door of the interview room and told David he had a phone call. "She says it's urgent."

On the other end of the phone Dana was almost hysterical. David could barely make sense of what she said.

Chapter 5

Two white cars with *Union-Tribune* logos on their doors were parked against the curb, and television vans blocked Miranda Street in front of the Cabot house. On the edge of the park neighbors and busybodies stood and stared and gossiped.

Between phone calls to the police and David and the appearance of the first reporter, Dana had hung a sheet over the broken window in the living room. Now there were police in the house and strangers under the olive tree, some of them flicking cigarette butts into the beds of white impatiens. Bailey loved every minute of it. While Dana sat on the stairs in the entry, the little girl kept up a vivid commentary from the dining room, where she stood on a chair watching the street through a pinched-back corner of the blinds.

The eleven o'clock news would show her elfin face peering out at the world as if the daughter of the man defending Frank Filmore were herself a prisoner.

"Daddy's home," Bailey cried as she jumped off her chair and ran across the tiled entry to the front door, ponytail flying. Dana grabbed for her arm. Screaming, Bailey twisted away. She was agile, too fast for Dana and twisty as a morning-glory vine climbing a fence-post. David opened the door and Bailey leapt for him. On cue, the flashbulbs flared, shutters clicked, and the video cams pressed forward.

David kicked the door shut behind him. His color was high, and his eyes flashed when he grinned at Dana and brushed back the thick hank of black and silver hair that had fallen across his forehead.

He loved being in the middle of things.

He lifted Bailey into his arms and held her. "What a scene, huh?"

"You squeeze," Bailey cried, shoving her hands against his chest.

Sweat beaded his forehead.

Dana said, "Don't look at me like that. I didn't call them."

"Roses? Big old red cabbage roses? Jesus Christ, Dana, can you think how that sheet's going to look on TV?"

"It's the only one big enough to cover that window."

"I had to park a block away. Felt like a tight end making it through the crowd to the door."

"DaddyDaddyDaddy." Bailey put her hands on David's cheeks and turned his head so he looked at her. "The s'cream man banged Moby and a rock crashed—"

David looked at Dana. "Ice cream?"

"Moby got broke."

"How's he do—?"

"Mr. Cabot?" The speaker was a moon-faced young police officer in a beige uniform stretched tight across his muscular chest and shoulders. "Patrolman Ellis." The men shook hands, and as they began to talk Dana headed for the kitchen.

She had already explained to the police about the white van and Moby and how she had left the dog for the night at the emergency clinic and come home just before five, driving fast all the way because while sitting in the clinic she had remembered the sound of shattering glass. Something thrown from the white van had broken the large, triple-arched window at the front of the house. No, she told the police, she did not get the license number of the van. No, she could not say how many passengers were in it or what they looked like. There was a bumper sticker on the back fender, driver's side; no, she did not remember what it said.

While Patrolman Ellis had asked Dana questions, Bailey tugged and hung on his arm. "The s'cream truck hurt Moby."

Ellis—no wedding ring, a bachelor unused to a nagging, dragging child—looked at Dana with eyes that cried, *Get this kid off me.*

Bailey patted Ellis's hand as he tried to write down Dana's answers. "Policeman, policeman, policeman," she chanted excitedly. "Policeman, policeman, policeman."

Dana sat on the couch in the living room and watched him suffer.

He managed to ask about the rock. "And you picked it up."

"Moby Doby got hurt."

"Of course I picked it up." She had not thought about fingerprints. "I saw the rock and the paper around it—"

"What did you do after you read the note?"

"I called 911 and my husband."

The boy cop made her feel guilty for doing what any person would, and she disliked him for ignoring Bailey. Television, she realized, had given her unrealistic expectations of police officers.

* * *

Dana hoisted Bailey onto the counter beside the sink. Bailey immediately began banging her heels against the cupboard, chanting, "Brown s'cream, white s'cream, pink s'cream," and so on through all the colors she knew, which were blessedly few.

Above the sink and along the speckled granite counter, a line of square windows the size of playpens overlooked a wide redwood deck and back garden separated from an alley by a six-foot wall overgrown with Carolina jasmine. To the right there was another wall and a gate between the garden and the driveway. A *Union-Tribune* truck was parked in front of the garage, and a man with a camera snapped pictures of the back of the house. The pots on the deck needed watering, Dana noticed. News at Eleven: Dana Cabot neglects her garden. She yanked the blinds down, plunging the kitchen into gloom.

"How you holding up, Number One?" David asked as he entered the kitchen. He kissed the top of her head.

Gratefully she turned and laid her head against his chest. She timed her breathing to match his and relaxed a little.

On the counter, Bailey held out her arms. "Me, Daddy, me, me, me."

"Come 'ere, Buckaroo." He held them both easily.

In college and as a pro, David had a reputation for being a quarterback who stayed cool in the pocket as three-hundred-pound, corn- and potato- and pork-fed Nebraska farm boys barreled down on him with mayhem in their eyes. She had worried about him before games. He'd told her, "They won't run me down if we don't let them." A team, he believed, could do anything if it worked together.

"How's Moby?" he asked.

"He'll be okay. He's in Emergency."

"Shit, that'll cost—"

She pressed her palms against his chest. "Please, David, don't start with the money." He would never see the bill; she would pay off the vet in installments.

Bailey tugged on David's earlobe hard enough to make him wince. "The window got broke and the policemens came 'cause the s'cream man wrote a bad note. I saw all the letters." She made a down-mouth, shook her head, and sighed. "No *B*."

For once Dana was glad that her seven-year-old daughter could not yet read. She asked her husband, "Did you see it?"

He nodded. "We'll talk about this later. You two go upstairs—"

"I want s'cream."

Dana scooped chocolate ice cream into a Babar bowl knowing that in thirty minutes she would regret giving her daughter sugar, but she could not face the inevitable screams if she played tough mommy right now. *Choose your fights, or at least postpone,* she thought as she settled Bailey at the counter with a dish towel tied around her neck.

"Eat up, Sweet Pea." She put the ice cream carton back in the freezer. "What happens next?"

"I guess I have to talk to the cameras."

Oh, you'll hate that, she thought sarcastically and then felt mean-tempered and small. The limelight was his natural environment.

"I wish you wouldn't encourage them," she said. "Some ambitious kid reporter'll be over tomorrow wanting to write a feature story about the family of the poor beleaguered defense attorney."

"I'm going to turn this around, Dana." He gripped

her shoulders. "Whoever threw that rock doesn't scare me."

"But he scared the hell out of me. And what about Bailey?"

"It'll take more than a rock and a note to get me off the Filmore case."

She wondered if he had even heard her say his daughter's name.

"What's more, we're going to make this work to our advantage. Filmore can't get a fair trial in a city where—"

"He killed that child," Dana said, whispering. "You know he did."

"The evidence is lousy, Dana."

Bailey banged her heels into the chair leg and clanged her spoon against the side of her empty dish. David said, "Hey, Bailey, you want to come outside with me and talk to the cameras?"

She cheered and lifted her arms, swinging her spoon wildly.

Dana took it from her. "No, David."

"You come too."

She shook her head and turned her back on him, staring down into the stainless-steel sink, where she saw a blurred reflection of herself and was thankful the image was unclear. "You're using her."

He waited a beat. "If you're not coming out, make me some eggs, will you?"

"At least wipe the ice cream off her face."

"And bacon if you've got any."

Chapter 6

Later she regretted everything: the saturated fat in the eggs and bacon and butter; the floral sheet; going to the emergency veterinary clinic when Dr. Talbot would have served as well and charged a quarter as much. Worst of all, she had forgotten what every defense attorney's spouse must always remember: the client is never guilty until the verdict is in. And sometimes not even then. She should have walked onto the front porch with David and Bailey; they should have stood together like a team.

As they prepared for bed that night, she thought how mean she was to David, how she withheld herself as if she wanted to punish him when he had done nothing but give his best. She thought of saying she was sorry, but she was no good at apologies.

Sometimes she let herself think what their life would have been like if Bailey had been normal. There would have been another child by now, maybe two. They had bought the Miranda Street house because Mission Hills was a safe neighborhood and they wanted a big family. As Dr. Wren told her every time she saw him, there was no reason not to have another child. Bailey's disability was no one's fault. Though she understood his words with her logical mind, another part of her felt responsible. She had soured on her body. Occasionally David brought up the idea of another child, though rarely in the last few months. She knew he hoped for a son, someone to play ball with and dream for. *So why not just say yes, let's have another baby?*

She did not want to think about what might be holding her back.

"You want to watch the news?" she asked.

"God, no. I don't even want to think how that sheet's going to televise."

She felt the blush of heat in her cheeks. "I used the only thing big enough—"

As soon as the police and press left, David had called his partner, Marcus Klinger, who appeared an hour later with a bag of nails and several large sheets of plywood that they hammered into place over the window.

"I'll call the glass man tomorrow."

"You won't have to." David got into bed wearing short-legged sweat pants and a T-shirt with the Miami of Ohio Athletic Department logo fading on the front. "They'll be lined up after seeing the mess on TV."

Dana's diaphragm tightened. "Did you tell the reporters what the note said?"

"Just that it was a threat."

PERVERT LOVER, YOU'LL GET YOURS.

"Maybe Marcus should take the case. If you were second chair—"

"I won't be intimidated, Dana. You know me better than that. Whoever did this, he's a coward. Only cowards and kids throw rocks and run away."

She grabbed a hairbrush off her dresser and dragged it through her thick dark hair.

"Frank Filmore deserves a fair trial just as much as anyone."

She nodded.

"I know you hate the work I do."

Her temper flared. "I don't hate your work. I believe in it. But couldn't you for once defend someone who's not a scumbag? What's wrong with a clean-cut bank robber?" She thought of George Clooney or Cary Grant. "Maybe a nice jewel thief?" She sat beside him and laid her hand on his chest, feeling the heat of his body beneath her palm. "Why does it always have to be the dregs of the earth? Can't you see how these people pollute our life?"

He couldn't leave them behind at the end of the day. He brought them home from the office and court and jail—the rapists and drug addicts, the thugs and derelicts. And not just their crimes and cases, but their agonized histories, too, all their rage and pain and deprivation. He couldn't help it.

"You weren't so miserable when I showed you that hundred-thousand-dollar retainer."

Giddy described them both when they'd counted the zeros on the check. And astonished when it didn't bounce, when it settled comfortably into the business account beside the two-hundred-and-fifty-dollar payments on time, the five-thousand-dollar checks for twenty-thousand dollars' worth of labor. Overhead at Cabot and Klinger was high, and the money was gone in less than a week; but for a day or two they'd both felt rich.

"If this trial goes the way I think it will, there'll be plenty more big retainers. You can pay off all the charge cards and Bailey's school and finish fixing the garage apartment and get yourself a new car. Think about it, Dana, no more pinching pennies, no more debt."

"This isn't about money."

It was about injured dogs, broken windows, and the danger Dana smelled in the air like a grass fire circling them.

"This is the Super Bowl, Dana. You don't walk away from—"

She stood. "It's not a goddamn game."

"Don't I know that? I have a man's life in my hands."

And he could not forget that any more than he could overlook his loyalty to his family. He was made that way, and Dana knew she should trust him. He would die before he let his family down. But there had never been threats before. And their home had not been violated.

He put his arm around her shoulders. As he pulled her to him she had to tell herself to relax. This man who meant everything to her: when had she begun having to work at loving him?

"Dana, I know this is rough on you, and I'm not much help. But I've had hard cases before. This is nothing new."

Except that the stakes were higher now because their life—stressful, trying, imperfect as it was but still theirs and precious—had been threatened.

"This isn't the time for us to fall apart, Number One. We have to make some plans." She recognized his take-charge voice. "I want you to check Bailey out of Phillips tomorrow. Tell the principal we'll be back when the case is over. She'll understand."

"Phillips Academy has a waiting list. Bailey'll lose her place."

"You explain it to the principal." A muscle moved in his jaw. "You can do that. Say you're going to home-school her for a while."

"David, she's a special child. She needs to be at a special school. I can't teach a kid like Bailey." And

Dana had a job and a thesis to write. There was a limit to the number of extensions her advisor could give her on it. And small as her salary was at Arts and Letters, it helped pay interest to the credit-card usurers so the Cabots could continue to live thousands of dollars beyond their means while they waited for the big cases to roll in.

"Bailey has friends at Phillips, and she loves riding the bus every day."

"You used to like teaching before you decided to study art history."

"You make it sound like art's not important. I should have stayed with teaching, that's what you're saying. What I want, what I care about, it doesn't matter?"

"Dana, who're you fooling? You haven't worked on your thesis since you got back from Italy. We spent all that money so you could do research—"

"I don't have enough time."

His jaw tightened. "This isn't about you, Dana. It's about Bailey's safety. Can we just stick to the issue?"

This was the way the defense attorney/husband argued. He got her off the subject, and she lost track of the point she had been trying to make and then said all the wrong things so that when they finally got back to the topic her confidence was gone.

"Dana, you're the one who's been going on—"

"I haven't been going on about anything."

"—about danger and risks."

"You want me to quit work, like what I do, *my life,* doesn't matter!"

"That's crazy. I'm the one made you go to Florence to do the research. But I don't believe you even care about getting your degree anymore."

A passing car cast light and shadow across the bedroom ceiling. "You don't know anything."

He sighed. She hated when he sighed at her.

He reached behind him and switched off the reading lamp on his side of the headboard. "If you can come up with a better plan, great. But I'll tell you, Dana, I'm through being the bad guy around here."

He fell asleep immediately while Dana tossed for another half hour. Fighting did not seem to trouble David. It was, after all, what he did for a living. She hated it, felt torn apart, her insides twisted. One day she imagined her loyal and steady husband would say he could not take it anymore, drive away and leave her alone on a porch in the dark. Dana thought this way even though she knew no one was less like her mother than David.

The night Dana had been abandoned, her mother had probably been high on something. Dana remembered her taking speedboat turns in the old Chrysler, sometimes jerking the wheel so hard Dana flopped from side to side. No seat belt. She was five years old at the time and already the grown-up in the family. She remembered asking her mother to slow down. Swift as a snake, the back of her mother's hand had swung off the steering wheel and slammed against Dana's mouth. Her lip burst and bled down the front of the Dead Head T-shirt she wore. She had been quiet then, squeezed her eyes tight, hung on to the edge of the seat, and waited for whatever came next.

Five years old, wearing a T-shirt to her knees, standing on the porch of an old frame bungalow on a dark city street, a bulging duffel bag beside her. Dana still remembered her mother's last words to her. "Ring the doorbell. Keep on until she lets you in. Tell her I can't take it anymore."

Chapter 7

Just before dawn Dana rose from bed, put on shorts and a hoodie, and ran the twelve blocks from Miranda Street to Goldfinch, passing unnoticed through safe and silent, sleeping Mission Hills, with its stately Spanish colonial residences, angular, Forties-style Hollywood mansions with carefully tended yards and pristine paths from sidewalk to door, and classic Craftsman homes built half of wood and half from river stones the size of footballs. A four-bedroom pale pink stucco Spanish colonial in Mission Hills proved how far Dana had come since that night on Imogene's front porch. In these days of hugely inflated prices the home they could really afford would probably be three cramped bedrooms baking under a flat roof on a treeless street in El Cajon. Dana wondered if Frank Filmore and more of his kind were worth the neighborhood's high price tag.

The spring night was clear and cool, and her nose tingled with the smell of jasmine and damp gardens. Overhead the sky glowed a yellow-gray from the reflected city lights. On Arboles she surprised three raccoons scrambling into a garbage can set on the street for morning pickup. They stared at her brazenly from behind their masks. A homeless person slept on the porch of the Avignon Shop. Embarrassed, Dana looked away too quickly to note if the figure was male or female. She thought of her mother and wondered what had happened to her. Margaret Bowen had been twenty-two the night she drove off.

Dana let herself into Arts and Letters and locked the door behind her. As she did she felt a jab of alarm between her ribs and turned around quickly, half expecting to see someone standing in the shadowy store; but of course there was no one there. There had never been a break-in on Goldfinch as far as Dana knew. Her knees were doughy with adrenaline as she felt her way upstairs and into the loft, where she turned on a small corner light and sat down.

She had just begun work on her doctorate in art history when a professor told her that Arts and Letters had the best collection of art books in San Diego County. Dana had seen the store dozens of times—it was in her neighborhood, across the street from Bella Luna, where she bought her coffee—but she had never done more than browse the best-sellers and deeply discounted remainders on the first floor. Once she saw the second-floor loft full of art books, she became an habitué; and two years ago Rochelle, the shop's eccentric English owner, had given her a key and hired her to work a few hours every week.

She dug a dust cloth from its place lodged behind an ancient edition of Tansey's book on the Sistine Chapel. Using a wooden step stool to reach the top of the six-foot shelves, she dusted the heavy books one by one as she reran her conversation last night with David. He was right. Bailey was not safe in school when there was someone out there making threats; keeping her home

was the logical course. Thinking this, Dana felt trapped.
And then ashamed. She did not want to be the kind of
woman who felt trapped at the thought of spending
more time with her child.

Margaret Bowen's daughter.

Imogene Bowen's granddaughter.

She lifted down and dusted a huge book of reproductions of works by Early Renaissance Italian painters.
This was Dana's period; and someday she would buy
the eight-hundred-dollar book, but for now she was
content just to look at it. She laid the heavy volume on
the refectory table in the center of the loft. Turning on
one of the brass table lamps, she bent its swivel neck so
a band of yellow light fell on the pages. Then she turned
to page four hundred and thirty-six, the Nerli Altarpiece.

Just six weeks earlier Dana had been in Florence
doing research for her thesis. While she was there,
Lexy's brother, Micah Neuhaus, who had lived in Florence for more than ten years, had taken her to Spirito
Santo to see the great painting.

In the immediate foreground pious-faced Nerli and
his wife kneel in profile facing each other. The Virgin
Mary sits between them with the baby Jesus, who is
mischievously eyeing his cousin, John the Baptist. The
gilded frame holds other figures, but what interested
Dana in Early Renaissance paintings were the background scenes—in this case, a village street scene and
a nobleman pictured embracing a younger woman in a
doorway. Scholars had determined those figures were
Nerli and his daughter. For Dana the detailed painting
opened doors into a story of ordinary lives that had
nothing to do with the sacred figures. It was the mys-
teries of the secular narrative present in many early

Italian masterworks that captured her imagination as nothing else in art had.

She closed the book and rested her head on her hands. She had to find a way to do it all. Somehow. Rekindle the excitement about her thesis; be a better, more loving wife; homeschool Bailey. *It will all work out,* she told herself. There had to be a way to make it all happen. She tried to pray, but her thoughts had frozen solid. She wondered if it made any sense to ask the God of Year One for help in modern times. Faith and prayer must have been simpler for Tanai Nerli and his wife.

When she was young prayer had come as easily as speech, as automatically as a language she was programmed to speak. Her grandmother had made fun of her devotion, and once she even hid Dana's good shoes on Sunday, but Dana went to church wearing rubber flip-flops. No one cared what she wore at Holy Family Episcopal—a royal name for a storefront church that housed, as well as Episcopalians, a congregation of Korean Methodists. In that shabby church she belonged not simply to the congregation—that was easy—but to something she felt in her bones but lacked the words to describe. Years later Lexy had helped her understand that what she'd felt was a hunger for transcendence. This soul-longing was a gift, Lexy said.

Dana lifted her head and listened. Someone was knocking on the door of Arts and Letters. She glanced at her watch and saw that it was not yet six A.M., much too early for Rochelle to appear, and anyway, she was the owner and had a key. Dana turned out the lights and sat still as the knocking continued. She heard a voice say her name.

"David?"

"It's me, Micah."

Her thoughts shut down.

"Let me in, Dana."

If she ignored him, Micah Neuhaus would bang with his fists until the neighbors called the police. He would like nothing better than to make a public demonstration. But if she let him in . . . He was a python curled in the darkest corner of her life.

This was ridiculous. He was an adult human being, nothing like a snake. She did not know what he was doing outside Arts and Letters, but she could guess, and it would not do. He had to leave her alone. She stood up, rubbing her damp palms on her running shorts, beginning to feel angry. What was he doing in San Diego? He had no business intruding on her life this way, and she would tell him so, and he would hear the steel in her voice and know that she meant every word.

But her knees were jelly as she went downstairs and fumbled with the doorknob.

He pushed past her into the dark bookstore.

In the weeks since they'd parted she had forgotten how young he looked, though he was almost forty, not much younger than she. He wore sandals, a pair of snug Levi's, and a baggy black sweater. His dark hair curled near the nape of his neck and was more untidy than she remembered it. But the piratical gold earring was still in his left ear, and the bruised, sensuous mouth had not changed. She remembered how his lips felt against the inside of her elbow, the pinpricks of pleasure, the half-drunk sense of simultaneously dropping into the center of her body and lifting out of it.

"Why are you here?"

"I saw your husband on TV."

"How did you know I'd be here?"

"I watched you leave your house."

"How dare you spy on me?"

"I'm really sorry about the dog. Is it okay?" He added, "I worry about you, Danita."

"Don't call me that."

"It's your name."

"No one calls me Danita." Except her grandmother. It was a memory of the old life, the life before she met David and began to live as normal people did.

"I'm glad the dog's okay."

For a few moments she had forgotten the terrible afternoon and night just past. Now the fear and panicky confusion, the tactless policeman, and her argument with David rushed back at her with the power of a flash flood.

He put his hands on her arms, and she jerked away. "Don't be mad, Dana."

"What do you expect me to be?"

"Just listen to me, okay?"

"What's the point? We've been over this a dozen times."

"No, I've got something new to say." His face was bright with conviction. "Where can we sit?"

"Say what you have to say, Micah." There would be no sitting down, no getting comfortable.

He laughed as if he read her mind. By the light of the street lamp outside the store Dana saw his blue-black eyes crinkle with amusement. "I've got this friend, he owns a great little house on the beach down in Mexico south of Ensenada, and he wants to sell it to me." As he talked, he walked back and forth between the rows of bookshelves, letting his fingers trail along the spines. His nervous energy filled the store, crackled through the bookshelves and along the countertops like heat lightning.

"You could come down sometimes. It's only a couple hours' drive, and David'd never have to know." He grinned at her. "I'll stay out of the way; you won't have to worry about me." Another grin. "I'll be a good boy."

Groaning, she slumped onto the stairs and rested her head in her hands.

"Dana, I've had time to think. I was way out of line before. I know that. But you're important to me."

He crouched before her, taking her hands.

"My beautiful Dana, I don't want you to suffer."

His back was to the window, his face in shadow; but a gray dawn light had begun to fill the store, and as he spoke she watched his mouth, wanting to trace the sulky outline of his lips with her fingertips.

She spoke to break the spell. "What about Lexy?"

"Forget my sister. Think about what I said."

"She loves you, and she worries, and you won't answer her phone calls."

His lips pinched in irritation. "I'll call her, okay? Okay?" He stood up and paced in front of her.

Dana felt her will strengthen.

"You never should have come back here."

"I want to be near you."

"Go back to Italy. You had a good life."

"First say you'll think about Mexico," he said.

"No, I won't." He was not a python. There was no lightning. "I told you, Micah. My life is in San Diego with David and Bailey. You can't be part of it."

She stood and pulled her back and shoulders straight. "I want you to go."

"What's wrong? Why did you change?" His question was almost a whine.

"This is a pointless conversation."

She expected him to argue with her, but instead he walked to the door. With his hand on the knob he said, "I love you. You either don't know what that means or you're fooling yourself. Either way . . ." He pressed his fist against his chest. "The pain, Dana, I can't stand it."

He waited, but she refused to speak. If she did not respond to his drama, he would leave.

"Okay, I'll leave, but don't tell me to go back to Italy. I'm not gonna do it until you come with me. In the meantime, if you want to see me, I'm living in that apartment house on Fourth and Spruce, second floor front."

And then he was gone, and it was as if a tornado had passed, sucking the air from the bookstore, leaving Dana with a bruised pain in her chest. She sat on the stairs again and by the gray light of dawn stared into the grain of the wood as if she hoped to read a message there.

Chapter 8

Florence

In January David had received a large bonus check, the first in Cabot and Klinger's history. He endorsed it over to Dana and told her to buy a ticket to Italy. No one got a Ph.D. in art history just thumbing through picture books, he'd said. She was both excited and fearful at the prospect of traveling alone. If she left her family for her own pleasure, fate might choose that time to punish her for being careless with what she had never deserved to have in the first place. She fretted about accidents, earthquakes, epidemics, and terrorists.

David said she was sweet and superstitious, but with the assistance of Phillips Academy and Guadalupe he would manage just fine. She had never been anywhere. Before she went to school in Ohio, she had not ventured farther from home than Los Angeles. She told Lexy she wished they'd used the bonus for a new roof.

"It's Europe," Lexy said. "And Italy's practically the cradle of civilization. You'll get there and you won't want to come back. But you do need some backup, and I've got just the thing. My brother'd love to show you around. He's been in Florence almost ten years. He's practically a native. Plus he's an artist. That can't hurt."

Dana did not want anyone to see what a klutz she was sure to be without David.

"He speaks the language—didn't you just tell me you're worried about not speaking Italian? He'll love you because he loves me."

Lexy persevered, and Dana gave in and let her call Micah.

"You have a right to have fun, Dana. Go for it."

David said almost the same thing when he saw her off at Lindberg Field. Friends and people she barely knew told her to have fun. It offended her, the way they tossed the word out—as if fun was a universal concept everyone but she understood. She did not remember playing games with the kids she grew up with. She had never owned a doll and never wanted one. Dana had been a loner, a quiet and bookish kid who'd had part-time jobs from the time she was eleven. The first "fun" time she actually remembered having was with David at the circus in Cincinnati. Even the barista at Bella Luna, the one with five rings in her left nostril, told her to relax and have fun. As if it were that easy. Just a wish and a click of the ruby slippers and she would be able to cast off the careful habits of a lifetime. Take some risks, Lexy told her. Life isn't about being safe all the time.

After three hours in the Atlanta airport and dinner thousands of feet over the gray Atlantic, she swallowed a sleeping pill, then until she fell asleep made lists in her head: places she wanted to visit, particular works of art she wanted to see. Before she dozed off she kissed the photo of David and Bailey she had shoved in the side pocket of her carryon. She missed them both and wished she'd stayed at home.

Micah met her at the airport brandishing his ridiculous and embarrassing sign, shocking pink, with her name in black Old English letters eighteen inches high. At the entrance to the four-star hotel where David had insisted she make reservations because it was only two blocks from the Uffizi Gallery, Micah had parked at an angle between a BMW and a Renault. He sprang from the car, grabbed her bags, and handed them to a bell-man. Another uniformed person opened her door and put a gloved hand under her elbow. Her head spun and her knees almost buckled. She'd barely slept in the last thirty-six hours. And eaten virtually nothing. She leaned against the desk for support as she signed the register and gave the clerk her passport.

As she followed the bellman to the elevator, Micah said, "I'll wait down here."

For what?

"If you go to sleep now, you won't wake—"

"Until I'm totally rested. That's the whole idea." She barely contained her annoyance. She did not want to offend Lexy's brother, but she knew what she needed. Her body was shouting that if she did not sleep, she would die.

They stood at the elevator while the bellman held it open. Micah said something to him in Italian, the man stepped into the elevator alone, and the doors slid shut.

"What did you say to him? I need to—"

"He's putting the stuff in your room."

She jingled her room key in front of him. "He can't get in."

"He's got a passkey."

She slammed the heel of her hand on the up button of the elevator.

Micah said, "It's just past five here. You need to keep moving until at least ten."

She leaned her forehead against the wall.

"I know some people, they got here about the same time as you and went right to bed. They woke up at one-thirty in the morning. Screwed their whole day."

The elevator appeared to have taken up residence on the third floor. She imagined the bellman going through her suitcase and finding the emergency five hundred dollars David had tucked in the pocket of her slacks.

"You can't give in to jet lag," Micah said, grinning. "It's the physical equivalent of terrorism."

She sighed. "Can I at least have a shower?"

"But don't lie down."

"Generally, I shower on my feet."

"You're done for if you lie down."

The elevator door opened. The bellman stepped out, and she stepped in.

"If I'm not down in thirty minutes . . ."

"I'll come get you."

"Ring my room."

"I'll pound on the door."

In the early twilight the Arno was a satiny olive-green. It lay to their right across a narrow cobbled street jammed with cars and motor scooters that filled the air with noise and stinking black exhaust. Micah told her, "If you know where the river is, you can't get lost in Florence. Not in the Old City." He pointed across the river to a red-tiled palazzo of pale gold stucco. "That's where I live, the place that looks like it's falling into the river, which it almost is. I rent the top floor from the princess who owns it."

"A real princess?"

"Italy's got hundreds of 'em. Mine's eighty and poor as a peasant."

He steered her out of the traffic onto a cobbled street wide enough for one car and stopped a block up in front of a shop selling upscale souvenirs of the city.

"That's me," he said, pointing to the elegantly precise pen-and-ink rendering of a Florentine skyline displayed in the window.

Dana was surprised by how good it was.

"One of these pays the rent," he said. "I generally sell a couple a month. More during the summer."

"I want to buy it and take it home."

"Nah, it's way overpriced. I'll give you one."

They followed the narrow street. As they stepped into the Piazza della Signoria Dana's knees went suddenly weak. She cried out inadvertently, surprising herself. There before her were the statues she had seen in books: the immense figure of Neptune rising from the sea, and Duke Cosimo astride a beautiful figure of a horse. No matter how fine the reproduction in a book, nothing could have prepared her for the size and life that emanated from the actual statues. She forgot about having fun, about David and Bailey.

In front of the reproduction of Michelangelo's *David,* Micah said, "I'll take you to see the original in the Academia. It's amazing, of course, practically a shrine, with camera Nazis all over the place and everyone telling you to be quiet if you raise your voice above a whisper." He looked disgusted. "I actually like this one out here better, even if it isn't the original. The *David* was meant to be public art, exposed to life. I understand all the practicalities, but I don't like it when people treat art like it's . . . holy. Mostly Italy doesn't do that."

They walked back toward the Arno through the imposing colonnade of the Uffizi Palace Gallery. "I love this city," he said. "Everywhere I look I see something beautiful."

His words awakened her. Until that moment she had
been seeing Micah as Lexy's eccentric and impertinent
little brother, as a wild driver and a source of restless
energy who would not let her sleep. But in the amber
twilight of the colonnade she shed her resistance like a
snake its tired skin. She saw that he was like an angel
in a Renaissance painting, with his dark and curly, untidy hair, his large blue-black eyes and sensual, sulky
mouth. Micah's high energy and enthusiasm had made
him seem boyish at first, but in the half shadows she
could see the sadness in his face. The lines around his
eyes had not come from laughing. She felt an instant
empathy, and vaguely remembered Lexy saying her
brother suffered from depression and had been unhappy as a boy. Happiness and grief were both written
in his face along with something renegade she could
not classify. As she stared at him, half mesmerized by
the contrasts, she lost her footing and stumbled. He
steadied her with his hand on the small of her back. His
touch excited her, and she jerked away. She had not
been prepared for that.

They crossed the Arno at the Ponte Vecchio, where
most of the gold- and silversmiths had closed their
shops for the night. It was the middle of the week and
not quite tourist season. Though there was plenty of
foot traffic on the ancient bridge, it did not feel crowded
to Dana. They walked up the hill past the hideous fa-
cade of the Pitti Palace until they came to the little Piazza Santo Spirito and a first-floor restaurant just large
enough for six tables. Micah had to duck his head as
they walked in. He was perhaps six-three or four and
slender; but he moved like an athlete, which surprised
Dana. Jock-artist was not a common type. David was
smart, but he had no interest in art.

Micah and the owner, Paolo, played together on a

recreational soccer team; they greeted each other with an embrace. Their conversation was incomprehensible to Dana, but she guessed the subject was soccer because the body language of men talking sports is much the same in any country. The heads turn from side to side, the shoulders and arms pump.

At dinner Dana and Micah talked about the city and art, and she went on about her thesis topic until she felt she had to apologize for talking so much. He said he was interested and asked more questions, informed questions that started her off again. Explaining, explaining: her thesis had never seemed more real than it did that night. It was thrilling to be in Florence on her own, talking art, without Bailey tugging on her, or David looking at his watch, never telling her where to go exactly but always with his hand on her elbow steering and supporting like she might fall over if he did not hold her up. She felt guilty for her thoughts.

It was after eleven and cold when they left Paolo's and walked toward the river through the almost empty streets.

Micah put his arm across her back. Tired and a little drunk after sharing two bottles of wine, she leaned into him and resisted his suggestion they find a taxi.

"Let's walk," she said.

In less than a day, this city has seduced me.

She woke up feeling headachy and slightly nauseated but ignored the symptoms, blaming jet lag and too much wine the night before. This was the day Micah was taking her to the Uffizi.

They walked past the tourists waiting in line and entered the gallery by a side door because Micah knew the right people. They made their way backward through the gift shop to the marble stairway where the guard waved them through with more jock body language.

Her stomach dipped as they entered the first rooms, the walls covered with iconic art in blue and gold and umber dating back to the early centuries of the second millennium.

After the third room she went into the long passage-way and sat on a bench, dropping her head between her knees.

"I'm going to be sick." She looked around for a sign directing her to the rest rooms.

Micah blinked and pointed over her shoulder, through the window and across the colonnade where they had walked the night before and into the corner of the gallery farthest from where they were standing.

It was more than half a mile away.

When it was all over and she sat in an easy chair in Micah's apartment wrapped in a duvet, Dana was able to laugh as Micah described in graphic detail how much worse it might have been. True, she had not made it all the way to the rest rooms, but at least she had gotten as far as the stairs leading down to them. And the line could have been worse. In the summertime there might have been fifty people staring at her while she threw up.

They talked of art and life, and Micah fed her dry crackers and soda water. As the afternoon waned, the light streaming through the tall, uncurtained windows of the palazzo changed from white to yellow to red-orange. Across the river, the bricks of Florence, absorbing the light, turned to rose gold. The room filled with long shadows and the dank smell of the river. Dana yawned and closed her eyes.

She sat up. "Do you have something I can wear back to the hotel? I need a nap."

"Sleep here," he said. "Later we can go out again.

Nothing starts in Florence until after ten anyway. On the other side of town there's a jazz club. You'll like it."

"You don't have to babysit me, Micah. You have a life—"

"Is that how you see me? As a babysitter?"

"What about clothes?"

"Give me your key. I'll go back to the hotel while you sleep."

His back was to the window; the falling sun outlined him like gold encircling a medieval icon. She held her breath. He turned, and they looked into each other's eyes. He held out his hand, then led her to his bed.

She knew exactly what she was doing. She was in a three-hundred-year-old palazzo owned by an Italian princess. She had been transported to a fairy-tale world, and she did not once think of David and Bailey or stop to ask if this was the way normal people behaved. In the Kingdom of Florence none of the old rules applied. Later, she recalled what Lexy had once said about life being full of crossroad moments, opportunities taken or lost forever.

Late that night, after jazz and slow dancing, he leaned her against a crumbling garden wall draped in wisteria, unzipped her Levi's, and entered her with his fingers. She cried in the dark from the thrill of it. Night and the city sounds, a few feet away the voices of men and women coming out of the club where they had been moments before. And Dana impaled on her lover's hand, crying because she had never had an orgasm like that, never knew it was possible.

She inhabited a small world that week. In the mornings Micah brought her hot chocolate and a croissant from the coffee bar at the corner. They made love amid the crumbs and might not eat again until dinner; but she felt full all the time. In mirrors and shop windows she saw the difference in herself, a look of slightly blurred and puffed fatigue, a languor in her arms and legs. Her hair was heavier, thicker, and darker than it had ever been; and she wore it loose, not tied as usual at the nape like a convent girl.

They went back to the Uffizi three times so Dana could study paintings rich in visual subtext. Da Fabriano's *Adoration of the Magi* transfixed her. In the faces of the crowd—suspicious, venal, good-natured, Mary's sly and gossipy attendants—she saw the emotions of living people. She walked through rooms full of two-dimensional medieval virgins holding infant saviors with the wizened features of old men, but in paintings of the Renaissance she saw faces as modern as those in the cafés and shops of Florence. This was the great breakthrough of Renaissance art. It brought mortals into art where before there had been only saints and gods.

One morning as she put her hairbrush down on the table in the bathroom she knocked a vial of pills to the floor. She picked it up and tried to read the label written in Italian, but the only word she recognized was depression. Hard to believe, easy to dismiss. During the short time she'd known him Micah had been ebullient and lighthearted. No one who was depressed could have so much energy. She thought about mentioning the pills but told herself it was none of her business. Besides, these days doctors prescribed mood-altering chemicals to almost anyone who wanted them.

In the afternoon they bicycled out of town to the Villa Reale di Castello, a sixteenth-century garden laid out with checkerboard formality. Descendants of plants gathered centuries before from countries as distant as China filled the garden with the scents and colors of spring.

They sat beside a fountain and ate a lunch of fruit and bread and cheese; and afterward they found a secluded spot and fell asleep until an ill-tempered guard rousted them and they hurried off, giggling like teenagers. Micah seemed so happy; she could not help asking him if he still got depressed.

"You know about that?"

"Lexy told me."

"Thank you, sister dear."

"It's nothing to be ashamed of."

"Did I say it was?"

"Look, it's none of my business—"

"Hey, I'm glad you brought it up." He did not sound glad at all. "What else do you want to know? Do I hate my mother? Am I constipated?"

She backed away from him, hands flattened in a "stop" gesture. "I asked a simple—"

"Yeah, well maybe it's not so simple; maybe it's so fucked up no one can figure it out anymore."

She had no idea what he was talking about now.

"Come on, Micah, I'm getting hungry. Let's get some of that hot chocolate at the bar. . . ." She held her hand against his cheek. "I'm sorry I pried. I never want to make you angry."

"I'm not angry. Do I look angry?" He smiled, and she didn't know what he was thinking. "I used to take pills for depression, but I don't need them anymore. You make me happy, Dana. You make me happier than I've ever been."

Another day they wandered through the Boboli Gardens in the rain giving names to the feral cats, getting soaked, playing chase and sliding on the wet grass. She remembered Lexy saying her brother was not a laugher. How amazing it was that now Dana knew him better than his own sister.

And every day, when they were not in galleries and churches and gardens and restaurants, they were in bed. Her vagina ached, and walking from one gilt-framed painting to another, she felt her clitoris as if it had permanently grown.

They made plans to visit Venice and Rome, Siena and Milan, where Dana had to see, must see, Bellini's *The Preaching of St. Mark in Alexandria.*

"There are camels," Micah told her, almost bouncing with delight. "And a giraffe and all these guys in fancy hats, and you hardly notice Saint Mark at all."

With his knowledge of Italian art, and his increasing understanding of what she was looking for, he plotted a trip that would take them as far south as Palermo, where he told her about a beautiful little museum and an extraordinary painting, loaded with subtext, called *The Triumph of Death.* She had to see it.

"Tell him about me," Micah said.

Not yet.

"Waiting won't make it easier on him."

It was Saturday. Her flight home was on Monday morning.

"It's not one of those things I can just say."

"What can't you say? That you love me?" He held her face in his hands. His palms were hot and dry, and she imagined she felt his lifeline mark her cheeks, making her his forever. "You do love me. You know you do. Say, 'I love you, Micah.'"

She whispered it.

"Tell him."

"Let me do it my own way."

"You want to leave me? You want to go back to that?" That.

She would starve without Micah, dry up and blow away like sculptor's dust.

She thought of a painting she had seen yesterday or the day before. Her days streamed together like watercolors. Or maybe it was a story she had read, or maybe she was making it up right now to explain how she felt, because only metaphor could make her emotions comprehensible. A maiden wandered into a dark and beautiful wood. She danced with a satyr and fell into a swoon. When he bent over her and asked for her will, she gave it to him.

Before they fell asleep that night Micah said, "Say it."

"I love you."

"Louder."

She laughed.

"I mean it. I want to hear you yell it out."

"I'll wake up the princess."

"Get up and go over to the window. Stand there and yell it across the river."

She sat up and stared at him.

"Do it and I won't ask you again."

She was tired, too tired to argue. She got out of bed and fumbled for her nightgown that had fallen off the end of the bed.

"Go like you are. Don't put anything on." He folded his arms beneath his head. "There's moonlight."

"What if someone sees me?"

"You have a beautiful body. Don't be ashamed of it."

"Micah, I'm not ashamed. I just don't like to make a public—"

"I'd like to put you on display in the piazza."

The gooseflesh rose on her arms.

"The women would envy you and the men would all want to fuck you. They'd offer me money."

She got back into bed. Pulling the blanket around her shoulders, she said, "I don't want to do this."

"Do what?" He bit her earlobe gently. "What don't you want to do?"

"Stand in the window."

He poked her gently in the ribs. "I was only kidding."

For years Micah had sold his drawings in the Piazza del Duomo marketplace on Sundays. These drawings were much less fine than those for sale in shops around the Old City but still better than most. If the weather was good he might make several hundred Euros selling his pictures. While he was doing that Dana would have the palazzo to herself. She could not talk to David with Micah in the room listening, feeding her lines, fluttering his tongue up her inner thigh.

She thought of the house in Mission Hills, the rooms she had lovingly painted and decorated, the hardwood floors she had stripped and sanded and buffed. She allowed herself to feel a pinch of regret for what she was abandoning.

She had not used that word before.

"Mommymommymommy."

The impulse to hang up was like a hand jerking her out the door and down the stairs.

Mommymommymommy.

She did not know what to say to Bailey. She had planned the words for David, scripted their conversation like a phone volunteer asking for campaign money. She had no spiel laid down for Bailey. "I love you" was all she could think to say that wasn't a lie she would choke on.

"Talk, Mommy."

She tried to swallow, but something had been added to her anatomy. At the base of her tongue there was a growth the size of a walnut.

"Dana." David at last. "Why didn't you call? I've been worried. Did you get my messages?"

"I'm fine."

"I called the hotel, but you were never there. Even in the middle of the night."

"I've been exhausted."

"Have you been sick? What's wrong with your voice?"

"I'm fine."

"You don't sound fine."

"It's been an incredible week."

"You weren't even there early in the morning."

"Don't be silly, of course I was there."

She had anticipated this line of questioning.

"It's a crazy place, David. The desk clerks are technological idiots. They probably rang an empty room."

"I thought it was a good hotel. Didn't you tell me it cost three-fifty a night?"

She had forgotten that digging out the truth was what David did best.

"It is a good hotel. Great breakfasts every day." She was winging it now. "But there was a mixup with the rooms when I got there. The clerks never did get it straight in their heads."

"I was worried." He sounded petulant. He wanted her to tell him he had been a good husband to whom apologies were owed. He had stayed home with a difficult child while she had a good time.

Fun.

"Dana?"

"I've been frantic to see everything. A week isn't long. In Florence it's no time at all."

"You sound like you've got a sore throat."

"Yeah. A little one."

The line buzzed in her ear.

"So," David said, "you've had a good time?"

"Better than I dreamed."

He laughed. "Gracie said I should watch out, you'd fall in love with Italy. Little old San Diego's gonna seem pretty boring."

"There's so much here, David." She wanted him to understand. "History and art. Just taking a walk, there's so much . . . beauty. You can be in a seemingly wretched neighborhood and there'll be an arrangement of pots or some tile or a wisteria vine . . ." Her thoughts spun forward through all she might tell him; but the effort seemed pointless. David would try to understand, but to him a picture was a picture and not much else.

She heard Bailey's voice in the background.

"How's she been?" She was far off her script now.

"Every day she asks me if this is the day we go to the airport to get you."

Bailey did not understand the concept of anywhere that was too far away to drive to. David had brought home a travel video of Tuscany. "That was a mistake. She got hysterical. I guess before then she thought you were staying at the airport for some reason. I didn't know what to do, so I called Miss Judy. She was great.

The next day she taught a lesson about vacations. She's a bloody genius, that woman, and I think Bay gets it now, that you're not living at Lindberg Field."

"I explained. I thought she understood."

"The house is lonely without you. Next time you want to take a trip, I'm going too."

She had prepared herself for guilt, but not for the sudden desire to see her husband and wrap her arms around his solid football player's body.

She had to get back to her script.

"That's what I wanted to talk about." She heard the silence on the line and the sound of David's breath. "There's so much to see, all the little towns around have fabulous art, not to mention Venice and Rome. . . . It feels kind of wasteful to fly over here, spend all that money, and not see more."

In the background, "Mommymommymommy."

"Is there something you're not telling me?" The lawyer was back in his voice. The trained interrogator.

She thought of the things she could say.

I love Micah Neuhaus and I'm never coming home.

Never that, never those words. They would hurt him too much; and no matter how much she loved Micah, she loved David too. And Bailey.

Dana, the smartest girl in her class, the girl who had always known where she was going and what she wanted: she knew her script and had learned her lines.

"Mommymommymommy."

But when she tried to say something, she was interrupted by her own small voice, weeping into the musty pillow in Imogene's spare room. For weeks she had worn shorts and a T-shirt to bed so she would be ready when her mother's lugging Chrysler turned into the driveway.

"Are you saying you want to stay longer? How much longer? Another week?"

"No."

"I don't get this, Dana. What's going on? Is there something I should be worried about?"

"I don't want to leave, that's all. But I'm fine, really. I just love it here, that's all. You're right, I fell in love. With Florence and Italy. David, I don't ever want to leave. I belong here. It's part of me now."

"Dana, sweetheart, it's a town, a city." He laughed fondly. "There'll be another time. One of these days I'm gonna get a big case, and when I do I'll take you back to Florence. I promise."

The open piazza was bright and bitter-cold and crowded with student groups. Hordes of boys and girls in signature black, mobs of young crows cawing Spanish, German, French, and guttural languages Dana could not identify, lined up to enter the Romanesque cathedral. To the right of the cathedral, Micah was one of a dozen artists who had set up tables and easels. Dana stood apart, so embarrassingly American in the yellow wool coat she would still be paying for this time next year. Bright as a target, she thought, aware that the crowds of young Europeans vaguely frightened her. Two days earlier she had ignored them and seen only the cathedral's pink and green and white marble façade like an elaborately decorated cake.

Micah wore his struggling-artist costume on Sundays. Black turtleneck, ragged at the cuff and throat, a Greek fisherman's cap, torn Levi's, and sandals. He hadn't shaved that morning and looked dissolute and pallid. As he spoke to a browser, Micah's gold earring flashed in the sunlight and a chill ran up Dana's legs. She wrapped her arms around herself, grateful for wool the color of midsummer lemons.

As she watched, he sold two watercolor-and-ink cityscapes to a pair of Japanese tourists. He could produce one of these in a couple of hours. He bragged that he had the Ponte Vecchio down to ninety minutes flat.

Micah looked in her direction. A wide smile opened his face, and he lifted his arm, gesturing her to him. She felt something move in her, move and stretch and snap.

She was too old, too married, too American.

And he was too young. Not in years but in the way he lived, thinking only of his pleasure, content to sell mediocre drawings in a piazza while other men erected bridges, negotiated treaties, and raised families.

Micah's hand cupped the air more urgently. "Turn around, let me see the back." He twirled a finger in the air. "That coat!"

Two men, passing with easels shoved under their arms, said something in rapid Italian, and Micah responded, and all three laughed.

"What?" Dana asked.

"They wanted to know if you were my American mistress. One called you Mistress Sunbeam."

"I'm going back to the apartment," she said. "I'm cold."

"You can't go. I won't let you. You have to stay." He motioned to a stool. "I'm sorry I teased you, honestly. It's a beautiful coat. Here. Sit down. You watch the store and I'll get you a coffee. Are you hungry?"

"My feet are frozen."

"What's the matter? What happened? Did you call him?"

Another group of Japanese tourists stopped at Micah's table. He turned his attention to them, though occasionally, as he smiled and laughed and cajoled and took their money, he glanced sideways at Dana. When they left he showed her the pile of hundred-Euro notes.

"Not bad, huh? Give me another hour and I'll shut down."

She covered her face with her hands.

"What did he say?" Micah waited for her answer. When she said nothing, he pulled her hands away from her face and peered into her eyes. "Okay. Go home. I'll close up here."

"You don't have to—"

"I'll load up the car and meet you back at the flat."

He brought fresh rolls and mozzarella, tomatoes, and blood oranges from Sicily. They ate a picnic on the bed. Dana was suddenly ravenous. Micah sliced a blood orange and nudged her onto her back, opened her mouth with his fingertips, and squeezed the fruit onto her tongue as his other hand lifted her sweater and cupped her breast. The juice was the color of raspberries and filled her mouth with sugar. Her nipples tingled as they hardened.

He shoved aside bread and mozzarella, clearing a space for them to lie. A knife clattered to the floor. He licked her sweet, sticky mouth.

I will always remember this. The smell of the fruit, the smell of him.

It was dark when she awoke, and cold. The wind was up, spitting rain against the window. In candlelight Micah sat across the room facing the bed, his sketch pad propped against his crossed knee. She pushed herself up on her elbows.

"What time is it?"

"Almost seven."

"You shouldn't have let me sleep. Why didn't you wake me up?" The remains of their meal still covered the bed and floor. An orange had bled onto the duvet, staining it brown.

"I wanted to watch you. Sleeping. You're so uninhibited," he said. "Awake you're always in control, or trying to be. But when you sleep your body lets go. You lie on your stomach with your legs apart. I can see all of you and you don't care." He held out his pad. "Here, look at yourself."

He had drawn her thighs and buttocks and her sex with the same precise detail as he rendered the rooftops of Florence. She handed it back.

"You don't like it?" His question sounded like a dare. "Why don't you take it home and show it to your husband?"

She went into the bathroom and sat on the bidet. He came to the door

"Go away. I want to be alone."

"You didn't care how much I watched you yesterday. You let me see anything, and now all of a sudden you're a nun. What did he say that's turned you against me?"

She splashed warm water between her thighs, then stood and dried. She still felt sticky and ran hot water in the old-fashioned tub so hard the room quickly filled with steam. She added cold and, when the temperature was right, stepped in and sank until the water covered her to the chin.

He crouched beside the tub and watched her. She slid under, her hair floating in the water as in Ophelia's suicide, and stayed there until her breath ran out.

His eyes shone with tears. "Tell me you're coming back to me."

His hand cupped the round of her shoulder. His thumb bore down into the soft tissue above her breast.

"You're hurting me."

"I could push you under. I could hold you under until you stopped breathing. You wouldn't have a chance." The steam had reddened his cheeks and brought up the wild curl in his hair. "You're not strong enough to stop me, Dana."

She was afraid.

"I've been waiting all my life for you," he said. "You don't know what it's like to be me. You're middle class to your core, Dana. You're a taker, a user. That yellow coat says it all."

"I've got to get dressed." And get out of the palazzo and back into the hotel. She would tell the man at the desk not to let him come up. The lock on her door would keep him out.

She grabbed for the towel draped over a nearby chair and wrapped it around her. In the palazzo's central room a triple-bar electric heater glowed near the couch. She stood in front of it and tried to dry herself without letting the towel slip. The heating element burned the back of her legs. She realized that she was barely breathing.

"Drop the towel."

"I have to pack."

"No. I want you to stay here, forever. I want to lock you in these rooms, feed you cheese and blood oranges and never let you out."

"Micah, you frighten me." His eyes drilled into her. "I can't leave my daughter. I know what that's like. My own mother . . ." There was no need to explain. They had talked about their lives until they knew each other's stories as well as their own. "If I stay with you I'll ruin her life. I can't do that."

Bailey needed her, and she needed Bailey. When Dana loved her, she also loved the little girl abandoned on her grandmother's front porch. How was it possible she hadn't understood that before?

Micah's expression brightened. "I thought you didn't love me."

"I don't know—"

"I've got a great idea. She can come here."

"It wouldn't—"

"How do you know? You haven't even heard what I've got to say." He followed her to the wardrobe where she kept her clothes. "We can make this work, Dana. I can earn plenty of money. We can move somewhere better if you want. Bailey'll love Florence." Dana thought of a top winding tighter and tighter. "God, wouldn't it be great to be a kid in Florence? She'd be bilingual in no time, and we'll send her to one of those convents—"

"David would never let it happen." Arguing only encouraged him. She must stop talking and dress, just dress and get out.

"She can stay with us in the summer, him in the winter. Whatever."

"You don't know about Bailey. She has special needs." Her voice was marbled with fear.

He stepped in close. It took all her will to keep from moving away.

"She needs *you*. You just said that."

"Yes, but more. A special school . . ."

"Florence has schools," he said angrily. "Italy isn't Borneo."

He had lost interest in everything but his plan. Good. He would not notice that as she dressed her hands shook. He paced around the bedroom, scheming about schools and special diets and tutors. He stopped finally and stared at her, as if surprised to see her fully dressed.

She had cleared away the mess on the bed and laid out her suitcase.

"We could work this out if you wanted to. Why don't you want to? What's happened? You were hanging on me when I went down to the piazza this morning and now you don't want me near you. What did he say to you? Did he threaten you?"

"He'd never do that."

"Why not? I would." He grabbed her wrists and drew her to him. She felt his fingers bruise her skin and heard David asking who had grabbed her and why. "I'd do whatever it took to keep you."

"You're hurting me." Her pulse roared in her ears.

He looked at her and stumbled back a step, throwing off his grip. He held his hands out before him and stared at them. "I want to hurt you," he said and began to cry. "I want to make you hurt like I do."

Chapter 9

Dana had expected Bailey to fret about being home-schooled; but she adapted well, and if she missed her friends at Phillips Academy and the cherry red mini-bus that took her there, she kept it to herself. This surprised Dana, but what had come as an even greater surprise was her own pleasure at teaching her daughter. When David was with the Chargers she had been a kindergarten teacher, and now the skills came back to her. Counting and alphabet games, story time, and field trips to the zoo and the bank and the supermarket: Dana had forgotten the way a young mind sponged up information, even one as challenged as her daughter's.

To be a successful mother, wife, gardener, cook, and teacher all at the same time, Dana had to be organized, and some days she just wasn't. Some days moved from confusion through chaos and into crisis with no rest in between. Not that Bailey cared; homeschooling and her mother's full attention suited her fine. She took charge of snack time, sometimes managing to pour more orange juice into their glasses than onto the table. They went for walks while she chattered about what she saw. She could not read, and numbers confused her; but her imagination was vast. She made up wonderfully intricate, amusing, and often violent stories about the evil disposition of the ugly gnome statue in the garden of the house at the end of the street.

Bailey was excited about the day's visit to the Birch Aquarium. In preparation she and Dana had spent the previous day at the library looking at books about fish and their habitats. For the last fifteen minutes Bailey had been sitting up straight in an easy chair in the living room with a picture book of ocean creatures open on her lap.

"I want to see a ee-ee-eel," she said, stretching the vowel out to show Dana she knew the long sound it made.

Standing in the entry, Dana sorted through the mail, not opening the bills, checking for letters without return addresses. The police had told her to set such envelopes aside. She was to leave them for the police to open.

"Time, Mommy, time."

"Soon, honey."

Finish sorting the mail.

Water and biscuits for Moby Doby.

Set the timer on the stove so the roast'll be ready at five-thirty.

Set another timer on the backyard sprinklers.

Turn off the answering machine so no one can leave threatening messages.

Two weeks had passed since the incident with the rock and note. Moby Doby was almost as good as new, the window had been repaired, the media had lost interest in the tribulations of the Cabot family, and there had been no further threats. Though the police had cautioned her against becoming complacent, Dana did not jump at the blast of a car horn anymore, or the telephone's sudden jangle. Micah Neuhaus had not attempted to contact her since the morning in the bookstore, and about him, too, she had begun to relax.

After their trip to the aquarium she and Bailey were going to La Valencia Hotel for afternoon tea—a dressup occasion. And risky. In a public setting Bailey might sit at the table and sip her chocolate milk and eat her cookies like a model child. On the other hand, if she became excited or frustrated for some reason, she could go off like a fireworks display and sling cookies at the waiter. But it wasn't fair to keep her cooped up in the house all day when she had done nothing wrong; she did not deserve to be punished. There had to be walks to the library and trips to the mall, and chancy outings like this one. She had to learn how to be in public places.

For the festive occasion Bailey had chosen to wear her favorite dress of lime green and pink dotted Swiss with a wide shiny sash striped in the same colors. And her shocking pink strappy sandals just back from the cobbler, who warned Dana his repairs would not last and the shoes were not worth fixing again. Obviously, he didn't know about seven-year-old girls and their favorite shoes.

Bailey dropped the fish book and jumped off the chair. She stood at the front door, kicking at the metal base of the screen. "Go-go-go."

"Quiet down, kiddo."

"Go-go-go."

Dana tossed the mail—all perfectly legitimate—into a basket. "I have to get Moby some water and put him outside. You stay where you are, okay? Wait for me and we'll go out together."

"I wanna see a ee-eee-eel."

"You will, Bay, you will."

If it were not for David and the stress in their relationship, Dana would have been happy. But they were so out of sync that nothing she did could make it better. He got home from work late, his complexion putty-colored with exhaustion. She fed him, he planted himself in front of the television, and fell asleep. He didn't even have time for racquetball or a pickup basketball game on Saturday afternoons. Their conversations had become more like interviews, with Dana asking the questions and David grunting the answers.

The last time they'd made love it hadn't worked. David had apologized. "It's the case," he said. Afterward Dana couldn't shake the image of Frank Filmore sprawled in the bed between them.

When they were kids and new to each other, she and David had talked and made love every chance they got. Best had been the humid Ohio afternoons before the start of football season when lightning cracked the sky behind mountains of blue-black and violet thunderheads and the moisture-laden air seemed too thick to breathe. Sex on those days had been like inviting the elements into their foreplay. Back then Dana had believed God had brought them together and that a special charm blessed their love and kept it fresh. These days she felt sad and foolish for having been such an innocent.

In the entryway, Bailey continued to kick the door.

"Don't kick," Dana yelled back over her shoulder. "Stop it now."

Moby made a soft, excited woofle in the back of his throat as Dana dug into the biscuit box for a handful of treats. In the backyard she checked the lock on the wall gate. As she did, she heard a car door slam and the screech of tires. The neighbor's kid had just gotten his driver's license.

She returned to the kitchen, set the timer on the stove

so the roast would be ready at dinnertime, closed and bolted the back door, then remembered she had forgotten to turn on the sprinklers and went outside again. Ready at last, she walked down the short hall to the front of the house. Bailey was not waiting for her there.

"Time to go, Kidney-Bean."

Hiding was one of Bailey's favorite tricks.

Dana checked the powder room under the stairs. Then she stood at the foot of the stairs and called up, trying not to sound irritated. "Come down now, Bailey, no more games."

Still nothing. Sighing, Dana looped her shoulder-strap purse over the newel post and went upstairs. Bailey's bedroom door was closed. She opened it.

"What are you doing in here—"

The pink-and-lime checkerboard comforter was pulled up over the pillows. A dozen stuffed animals—bears and pigs and a funny-looking gray and black warthog— sat in a circle the way Bailey currently liked to arrange them. The room was as clean and empty as it had been when Dana tidied it an hour earlier.

Dana flew down the stairs and opened the screen door, ran down the path and looked up and down the street and across the park. No one was about; the neighborhood was peaceful. She opened her mouth to call Bailey's name, and then she saw the shoe. The strappy sandal had broken again and fallen off. It lay in the muddy gutter beside a set of tire tracks.

Chapter 10

Bailey had been gone more than three months.
To Dana that was ninety-plus bed and bath times
and one-hundred-and-twenty mealtimes, not counting
snacks. It was fifteen Sundays at St. Tom's, one hundred tantrums give or take, thousands of small jokes, a
million hugs and kisses.

In the parking lot between St. Tom's and its offices,
Dana sat in the 4Runner, staring down at the keys in
the palm of her hand. She saw her ragged nails and her
dry skin. So many things she had done for years without thinking, like filing her nails and moisturizing her
skin, had fallen aside since Bailey vanished. Days passed
and she wore the same Levi's and shirt or sweater. Meals
were a mouthful of cottage cheese, an apple or an ice
cream cone. Nothing tasted good anymore.

She did not remember brushing her teeth that morning.

She stared across the street at the Mission Hills Nursery where a female employee arranged tubs of spidery
yellow and white lilies along the edge of the sidewalk.
Behind them, grappling up the chain-link fence, blood
red bougainvillea was in full bloom. Blue sky, vivid

colors: Dana felt invisible amidst the brilliant life. And she did not care, not even when she saw her face reflected in the rearview mirror. There were vertical lines bracketing her mouth that had not been there three months ago, a pinch at the corner of her mouth. Her eyes were so tired they seemed to have faded from brown to beige. But she had not, would not, cry.

Early in life she had learned tears made her mother angry, which meant a face slap. And because she knew her grandmother wanted to see her whining and pitiful, Dana had refused to give her the satisfaction of showing any weakness. Now, when she wanted to cry, she could not. She understood that the Bailey Committee had to move. And she knew Lexy loved her and felt frustrated by her inability to comfort her. There was nothing anyone could do. The loss of a child to death might become, with time, bearable. But a disappearance was a mystery and fed the imagination with grisly pictures and suppositions. And guilt: the conviction that if she had kept Bailey glued to her hip this would never have happened.

She reached into the backseat for her purse, opened the outside flap and took out her cell phone. Three months ago she had programmed in the number of Lieutenant Walt Gary, the officer in charge of the Bailey investigation. Though an improvement over kid-phobic Patrolman Ellis, neither was Gary a rock of empathy.

An electronic female voice told Dana to listen to everything because the police department had made changes in its menu. She stabbed the zero key; after a moment the voice of a live human being came on the line.

"This is Dana Cabot," she said, trying to sound like the kind of woman who got what she wanted. "Connect me to Lieutenant Gary, please."

"I'll check if he's in."

As Dana waited, three different customers came out of the nursery pulling American Flyer wagons loaded with seedlings that would bloom at Christmas. Dana had already decided she would not celebrate Christmas without Bailey. Lexy told her not to look ahead. She should live one day at a time.

She felt a quick impulse to go back into the office and tell Lexy she was sorry for being mean. It made no sense to be angry with her best friend, but when Dana looked at Lexy she thought about God, and she was mad at God. She had been tricked by religion, beguiled into believing God loved his creation. Which he didn't. If he did there would be no murdered Lolly Calhouns, no kidnapped Bailey Cabots.

The woman on the phone was apologetic. "I'm sorry, Mrs. Cabot. The roster says Lieutenant Gary's on a call."

Dana had seen the room where Gary worked. She knew that his phone sat on the right side of his gunmetal gray desk beside a picture of his mother and father and a pit bull named Louie. She knew he sat at his desk right now avoiding her call because he had run out of positive things to say to her. He was too honest to pretend hope when he felt none.

In the beginning, however, he had encouraged her to be optimistic and talked about how efficiently a search could be mobilized since the passing of the Amber Act. He spoke of something called NCMEC, the National Center for Missing and Exploited Children. Dana did not ask what exploited meant.

The media and police had moved into action so quickly it was impossible not to feel hopeful at the beginning. Twenty minutes after Dana reported Bailey missing a description of her had been broadcast on multiple radio stations throughout San Diego County.

On all the news shows that night and every night for a month afterward Bailey's picture was on the screen, and throughout the newscast a scroll ran along the bottom of the screen with a number viewers could call with information. Almost immediately the phones had begun to ring. A brown-haired child had been sighted crying in a restaurant in Yuma; a little girl was seen struggling with a man in a truck in Barstow. Strong leads, weak and crazy leads, plenty of dead ends, and even a couple of calls saying David Cabot was just getting what he deserved. Walt Gary was convinced that David's defense of Frank Filmore, the rock through the window, and Bailey's abduction were all related.

Dana sensed Gary did not approve of David defending Frank Filmore. Well, neither did she. Some days she was so angry with him she had to leave the room to keep from blurting what she thought, that it was *his* fault Bailey was gone.

Police, sheriffs, and the highway patrol were on the lookout for a white van like the one that had run over Moby Doby. One had been seen in the neighborhood right after Bailey disappeared, but there were tens of thousands of white vans in San Diego County. The rock and the note attached to it had been examined and yielded information Gary called valuable. The rock was of a sort most commonly found in the Sweetwater River bed; the note had been written on the kind of cheap paper used by schools and churches and for bulk mailings.

From a friend, an attorney with a brother in the sheriff's department, Dana and David learned that for several months officers in the area of the Sweetwater School District had been watching an elementary school teacher about whom a parent had made a complaint. The accusation of abuse had proved to be a malicious response to a child's poor grade, but the authorities weren't quite convinced. *Probably another dead end, but don't give up hope, Mrs. Cabot.*

Dana thought hope wasn't all it was cracked up to be. Sometimes it was harder to fight against it than for it.

The operator asked, "Do you want to leave a message?"

Tell him and the other police officers not to abandon Bailey just because her father is defending Frank Filmore. They should not hold the father's job against the little girl. "No. Thank you." She had no more to say to him than he to her.

She keyed in David's number and waited for someone in the office to answer, drumming her bitten-down nails on the steering wheel.

Barbara, the firm's receptionist, said, "Cabot and Klinger, Attorneys for the Defense."

That was new. Probably Marcus's idea. She asked for David.

"He's in court, Dana. Can I take a message?"

He was always in court; he was only happy in court these days.

The unstoppable memories rolled over Dana as if something in her wanted to be more miserable than she already was.

When she met David Cabot he was only nineteen but already a star in the world of college sports. A hustling quarterback tall enough to see over the line to his receivers, a basketball player, and a better than average third baseman. She never got tired of watching him throw a ball or catch one. She saw that more than anything else games were fun for him; the joy he got from competition lifted him and gave him wings. And the miracle was, he loved her and lifted her with him. He had seen not a quiet, studious girl with a crummy wardrobe and only two pairs of shoes, not Margaret Bowen's abandoned daughter or Imogene's unwanted grandchild. He had seen straight through to the heart of who she really was, the laughter in her, the courage, the dogged determination to succeed that perfectly matched his own.

Sitting in the parking lot with time on her hands and resting on her shoulders like a bag of cement, she tried to remember what that love had felt like. She thought of a story she had read to Bailey about a train making it over a steep mountain, thinking it could, it could, it could, and then it did. If only she could apply her will and think herself back to the way it had been just a few months ago. But love and trust and loyalty were not cars behind a locomotive. No matter how much she wanted to make things better, there was nothing she could do.

Just as well David was not in his office because a part of her mind knew the sound of his voice would only irritate her. It was so clearly no longer the voice of the boy who loved games for the sake of the play. The boy had vanished beneath layers of ambition and professional pride. Bailey's disappearance had smothered the last of him entirely.

No message, she told Barb, and put her cell phone away.

She envied David being overworked and stressed for time. All her days were empty. There were things she should do but nothing she wanted to do, and so she did nothing. She sat and stared out the front window; she lay in bed and stared at the ceiling. She sat through terrible movies she forgot the instant she stepped out of the dark and into the sunlight. Since May she had lost fourteen pounds. Levi's that had been snug and sexy hung on her hips like a punk's. Once she had loved food, loved cooking and serving; and even cleaning up had never been the grind for her that it was for some. But the kitchen had become no more than a room she walked through on the way in or out of the house. She had stopped making coffee and instead drank hot water from the tap or drove twelve blocks to Bella Luna, where the barista comped her cappuccinos and avoided her eyes.

She turned the key in the ignition and backed the big SUV around the tail end of the church sextant's rusty old Beetle and out onto the street.

She would take a nap; a nap was always a worthy option, since at night she rarely slept more than three or four hours. David was just as bad. Closed within their individual cells of fear and guilt, they were awake at four A.M. in their own silent corners of the house. Dana had begun to knit during the dark hours. She knit stocking-stitch rectangles in shades of lime and pink. The rectangles were all sizes and done on several different pairs of needles. Whatever suited her from night to night, and of no practical use at all except to occupy her hands. She did not know what David did in his wakefulness. Played solitaire perhaps or went on-line.

Despite his sleeplessness he bounded out of bed at five-thirty, ran four times around the park with Moby at his heels, and left for the office before seven. Sometimes he slept in the living room and she did not hear him leave, showered, shaved, and dressed in one of his beautiful suits. She knew he was eager to escape the house. Lexy said he filled up his life with work so there would be no room to think about Bailey. Dana believed he loved Bailey less than she did. It would take more than a job to make Dana forget their daughter.

At a stop sign she let the car idle longer than necessary as she watched a pair of girls in Arcadia School uniforms. They crossed the street, ignoring the 4Run-

ner, and ambled up the sidewalk with their heads together, laughing.

She wished they had been taken instead of Bailey.

She turned onto Miranda Street, looking ahead to
her house, fourth from the corner. There was someone
sitting on the front steps.

Chapter 11

An hour later Dana barged into Dr. Wren's office with Bailey in her arms.

The receptionist stood up, looking alarmed. "You can't come in without an appointment. If you have an emergency you need to see the doctor on call."

"It's not an emergency. It's a miracle!" Dana cried as she pushed through the door to the inner office.

Before the receptionist could do anything, Dr. Wren's nurse appeared around the corner, saw Bailey, and screamed. Dana began to laugh and then to cry as the office staff converged at the front desk, all of them either laughing or crying, all of them wanting to hug Dana and Bailey. Dr. Wren invited Bailey into an examining room immediately, where he checked her for external signs of abuse or injury, weighed her, and found that she had actually gained a pound during her absence.

"As far as I can tell," he said in his quiet, gentle voice, "Bailey is in fine condition." He grinned at her. "Roses in her cheeks."

"Thank God," Dana said and hugged Bailey tighter.

"There is one thing, of course. It's difficult . . ." The

thoughtful lines between his eyebrows deepened. "Would you like me to do an internal exam?"

"No," Dana said quickly. She would be able to tell if her daughter had been sexually abused.

"If you change your mind—"

"I won't."

"Well, let me know if I can be of help." Dr. Wren walked them out to the waiting room. At the door, he kissed Bailey's forehead. "Welcome home, little angel."

She had seemed perfectly healthy, but she had changed. She was subdued and watchful.

Little silent angel.

When the media learned of Bailey's return the public outpouring of love overwhelmed Dana and David. Cards and flowers from friends and strangers, toys for Bailey, gifts of potted plants, and from someone they didn't know a dreadful pink plaster statue of a cherub that Dana put out in the garden hoping it would only last a season. Occasionally strangers knocked at the front door. Dana thought there was something ghoulish in their eagerness to see Bailey, and she learned to ignore the doorbell unless she recognized the car at the curb. Once or twice a white van drove by slowly. Behind the smoked windows she thought she saw two heads but could not be sure. Nor could she tell if there was a bumper sticker on the back driver's side. She told Lieutenant Gary anyway.

The policeman wanted Bailey to be examined by a doctor to determine if she had been molested.

"I'll find out myself," Dana said.

"Begging your pardon, but you're not a professional, Dana. You won't be able to tell."

"Don't be ridiculous. I'm her mother."

Gary also wanted Bailey to speak with a psychologist to get her to name her abductor and describe him or the place where she was taken. Dana was opposed to this too, and at first David supported her.

At night they lay in bed, their faces inches apart, and whispered that they wanted to put the whole nightmare as far behind them as possible.

One evening after supper Dana took Bailey into the bath with her. In a tub full of warm water and clouds of grapefruit-scented suds, she soaped her daughter's body, pausing to enjoy the pleasure of her silken skin, the feel of slender arms and legs under her hands. Dana had feared she would never see her again, and when she touched her now, it was as if the world had been made new. Bailey was bony and straight, with valiant little squared-off shoulders, and her skin was the warm, dark color of eucalyptus honey except where her bottom had been covered by shorts or underwear. Though she had not lost weight during her months away—had, in fact, gained a pound—she had grown taller, causing her knees and elbows to lose their pillows of flesh, and when Dana ran her hands up Bailey's side, her daughter's ribs felt like a xylophone.

"Stand up, Bailey."

She was a water sprite with two new teeth, huge, unblinking brown eyes, and hair made dark by the water, plastered against her head, dripping down her face.

"I need to look at you, Bailey. I need to touch your private places." The moment was delicate as old parchment. One careless touch and all would crumble. "May I do that, Bailey?"

Bailey blinked and nodded once.

"And you must tell me, just nod your head, did any-one hurt you, Bailey, while you were gone?" It was not a matter of being gentle; the question itself was an assault.

Bailey blinked and looked at Moby standing guard at the bathroom door.

Dana rested her hands at her daughter's waist, the butterfly bones where her hips would be. She smoothed a hand across the pout of her tummy and kissed her belly button, this place where they had been connected for nine months. Bailey had swum in the waters of Dana's womb, rocked and jollied there like a dolphin baby. She had been warm and secure in the dark one moment and then expelled into the glare of an electric sun, hung by her heels and slammed by sound. And then in May it had happened again. Someone had ripped her from the home where she knew only warmth and love. She had been dragged off and forced into a strange van. It was too easy to imagine Bailey's fear. If her kidnapper had done more than steal her, Dana almost did not want to know.

But she had to know.

At eye level Bailey's labia was innocent and tender as a folded rose, as sweet as anything Dana had ever seen. She thought of a man's hands resting where hers did now, the heel of her hand on the small mons, and a sob choked her and she forced it to the back of her throat.

A man with bright white hair and starched black eyebrows had lived alone three houses down from Imogene and Dana. He gave the children of the neighborhood generous treats at Halloween, and one October he said his house was haunted and dared the kids to come inside. Dana took the dare first. The place did not scare her at all, but something in that house must have frightened some little girl, because right after Halloween there was a furor up and down the street and a policeman came to the house and stood in the kitchen talking to Imogene. He asked Dana questions, and she thought he had a mean voice so she was not very cooperative. Then Imogene stepped in, angry with her, saying she was *as stubborn as your mother.* Eventually Imogene took her to a doctor, and Dana was made to undress and put on a voluminous cotton gown. She lay on a table and the doctor told her to stop shaking and open her knees, but she couldn't or just as likely wouldn't, so the nurse and Imogene held them so far apart Dana thought she would split in two.

No one would force Bailey to do anything.

Bailey stood in the tub, and Dana asked her to turn around. The only marks on her body were a scab on the knee and another on her elbow. Ordinary kid scrapes. No rope burns or bruises.

Dana's hands slipped down to Bailey's thighs and gently, barely, parted her legs. As she soaped her, she keyed her senses for a flinch or shudder; just the ripple of a muscle beneath her hands might indicate a tender spot. But Bailey let herself be washed as she had done all her life, without shame or apprehension, with heartbreaking trust and perfect innocence.

"Turn around, sweetheart."

Dana ran her soapy hands down Bailey's back, along the straight knobbed spine, feeling each bone as if she suspected the crime against her daughter might even be this, the theft of a vertebrae. She spread Bailey's buttocks so she could see the dark pink circle of her anus, and again her child submitted without shying. No bruises, no tears. Dana drew her down onto her lap in the water, holding her tight against her breasts, trembling with relief as the water sloshed about them.

* * *

For several days after Bailey's return Dana kept her indoors. David spoke to the press gathered around the front steps, holding his daughter in his arms. Reporters asked him how Mrs. Cabot was holding up and wasn't she thrilled to have Bailey back.

"Say I'm an emotional wreck," Dana told David, laughing as she prodded him toward the front door. "Tell them I'm dead-drunk with joy."

She watched the scene from a window.

A female reporter put a microphone in front of Bailey and asked, "How's it feel to be back with your mommy and daddy, Bailey?"

Bailey hid her head against David's shoulder.

David did not say that though Bailey was healthy, eating and sleeping well, watching her old favorite videos and hanging her arms around Moby's neck whenever the dog would let her, she had not spoken a word since Dana found her on the steps.

The blonde asked David, "Is she all right? Have you had her examined by doctors?"

"She's seen the family doctor and she's fine. We're all happy and relieved to have our girl back with us."

Another reporter shoved a microphone in David's face and asked, "Do you think Bailey's kidnapping's connected to the Frank Filmore case?"

"I really couldn't say." David looked behind him at Lieutenant Gary. "You'll have to talk to the police about that."

Gary stepped forward. "It does seem pretty clear that the crime was part of a pattern of harassment designed to intimidate Frank Filmore's defense team. The fact that Bailey appears to be unharmed supports our theory."

"Do you have any leads?" the blonde asked.

"I can guarantee it's only a matter of time until we get whoever's responsible."

A matter of time. It could take the rest of Dana's life and make little difference to her. Bailey was home, Bailey was safe, and nothing else mattered. She wondered why she did not feel the need for revenge expressed by almost everyone she spoke to. For a week the letters in the newspaper had been about catching the perp and making him *pay.* She remembered that when she taught school she had always liked the look of a clean white board on Monday mornings. The blank surface and the morning faces of the children had encouraged her and suggested wonderful possibilities for the week ahead. If Dana had spoken to the press, she would have said, "Leave us alone. Let us get a fresh start on our life."

Ten days after Bailey's return St. Tom's hosted a gala luncheon in the undercroft following the Sunday service, where Lexy preached eloquently about gratitude and grace and the choir sang Dana's favorite hymn, the words, *Joyful, joyful, we adore thee, God of glory, Lord of love,* ringing loud in the little old church. The Sunday school had decorated the undercroft with pink and lime crepe paper, balloons and streamers—Bailey Cabot's signature colors. Above a long table dressed in linen and crowded with dishes of food, hugely enlarged photos of Bailey smiled down as people loaded their plates with Konnie's Mexican casserole and Mrs. Lindley's homemade peach pie. Others pressed in around the old oak upright piano that served the Sunday school classes and sang along as Imogene—David said they had to include her in the celebration—played rousing hymns. *I sing a song of the saints of God, patient and brave and true.* Dana tried to enjoy the occasion, but she was only going through the motions, as if anesthetized. The undercroft would always remind her of the Bailey Committee and three months of desperate days.

The guests drank a champagne toast to Bailey and then one to Dana and David and a third to the committee for its hard work. Dana wondered if she was the only person at the party who remembered it was nothing the committee did that brought Bailey home. She had been returned for reasons none of them would ever understand, though everyone had a theory. Dana believed the kidnapper felt remorse and shame and wanted to undo his crime.

"Where's Jason?" she asked Beth. "He did so much for the committee, I want to thank him."

Beth beamed with pride. "He's working in the kitchen, didn't want to come out. He'd be so pleased if you went in and said something."

"Of course I will."

"He's got a bit of a crush on you, I think."

She found Jason and another boy on the edge of the parking lot behind the kitchen. Three white vans nosed into the diagonal spaces not twenty feet from him. Each had bumper stickers. She did her best to ignore the alarm that clicked on in the pit of her stomach. David was right, she was becoming paranoid about white vans; if she reported every one she saw to Gary, he would dismiss her as a flake. Jason hid his cigarette behind his back when he saw her.

"I don't care if you smoke, Jason," she said. "I just want to thank you so much for everything you did, all those flyers and posters. I wish you'd come in and see Bailey."

He bobbed his head, took his baseball cap off, smoothed his hair, and put it on again. "Nah."

A piece of cherry licorice dangled from the mouth of the boy beside him. He kicked Jason in the shin.

Jason said, "This is Bender." Another gawky boy with bad skin and baggy clothes. "He helped too."

"Then why don't you both come inside? My husband would like to meet you both and thank you."

"Not me," Bender said.

Jason's shoulders squirmed.

Their shyness touched Dana at the same time she found it mildly irritating. "Shall I bring him out here, then?"

"We gotta go." Jason's cheeks were the color of the licorice vine.

"You're sure?"

Jason dropped his cigarette and ground it under the toe of his Dr. Martens.

"We're cool," Bender said.

As Dana turned to go back into the kitchen, Bender said, "Your husband, when they get the guy, he gonna be his lawyer?"

Dana took a second to untangle Bender's syntax. "No. That would be called a conflict of interest."

"But he's that other guy's lawyer, the one did the little girl."

Did. The way Bender used the word freighted it with ugly meaning.

"David's defending Frank Filmore because it's his job. He's a defense attorney. It's nothing personal."

Bender shoved the licorice deeper into his mouth. "I don't get how he can do that."

Jason said, "You won't tell my grandma I was smoking?"

"No, Jason," she said, laying her hand against his cheek and ignoring Bender. "Not a word."

* * *

That evening, as they moved through the house, closing it down for the night, Dana told David about her conversation.

"What kind of a name is that? Bender?"

She shrugged. "Don't ask me. He was a creep."

"So's Jason."

"No, he's not. He's just gawky and awkward." Dana twisted the front-door lock. "Plus, Beth says he's got a crush on me, which explains why he can barely put two words together when I'm around." She looked behind her. David had dropped onto the couch in the dark living room. "Come to bed," she said and held out her hand.

"God, I'm glad that thing's over." He patted the cushion beside him. "I hope everyone's just going to ignore us from now on. Let us get back to ordinary."

She sat next to him. "You seemed to be enjoying yourself."

"Yeah, well, Bay wasn't. If I'd let her, she'd of cut and run. You notice how she sort of zones out?"

"It'll pass," Dana said.

They were silent for a few moments.

"Maybe Gary's right. Maybe we should get her to talk to someone."

"Talk?"

"I mean someone who'd make her talk."

"Hasn't she suffered enough? You want to make it worse?"

The radio was on, tuned to a classical station. Bach, Dana thought. Orderly music for a more orderly time.

"If I hadn't taken the Filmore case it never would have happened."

David was probably right, but she told him he wasn't. It was the same when he had a bad game. The quarterback's wife never mentioned the slow footwork, the wobbly passes or fumbled snaps.

"It was my fault," she said. "I shouldn't have let her out of my sight. She was too excited. I shouldn't have trusted her alone."

"When I was in law school Gracie and I used to talk about the risks a defense attorney has to take. Back then it sounded kind of exciting. When you're young you don't think about how everything changes if you have a kid."

"You do good work, David; you know you do. Think about that boy last year; he would have gone to prison for something he didn't do—"

"Shit, Dana, he was guilty."

"Well, even so, it was his first offense. He didn't deserve to go to prison."

"Youth Authority can be just as bad."

She put her arms around him. "Don't be so down on yourself. You're a good man and a good attorney. Even someone like Filmore deserves a fair trial."

He lay back on the couch, drawing her down beside him. "I love you, Danita."

"Don't call me that." She remembered Micah using her full name.

"DanitaDanitaDanita." He pulled her closer. "Kiss me and I'll shut up."

Bailey's abduction had driven Micah from her mind. Now all at once he seemed to be standing in the room with them, leaning against the doorjamb, watching David tug down the zipper of her slacks and slip his hand down the front of her panties.

She pulled away. "I'm tired, David. Let's go to bed."

"Come on, Dana. I miss you."

"I know. I miss you too. But I just can't do it yet."

He groaned and sat up. Resting his elbows on his knees, he ran his fingers back through his hair. She was surprised by how much gray there was.

"It's been weeks."

"Don't guilt-trip me. Please."

He said, "When Bailey was gone it made sense. I got that. But she's back now. We've got our life back. We should be fucking our brains out to celebrate."

"I just need a little more time." She stood up and zipped her pants. Her body ached with fatigue that ran clear through to her bones. She doubted she had the energy to climb the stairs to bed. "I'm not ready."

"Sometimes I feel like . . . What's happening, Dana? Where've you gone? Where's Number One?"

She looked down at him from halfway up the stairs and told the truth. "I don't know."

Chapter 12

In David's oversized office chair, Marsha Filmore looked like Alice after too many bites of the cookie.

"I'm sorry," David said as he stowed his briefcase in the well of his desk. "I didn't mean to keep you waiting."

He had been in court all morning on a too-good-to-be-true personal injury case involving a child, a crossing guard, and a San Diego Gas and Electric truck. David would have liked a break for lunch between court and this interview, but Judge Wellman had started late, as he often did. Hungover, from the look of his trembling hands, he had embarrassed everyone while he figured out where he was and why. Incompetence and irresponsibility heated up David's stomach acid and made him want to punch someone. Not the best time to see Marsha Filmore.

"I don't know why I'm here at all," she complained. "Frank says I've talked to you enough already."

David sat down and pressed a button on his phone. "Barb, ask Allison and Gracie to come in, will you?"

"I have a doctor's appointment."

Marsha put her long, bony hands over her stomach.

Behind the big knuckle of her ring finger she wore a plain gold band and a diamond solitaire so big David would have guessed it was a good fake if Filmore had not declared it among his assets.

"In an hour."

David smiled in a way that made his jaw ache. "No problem."

"I'll have to get a taxi," she said. "There are never any taxis in San Diego. It's such a burg."

"We'll take care of you, Marsha. When's the baby due?" He did not want to begin the serious questions without Gracie and Allison. "I should remember, but—"

"Men never remember," she said and suddenly became disconcertingly chatty as if his question had flipped her animation switch. "Last week I went to see Frank, and he acted like he didn't even know I was expecting. He's so smart, but he forgets the little things." She smoothed her hands over her stomach. "Six weeks. Six weeks to go."

"You're feeling okay? Everything going okay?"

She gawked at him. "Oh, yeah, sure. Dandy as candy."

David felt a rush of dislike as powerful as it was sudden. His inability to warm to her, to feel even vaguely empathic, reminded him of his father's attitude toward the men he sentenced. Since David was ten and began spending the school year with his aunt and uncle in Texas, he had made a hero of his uncle and trained himself to be like him; but unwanted aspects of Claybourne Cabot still crept into his personality like enemy mercenaries nosing under the tent. The judge would have hated Marsha Filmore. His uncle would have recommended tolerance and reminded David that he could not guess what hells Marsha Filmore had walked through.

In the big wing chair—David wanted his clients and visitors comfortable, because comfortable people were more likely to speak freely—Marsha Filmore did not look like the competent businesswoman she had been before her husband's arrest. A few months ago this lank-haired, skinny little woman smelling of nicotine and hairspray had been chief accountant for a chain of local drugstores. David wondered which woman was the real Marsha Filmore, the mouse or the manager.

The office door opened, and Gracie stepped in wearing a tiny, tight skirt and very high heels. David smiled.

"Afternoon, Boss." Blond, bouncy Allison followed her, similarly dressed. David thought, *Thank God for pretty women.* He said, "Let's get started. When we finish, Allison, you go down with Marsha, help her get a cab."

"Right, Boss."

Since the days he had quarterbacked the Pinewood High School Patriots, Boss had been his nickname, one he encouraged.

He glanced at the notes he had written that morning at just after six A.M. in anticipation of this interview. Despite multiple interrogations, he could not shake the sense that there was more he should know about Frank and Marsha Filmore. The prosecutor, Les Peluso, would leave nothing to chance.

"I know this is repetitive, Marsha, and going over the same ground can seem—"

"Pointless. I've told you everything I know. Frank didn't do it. He never would do such a thing." She squirmed in the big chair. "He is a very smart man, you know. Probably smarter than all of you combined."

Gracie said gently, "Just tell us again about that morning."

"He's not a monster."

"Of course not," Gracie said and laid her large hand on Marsha's forearm.

Marsha shook it off. "I was in the supermarket the other day, and a woman saw me, recognized me from the television. I'm going to have to move. Out of town. Everyone knows me. I'm like a pariah. What about my baby?"

This was the fourth time David had interviewed Marsha Filmore, and at each meeting she seemed more rattled and uncertain.

"You don't have to worry about your baby," David said. "Your baby's going to be fine, and we'll get you somewhere to live."

"There's nowhere I can go where I'm not recognized. If I went to the movies no one'd watch the show."

Gracie said, "Tell us again what happened that morning."

Marsha cupped her palms over her face, her fingertips pressing on her eyelids. "Oh, all right. I was talking to Sandra Calhoun, hanging over the fence and laughing." She made a sound into her hands that was half laugh, half sob. "You go your whole life and you laugh all the time and you never think about it, and then you realize . . . Last night I tried to watch a Robin Williams video, that one where he's in Vietnam? I barely even smiled."

"What were you and Sandra laughing about?"

"How should I know? Jesus, the questions you ask. Something about Mexico, I think. About when Frank and I lived down in Rosarito Beach."

David thought he saw Gracie's pupils widen.

"When was that, Marsha?" she asked.

"God, years ago. In the early nineties."

"How long did you live there?"

"Why? What do you care about Mexico?"

David leaned forward a little. "I always thought it might be cool to live in Mexico," he interjected. "Commute to San Diego. 'Course the line at the border would drive me crazy, but I guess it wasn't so bad back in the nineties. What took you down there?"

"We lived there. I told you."

Expectancy feathered up behind David's ribs.

"It's gotta be cheaper than here," Gracie said.

"We had a little house on the beach." The chatty switch clicked on again. "It was a good life. We had plenty of room and a nice, safe, fenced yard."

"You had a dog, huh?"

"Oh no, never. Frank hates animals."

Her hands fluttered, and she smiled like a girl on prom night. "The best thing was the help we could afford. Frank had a man to drive him to the border every day—traffic irritates him. A man of his intelligence couldn't be expected to cope with that confusion every day. I had a live-in maid to help me with—" Marsha stopped, looked at David, and then down at her watch. A jewel-studded Rolex. "If I miss my appointment the doctor makes me pay anyway."

"It must have been great," David said, "having live-in help with the baby."

From the corner of his eye David saw Allison's hand pause over her laptop. Marsha was silent.

"You said you had a live-in to take care of the baby."

"No, I didn't. I never said that."

David laughed. "I think I need my ears checked."

Gracie said, "So you were talking to Sandra Calhoun that morning. Then what?"

David turned his chair enough to see out the square office window behind his desk. He used to have an unobstructed view of the bay and Coronado Island, but in recent years construction in the part of town called Little Italy had filled up most of the gaps between the old two- and three-story buildings, the mom-and-pops left over from the days when San Diego was a navy town. On a typical day he could count three construction cranes and a half dozen condominium and office buildings in progress. He liked the urban view and the feel of being at the center of a city that was doing something, going somewhere.

If there was a baby in Mexico, where was it now?

He listened as Gracie continued to question Marsha Filmore and made a mental note to send her flowers for stepping in and giving him a chance to gather his thoughts. Against the background of the women's voices—Gracie's low and smooth like a deep river and Marsha's like shallow rapids—he let his thoughts drift.

He was certain Marsha had been about to tell them she had a Mexican maid to help with a baby. When she denied it she looked caught. Yet Frank had made a big thing about the expected baby being their longed-for first.

As she was leaving the office Marsha Filmore said, "I read in *People* magazine you got your daughter back. I saw the picture. Do they know who took her?"

Bailey wasn't a subject he wanted to discuss with this woman.

She stopped at the door. "Why do people—men— do things like they do?" Her eyes lost focus for a moment. "The man who took your little girl, did he hurt her? Did he violate her?"

Gracie said quickly, "Taxis are tough to get in this town. Allison?" She practically shoved Marsha forward.

Marsha shook her off. "You bring a baby into the world now, you take such a chance."

Gracie held Marsha by the upper arm and steered her out of the office. When the door closed behind them, David sank back into his chair and closed his eyes. He felt his eyelids trembling.

Chapter 13

Dana wondered if the sharks in the tanks at the Birch Aquarium knew they were swimming in a sea the size of a backyard pool. What went on in their brains and nervous systems? A kind god would have created them without a sense of space and time.

The Birch Aquarium, part of the Scripps Institute of Oceanography north of La Jolla, is a strikingly handsome building perched on a bluff overlooking the northern portion of La Jolla Shores Beach. On a Wednesday in early October the crowd was thin, just a few tourists enjoying the hot fall weather, nannies and mothers pushing strollers the size of whales, a noisy school of preadolescents led and lectured to by a teacher wearing shorts and a tank top.

Dana and Bailey had visited the library the day before; and as they had done prior to Bailey's disappearance, they spread the fish books on the table open to the full-color pictures. Dana had turned the Technicolor pages slowly, pointing out fish she knew anything about, commenting on all the colors, hoping for some sign of interest, waiting for a smile.

In the first days after her return, Dana had not been

deeply troubled by Bailey's lack of speech and her flat-line emotions. The shock to the little girl's system had been seismic, and Dana reasoned it would take time for her happy nature to recover itself. But Bailey had been home more than three weeks now, and there had been no improvement. She still watched Dana and David with disconcerting intensity. Her lethargy was pervasive; even pictures of predatory eels failed to kindle a response from her. Gone entirely was the mania that had once singed Dana's nerve endings. Bailey no longer airplaned from room to room caroling her favorite words: *smellybellyjelly, stinkypinky.* These days she clung to Dana or sat pressed against her or lay on her bed or in front of a video sucking her thumb. And never spoke.

In the aquarium they stood before a vast glass tank where sequoias of kelp grew up from the bottom and swayed in the artificially created swells. In and out, like birds through a forest, the popeyed fish glided, kissing the water. Dana recognized the groupers, fat brown gentlemen and ladies of substance and propriety, and their gaudy cousins, the golden Garibaldi damselfish. But the small fish she could not name were her favorites, the darters and jerkers that flashed by in a blaze of electric blue, yellow, and scarlet.

Dana crouched beside Bailey and told her about the time she and David snorkeled in Hawaii and schools of tiny fish nibbled frozen peas from between her fingers.

At the end of the story, Bailey held up her arms. *Carry me,* her eyes said.

"Ask me, Bay. Say the words."

Bailey stood on tiptoe, her slender arms outstretched, making soft animal noises at the back of her throat.

Dana wanted to sob with frustration. She did not know who irritated her more, the other visitors to the aquarium watching them with sideways glances, or herself for having thought the excursion could be anything other than an ordeal. She was sick of Bailey's silence and her neediness. Instantly, she cut off the thought. She would not allow herself to be upset with her daughter. To do so would be to risk losing her again. David called this magical thinking, but she believed it anyway.

Dana suggested they leave the aquarium and drive down to the beach. "I brought our swimming suits."

No response.

There was nothing wrong with Bailey's hearing. She came when she was called, she turned at sudden noises. But in reaction to her abduction some part of her had shut down, and now that she was home she would not or could not turn it back on. As Dana read books on voluntary mutism, she told herself that eventually her daughter would speak again; they must all be patient. Lieutenant Gary admired her tolerance but still urged her to send Bailey to a child psychologist. David had begun to think it was a good idea as well, and Lexy had given him the name of a psychiatrist experienced with traumatized children. Everyone had an opinion of what was right for Bailey.

Dana pulled into a parking place at La Jolla Shores and unloaded the car. She handed Bailey a towel, bucket, and shovel to carry.

"Mommy's got lunch and the chairs." Plus the umbrella and a backpack full of beach miscellany.

These days David was much too busy for the beach. He claimed he missed family time, but Dana knew he thrived on the demands of his work. The pressure of a coming trial made him feel alive, as he had on game days.

The reporter from *People* wanted to do a happy ending follow-up to his earlier abduction article that had focused as much on the Filmore case and the perils of being a defense attorney as on Bailey herself. Dana had been against the interview, but David said it would be good for business. To coax a smile from Bailey the photographer had clowned and courted her. But she would not satisfy the public hunger for simple solutions, and Dana felt perversely proud of her daughter showing the world that for a stolen child and her family there was no such thing as happily ever after.

Having given up on Bailey, the reporter spoke mostly to David, who had said all the right things, remembered to thank the Bailey Committee, the police, all the kind folks who had come forward to offer their good services. Dana had been too numb to do more than nod through the interview. Obviously the reporter had expected her to bubble with relief and joy, as if three months of terror could be cast aside like a frumpy coat.

Later she wished she had just told the reporter the truth. Perhaps he would have printed it, and then people might have understood what it meant to lose and regain a child, how it changed everything. David's hair was grayer. Dana's body had become stiff and awkward. She could no longer run without feeling as if her arms and legs might fly out in opposite directions unless she exerted extreme control. She felt conspicuous in public; and even if people in line at the bank, the grocery store, at Bella Luna, and the Birch Aquarium did not recognize her or Bailey, it was enough that she imagined they did. On the beach in La Jolla she thought the bikini-clad girls and the couples walking hand in hand along the waterline must know and would later speak of having seen *that poor child and her mother.* She felt as if guilt had become the most obvious thing about her, what people would remember if they were introduced. *That beautiful child. Her mother should have taken better care of her.*

Dana had always been awkward in her skin. Time and experience had built her confidence; but since Bailey's return the old insecurity had reasserted itself. There was nowhere safe anymore. Moby had been run down in front of their home, a rock had shattered their front window. Bailey had been stolen from her own front yard.

What kind of a mother lets that happen?

They stopped at the showers to put on bathing suits. A few feet above the rickrack of seaweed that marked the waterline, Dana set up her beach chair, laid out Bailey's towel, and drove the base of the umbrella deep into the sand. She unbuckled Bailey's sandals and put them in the backpack. In a pink and green one-piece suit, her long legs stretched out before her, Bailey sat with her back to the surf, digging her heels into the hot sand. She had been suntanned to a golden brown when Dana discovered her sitting on the front porch. She still looked as if she had just returned from a tropical holiday. Gary said she had probably been taken to Mexico.

It made Dana physically ill to think of it. The murkiest corner of her nightmare had been that Bailey was taken out of the country into whatever hell awaited beautiful little girls with no one to protect them.

Dana unpacked a lunch of sandwiches and fruit and laid it out on a towel. "Want to get your feet wet before lunch?" Bailey was fearful in the water, but she liked to feel the tide suck the sand from under her feet. "Bailey?"

Dana looked toward the parking lot to see what had captured Bailey's attention. On that warm weekday in early October the beach was not crowded, so Dana had a clear view twenty meters to the low cement wall that divided the beach from the boardwalk and parking lot. In the lot, double-parked, was a white van.

You're paranoid. The city's full of white vans. But this was the one. Lurching to her feet, she ran toward the wall, barefoot across the scorching sand. On the wall a bronzed young man with a head of thick curly brown hair watched her run toward him.

The van pulled away. No bumper sticker and, she saw now, lettering across the back: MOBILE LOCKSMITH. And a number to call.

"Shit."

The young man laughed.

She stared at him.

"Sorry," she said.

He spoke to her. At first she thought his language was Italian, but then she realized he spoke Spanish. She felt like an idiot for running across the sand to stare at a van when there were thousands of them in the city. Swearing aloud. Talking to strangers. Leaving Bailey alone.

Dana held Bailey's hand as they waded through the curling foam. The breakers were low and easy, and the hot Indian summer weather had kept the ocean warm enough for swimming. Bailey stopped, planted her feet, and watched the retreating tide suck the sand away from her feet. She fell over, got up, and did it again. When they had waded out to where the water reached Bailey's waist, Dana tried to lift her up, but Bailey pushed her away and went a few steps farther, into deeper water. She turned her back to the waves, glanced over her shoulder, and then, at the perfect moment, raised her arms in front of her, lifted her feet, and rode the little wave a few feet to shore. Dana ran to her, expecting tears. Instead Bailey broke past her and ran back into the waves, lifting her knees high and clapping her hands.

Someone had taught her to bodysurf.

Chapter 14

"Someone taught her to bodysurf?" Lexy asked. "What kind of kidnapper does that?"

It was later the same day, and Dana and Bailey had met Lexy at Bella Luna. They sat at one of the round metal tables at the edge of the outdoor terrace but mostly hidden from the sidewalk and busy street by a hedge of red cape honeysuckle. The sky was a flawless Della Robbia blue, and Lexy's red hair flashed like polished copper.

At the other tables, the late-afternoon crowd getting its coffee fix was mostly men and women from the offices and shops up and down Goldfinch Street. Dana recognized the owner of the Avignon Shop giggling with a man wearing a backward baseball cap; and a few moments after they sat down, Rochelle dashed across from Arts and Letters, pausing at their table only long enough to say, "Watch the shop, darlings. The loo's out again."

The baristas at Bella Luna had made a fuss when they saw Bailey and concocted for her a chocolate drink topped with enough whipped cream to ski on. They invited her to stand on a stool behind the counter and help them serve customers. As Dana was about to thank them for the kind offer and make apologies for Bailey, her daughter astonished her by nodding her head. Yes, she wanted to help. As Dana talked to Lexy, she watched her daughter perched near the cash register. The barista handed Bailey the customer's receipt, and she handed it to the customer.

"This is the first time she's left me." Dana had a light, leafy feeling that was almost giddy. "Being at the beach helped her."

Every few moments Bailey came out from behind the counter as if to make sure Dana was still there, as if she did not trust her eyes alone but had to touch her mother's hands and stroke her hair before running off again.

On one of these occasions Lexy reached across the little table and lifted a lock of Bailey's sun-streaked, salt-stiff hair off her forehead. "You know how to swim, don't you?"

Bailey looked from Lexy to Dana and back. She nodded.

"Do you like swimming?"

Another affirmative nod accompanied by a wide smile. This was more communication from Bailey than since the kidnapping. Dana wished she were a ballerina. She would pirouette down Goldfinch Street.

"You had a good swimming teacher," Lexy said.

Bailey licked whipped cream off her upper lip.

"Can you remember your teacher's name?"

She looked at Dana and at Lexy, then ran back to the counter. Dana watched the barista lift her onto the stool and lay her hand on her head affectionately.

Lexy said, "One of these days I believe she's just going to open her mouth and start talking."

"The surf jarred her memory some way. It's like she's

got this combination lock inside and today something clicked."

Lexy nodded. "If he taught her to swim, don't you think she must have trusted him?"

It hadn't occurred to Dana that Bailey might have had a relationship with her kidnapper.

"How could she trust a man who'd steal her?"

"Three months is a long time in a little kid's life, Dana. And maybe it was a woman. Someone who wanted a daughter."

"Lieutenant Gary doesn't think so."

"Well, you know what I think, and you don't want to hear me say it again. But. She's got to see someone who knows how to question kids. She's ready to talk."

"I won't push her. She's been through enough."

"But if she's been sex—"

"I told you, that didn't happen."

"A professional—"

"She doesn't need a professional." Dana waved at Bailey and blew her a kiss. "You and Detective Gary are on the same side."

"It's not about taking sides." Lexy looked tired. "But don't you wonder who did it? Doesn't it alarm you that he's still out there?"

"Why do you think my pulse jumps every time I see a white van? Look, there's one at the end of the street. And it happened at the beach today. I got up and left Bailey alone—alone on the beach, for God's sake!— and it was just some locksmith."

"Oh, Dana."

Time to change the subject. Time to pretend we're normal people leading normal lives.

Normal was all Dana had ever wanted, to be like everyone else, like the cliques of blond girls at Bishop's School. She had believed when she was fifteen that such girls knew a secret she did not. It was a class thing, she finally decided. If your father had the right kind of job, if your mother only worked because she wanted to, if you took vacations in Hawaii and your grandmother took you to Europe the summer before high school, and if you got a convertible for graduation, then you knew the secret of feeling normal in your skin.

"What's up with you, Lexy? Let's talk about your life for a change."

"Well, mostly the same old stuff, but I did have dinner with Micah last night."

Dana had been telling herself that he had gone back to Italy.

"Mind you, I had to go over there and drag him out of his apartment. He was in one of his moods."

After Italy she had let Lexy think she and Micah did not like each other. She buried the truth in silence not because Lexy was a priest but because her friend's feelings about her brother were so possessive and protective.

"I told him he had to keep me company or I was going to go wacko." Lexy groaned, "I think I'm in burnout. I used to have enough energy for two women, but now I fall into bed and sleep like the dead and wake up just as tired as I was when I lay down. I tell my therapist I haven't got time for coffee breaks. She says I have to make time."

"Since when are you in therapy?"

"She's a clergy member up in Orange County. Lutheran, actually. Eleanor."

"How could I not know that?" Dana asked, feeling as if she had let Lexy down. "Why are you in therapy?"

Bailey appeared at Dana's elbow and rested her head against her shoulder for a moment. "Are you having a good time?" Dana asked her. "Do you want to sit on my lap now?"

She darted off, back to her friends behind the coffee bar.

"She's so beautiful," Lexy said, watching her. "But I worry . . ."

"We're talking about you. I know your problem. You don't have a life except St. Tom's. You've got to stop hiding behind that collar; it's not big enough."

Lexy sighed, tilting her head to the sun, letting her hair drop back like falling fire. "It's work, and it's Micah. And it's me. Mostly, lately, it's Micah."

Dana stared over Lexy's shoulder at the street where a white van with darkened windows was stopped at the light.

Lexy said, "When we were kids he'd have these spells. . . . He'd set his tent up out in the yard and sleep there, eat out there for days and days. No one ever told him to come inside. I think our folks forgot about him. Sometimes I'd go out and try to make him come inside and he wouldn't even talk to me. He loved me better than anyone, but he wouldn't say a word."

"You can't be responsible for everyone, Lexy. He's a grown man."

Lexy smiled. "Sometimes I forget you met him."

"Yes."

"I wish you two had gotten along."

Bailey scrambled onto Dana's lap, and she was grateful for something to hold on to.

"Maybe when he's feeling better I'll have you all to dinner. Try again, huh? You and David and Micah." She sighed and stood up. "Sometime when we have a whole afternoon I'd like to talk more about this. It'd do me good, but now's a bad time. I've got an appointment at

ECS in fifteen minutes." She straightened the lines of her forest green moleskin jumper. "And after Evening Prayer I've got to go by and see Dorothy Wilkerson. Do you know her?"

Dana remembered an upright little woman with a formidable jaw sitting rigid as a bookend in a back pew.

"She's a hundred and two years old, but she walked to church twice a week until five years ago. Last Easter she gave me her power of attorney, went to bed, and said she was finished, ready to die." Lexy swung her leather bag over her shoulder. "I expect every night to be her last, but come the dawn she wakes up and drinks a cup of black coffee, calls me on the phone, and says she's still alive. I'm never sure if she's glad or disappointed."

Dana would not live to be one hundred. Sometimes it was a stretch making it to the end of a conversation.

Dana sat with Bailey for another half hour, watching the traffic through the red flowers of the cape honeysuckle. At least six white vans went by. She tried not to think about Micah.

When David learned that Bailey could bodysurf he would say it was time she saw a psychiatrist. They would argue and go to bed angry again. He did not need to know. She would tell Lieutenant Gary instead.

She thought of the ways she continually failed people, those she loved the most, like David and Bailey and Lexy. There had never been a time when she had not been trying to be good. She had believed if she pleased people her reward would be a normal life. But the older she became the less sure she was that she would recognize normal if she ever got a chance to live it.

Micah had been strange from their first meeting, the

furthest thing from the normal she admired. He was
waiting in the little Florence air terminal when she stag-
gered off the plane, jet-lagged and stiff as a cheap shoe.
He waved and called out, and the sign he held with her
name written in huge Old English letters was like a
dozen fingers pointing at her. If it weren't for Lexy she
would have walked right by him. No one else had such
an ostentatious greeter. She did not like the way other
travelers smiled at his enthusiasm. He drove a car the
size of a telephone booth, a Mercedes of a variety never
dreamed of in Mission Hills. With her two bags jammed
behind the front seat, they flew through the outskirts of
Florence, creating three lanes of traffic on streets only
wide enough for two. In gridlocked intersections Micah
laid on his horn and stuck his head out the window,
yelling in flamboyant Italian.

When the sun inched around to their little table on
the terrace at Bella Luna, she and Bailey got up and
walked to the 4Runner parked around the corner. They
held hands; Dana thought she detected the hint of a
skip in Bailey's step.

She *was* getting better.

Dana had left the car windows down a few inches,
and the interior was cool when she opened the rear door
and fastened Bailey into her car seat. When she opened
her own door she saw a rock on the driver's seat with a
piece of paper around it, held in place with a rubber
band.

She jerked back as if she'd seen a snake. For a moment she stared at it, not quite able to believe what she
was looking at. She had thought with Bailey's return the
trouble was over. David and Gary had said she couldn't
count on that, but she had.

A scream came up from her stomach and twisted in
her throat. She ground her teeth together, held on to the

door frame, and told herself not to frighten Bailey. The street seemed suddenly, strangely empty.

She picked up the rock and pulled off the rubber band. The paper fluttered to the asphalt, and she stared down at it with raw eyes. Then she got in the car and slammed the door, jerked her seat belt across her chest, and turned the key in the ignition.

Roaring out of the parking place and down the street, she left on the pavement both the rock and the note with its cutout letters glued onto ordinary white paper. But she had seen the message and read it.

DON'T BE AFRAID. I LOVE YOU BOTH.

Chapter 15

Dorothy Wilkerson was one hundred and two years old and dying of exhaustion.

"Any changes?" Lexy asked Alana, the home nurse on duty.

"She told me this morning she'd had visitors in the night and I shouldn't be letting people into her room without her permission."

Lexy knew many old people near death had night visitors, some friendly and comforting, others threatening and dreaded. Two gentlemen had talked to Lexy's grandfather every night for several months before he died. When she asked him what they talked about, he said they explained things he needed to know. She had been small at the time and a little afraid of the old man with hairs sprouting from his nose. Now she wished she'd asked him what those things were.

"She called me a heathen." Alana, a graduate of San Diego's large Roman Catholic university, had married a Jordanian and converted to Islam. Her distinctive head scarf had given her away to cranky old Dorothy Wilkerson, who, despite her fractional eyesight, could see enough to make an insult stick.

"Other than having visions and being abusive, how's she doing?"

"She has incredible stamina, Lexy. And such will." Alana raised her eyes to heaven. "I know her joints give her pain, but she won't take anything. I think she's afraid of not thinking clearly. And I know she wants to tell you something."

"In that case," Lexy said, "in I go."

Alana touched her arm. "Allah is good."

"Amen to that, sister."

Though she was almost blind, Dorothy claimed to hear better than she ever had. Her muscles had atrophied to the point of being virtually useless, arthritis had cemented most of her joints, and osteoporosis had made her bones so brittle that if she turned over in bed she could break her hip, so she slept in a contraption that made it impossible to move without assistance. To a woman who in her youth had been a talented horsewoman and ocean swimmer, this confinement might as well have been a barbed-wire wrap.

She had the right to be curmudgeonly.

Dorothy's husband had left her sufficient money to be cared for at home in the same bedroom in which she had slept for seventy years. If one had to die alone and slowly, this room on the second story of a gracious old Craftsman at the edge of a pretty canyon, tree-shaded and, now, at twilight, full of the songs of birds, was not a bad place to do it. Someone had brought in a large, untidy bouquet of homegrown roses and put them on the table under the window. From across the room Lexy smelled their spicy-sweet fragrance.

She had sat at so many bedsides where the dying shared unpleasant quarters with strangers. Once, in such a place, the loud voices of two orderlies in the hall discussing the intimate details of their dates had interrupted her prayers. The noise continued until Lexy, at the end of her patience, charged out into the hall and with all her priestly authority reminded them that people were dying and if they didn't have respect for that, would they at least go outside so she wouldn't have to hear about their escapades.

A six-foot-tall redheaded female priest could kick a lot of butt when she wanted to.

"It's me, Dorothy." She pulled up a straight-backed chair and sat. "Lexy Neuhaus."

"I know who you are. I recognize your voice. Where've you been?"

"Evening Prayer."

She had been the only person at the short service. At the end of the day people wanted to be home with their families or off with friends. Solitude did not bother Lexy. She loved St. Tom's. From within its shadows and musty twilight she imagined she heard the murmur of old prayers and petitions. As she read aloud the names of the sick and dying, the travelers, the troubled and the weary, she tried to envision each person. That evening her favorite prayer of intercession had been chosen with Micah, Dana, David, and Bailey in mind.

Keep watch, dear Lord, with those who work, or watch, or weep this night, and give Thine angels charge of those who sleep. Tend the sick, Lord Christ; give rest to the weary, bless the dying, soothe the suffering, pity the afflicted, shield the joyous; and all for Thy love's sake.

She improvised a prayer for herself, asking God to help her overcome her anger, deal with loneliness, and take greater joy in her work. The priesthood was an isolating job. She had known that from the start.

"What are you thinking about?" Dorothy snapped.

"A family at St. Tom's, the Cabots. Their daughter was kidnapped."

"I don't pay you . . . to think about whoever they are."

"My dear, you don't pay me at all."

"You're . . . only here so I'll give money to the church."

"Wrong again, Dorothy. There are a few things money can't buy, and I'm one of them."

Women from the church came by every day and sat with Dorothy, but volunteers for the job were few because Dorothy was not a likable woman and probably never had been. At coffee hour a few Sundays back, Lexy had overheard someone say that it was well beyond time Dorothy Wilkerson died. The endowment needed her money, and one hundred and two was more years than anyone deserved. Lexy had flinched at the words. Sometimes the truth was too ugly to speak.

A tear made its slow way from Dorothy's eye down her crevassed face. Lexy pulled a tissue from the box on the bedside table and touched it to her cheek.

Dorothy winced and jerked her head aside. "Don't . . . put paper on my face." She lifted her hand a few inches off the blanket and wiggled her fingers. "In the dresser. Handkerchief."

In a cream-colored, quilted satin box lay four piles of ironed handkerchiefs of fine cotton and linen, lace-edged and embroidered.

"Oh my," Lexy said, "these are beautiful. I've never seen hankies like this. It seems a shame—"

Her phone vibrated against her hip.

"Nonsense," Dorothy croaked. "Bring me the . . . red poppies."

When Lexy laid the handkerchief on Dorothy's upturned palm, the old woman's fingertips skimmed the raised red embroidery as if reading Braille.

Lexy said, "I couldn't blow my nose on that. It's much too beautiful."

The vibrations stopped.

"When I was a girl we always had . . . like this. Now everything's paper . . . plastic." She lifted the handkerchief to her face, holding it a few inches from her eyes.

Lexy used the moment to glance at the printout on her phone. The call had been from Micah. Much as she wanted to talk to him, she could not leave Dorothy now.

"I sat . . . on Mother's bed and played with these. She had more . . . more beautiful." She lifted the red poppy-embroidered handkerchief an inch.

"Do you want your medication, Dorothy?" When there was no response, Lexy asked, "Do you want to tell me why you're crying?"

A single light on the table beside the bed cast an ashy golden glow across Dorothy's face. Lexy rested her hand on the pillow. She rarely urged medication on a dying person, believing that at the end of life pain was sometimes less important than the need to communicate with a clear mind.

Why had Micah called?

"Doctor Neuhaus . . ."

"I'm not a doctor, Dorothy. Call me Lexy."

"Reverend Neuhaus . . ."

Even when she was healthy Dorothy had not known what to call her female priest.

"I'm listening, Dorothy."

"Something . . ." Lexy saw her fingers twitch in agitation. Lexy held them gently. "I . . . Before I was married there was . . . a man . . ."

There was so often a man.

Lexy shut her eyes and focused Dorothy's image in her mind as she imagined that a narrow band of light connected the two of them. She felt the light pour into her palms and heat them.

"I'm here, Dorothy. I'm listening."

"I had . . . abortion. Mama took me . . . Kansas City, and then I married Forrest . . . never told him."

Most of the sins men and women carried with them all their lives were in the end so mundane; and yet, as the liturgy said, the burden of them was intolerable. Lexy felt a heavy sorrow pressing against her heart and lungs like a shadow-being filling her up inside. Dorothy probably thought she was the only person at St. Tom's with a dark story to tell, but Lexy knew everyone's secrets, and there were far worse tales. George Willits killed a child in Vietnam, and no amount of absolution could banish her face from his dreams. Another man made love to his sister until they went away to separate colleges, and he still yearned for her though he was married and a father several times over. A woman put a pillow over her suffering husband's face and held it there until he died. She felt guilty for not feeling guilty, for being glad she'd done it. Lexy had heard these stories whispered in her office, in the church; a confession of murder had come in a letter. Each case had deepened her understanding of what it meant to be a child of God. Dorothy's body was, ultimately, as disposable as one of the paper tissues she so despised. Despite age and illness, and no matter what tawdry things occurred in the course of a lifetime, the child of God remained unsullied.

In each of the unattractive, the grumpy, irrational, and difficult men and women she dealt with every day, Lexy tried to see that child of God within. This was central to all she believed; it was what enabled her to love and forgive the imperfect individuals around her. But love and forgiveness required a particular kind of emotional energy, supplies of which often ran low in her. She had learned to playact at such times and disliked herself for doing so.

Lexy settled Dorothy's hands on the coverlet. "None of it matters now."

"A boy . . . I believe . . . was . . . a boy."

"You don't have to be afraid or ashamed or worried. Your husband isn't angry with you, and God loves you just the same as the day you were born, just as much."

Lexy opened her prayer book to the Office of Reconciliation and read the reassuring old words. "Now there is rejoicing in Heaven, Dorothy; for you were lost, and are found; you were dead, and are now alive in Christ Jesus our Lord. Abide in peace. The Lord has put away all your sins."

After that Dorothy seemed to sleep awhile. In the dark room smelling of roses and medicine and old age, Lexy closed her eyes. She doubted she had said and done enough to ease Dorothy's guilt and agitation. At this most mysterious and important time in her one hundred and two years, Dorothy deserved a priest who was wiser than Lexy, more loving, more deeply and profoundly faithful. The needs of people were so many and so great, and by comparison, her gifts were so puny and unreliable. What the world needed was saints, men and women with unshakeable convictions and a genius for giving of themselves. And what did the poor world get? Lexy Neuhaus and her coat of many flaws.

She wondered if she should leave now and call her brother.

Dorothy jerked awake suddenly, her faded blue eyes wide with alarm. "They were . . . here again."

Lexy remembered the nighttime visitors.

"Three of them." Dorothy looked at her right hand and raised three shaky fingers. "They have hats . . . big. With feathers."

Great. The Three Musketeers.

"They say . . . call . . . Ellen."

"Who is Ellen?"

Dorothy turned her head aside and muttered something.

"I didn't hear you, Dorothy."

"Daughter."

"Dorothy, you've told me so many times, you and your husband were—"

"I . . . lied."

Of course, Lexy thought and almost laughed. Everyone lies. About everything. Still, it was a surprise to hear Dorothy say it. She belonged to what Lexy thought of as a more honest generation. But that idea must be a myth, another lie. Perhaps everyone had always lied, when and as it pleased them.

"Where is she?"

"Del Mar." A beach suburb a few miles north.

"How long is it since you saw her?"

"I have . . . phone number."

On the pillow Dorothy's old head was small and fragile as a newborn's, but gray-skinned, the eye sockets deep and shadowy as those of a Halloween mask. It was as if her body, unable to die, had decided to implode. One day Lexy would come into this room and find Dorothy had vanished into herself.

"In . . . drawer there." Her cracked voice still managed to sound imperious. "Yellow sticky thing."

Among the pencils and bookmarks and bottles of aspirin and tubes of dried-up ointment, Lexy found a square of yellow paper with a name—Ellen Brownlee—and an 858 number written in a shaky hand.

"Tell her I'm . . . dying. . . ." A profound sigh rattled up from Dorothy's throat, and she began to weep.

"I'll talk to her," Lexy said. "I'll do it tonight."

As Lexy got up to leave, Dorothy became agitated. She shook her head rapidly from side to side, her mouth twisting into a grimace, and said something too softly for Lexy to hear, so Lexy moved closer to the bed and leaned in.

"I won't know what to do," Dorothy said, gasping. "Who will . . . help me? I want to do . . . right thing."

She was talking about death. And having performance anxiety. Suddenly Lexy felt swollen with love for Dorothy Wilkerson.

"You won't be alone," she said. "Christ will be there. He'll show you the way, Dorothy. You can hold out your hand and He'll take it."

"You . . . stay."

Lexy would have to miss the ten P.M. Pacific Beach AA meeting. She had been looking forward to it, needing it, but Dorothy was more important.

"Reverend?"

"Yes, Dorothy."

"Will it . . . hurt?"

Lexy blinked the tears from her eyes and put her lips near Dorothy's ear. Before speaking she took a moment to inhale the scent of old skin under the sweet fragrance of rose-scented powder, the smells of age and death and dying. It was important not to flinch from them.

"It will be a sweet thing, Dorothy." Lexy thought of Bailey Cabot sitting on the steps and Dana seeing her as she turned the corner. "It will be like returning home. At last."

*　*　*

When Lexy returned to her office she sat in her desk chair with her long legs on the windowsill. She had a bad feeling about calling Dorothy's daughter. Instead she called Micah, letting the phone ring twenty times before she disconnected. She sensed that he was in his apartment. Listening to the ring, knowing it was she, not answering.

She had too much on her mind to have to nursemaid her brother. He made her cross.

She had promised Dorothy she would call her daughter Ellen that night. This also made her cross; she wished she were in Bermuda at a five-star hotel.

On a particularly dark day the previous winter, Lexy had an attack of martyrdom and misspent the better part of a drizzly Sunday afternoon tallying up how many hours she worked each week, multiplied by fifty-two and divided into her salary. The result was an hourly wage pitifully low enough to gratify her sense that day of being overworked and underappreciated. The mood didn't last long. No one became a priest to make money, and she was hardly suffering.

She lived rent-free a block from the ocean in a condominium owned by the church. Her insurance premiums and retirement were paid; and she drove an almost new Japanese import, compliments of a parishioner who owned a car dealership.

And then there were all the immaterial things she could never reckon in terms of dollars and cents. Hers was often exciting work, rich in surprises and challenges, with very little that was routine. She spoke to people at their most needy and vulnerable—like the stranger who wandered in one day needing to talk about his son who had died in Iraq. Afterward she saw that she had helped him by listening without judgment. It was the promise of such unexpected encounters with the Holy Spirit that got her out of bed and onto her knees every morning; it was the lift of her heart when she held a baby over the baptismal font and claimed it as Christ's own forever.

And then there were the things she never wanted to do. Like call Ellen Brownlee.

She fished in her purse for the yellow paper and stared at the number written there. She put her hand on the telephone, then withdrew it, looked at her scarlet nails, at the dark, empty street. In a few weeks it would be Halloween, which meant a return to Standard Time. The world would seem colder as it turned toward the Advent season.

She heard her mother's voice in her head, the atonal western voice parched of emotion, the voice of empty spaces and immense skies, telling her to get on with her work and stop dilly-dallying. She wondered if her mother ever talked to anyone about her two youngest children, the odd ones who had left Wyoming and carved out lives so different from those she had chosen for them. Lexy imagined her telling people about her three strong Montana sons with handsome families and steady jobs. She probably never mentioned her other son, an artist, a peculiar, moody boy, and her daughter, who was of all things—a priest.

Lexy called the number on the yellow paper.

Ellen Brownlee's voice was clipped, without lilt or laughter.

"I'm Lexy Neuhaus, the priest at your mother's church, Ellen."

A pause.

"She asked me to call you."

"Okay."

"She's dying."

Another pause, and this time Lexy waited, listening to the buzz on the line.

"I thought maybe she'd gone already. She'll be a hundred and two next April."

"Actually she's a hundred and two now."

"No kidding." There was a moment of silence. "I thought I'd probably know if she was gone. I mean, isn't that what happens in movies? Someone dies and another person senses it?"

What Lexy sensed was that Ellen didn't know what to say.

"Does she have cancer? Is she suffering?"

"She's remarkably healthy. She's almost blind, but her hearing's as good as mine. She's tired, though."

Ellen's laugh reminded Lexy of a small dog's yap.

"She'd like to see you."

"Would she?"

"Do you have a way to get here?" Lexy had a meeting the next morning, but she could be late, drive up to Del Mar and get this woman. "I could come—"

"Of course I have a way to get there. I have a car. I have a garage full of cars. That doesn't mean I want to see her."

An Alaskan chill came down from Del Mar, but Lexy persisted. "I wish you'd reconsider, Ellen. I believe your mother would like to let go of life, but there's apparently some unfinished business."

Again that laugh. "You bet there is."

Whatever had made Lexy think she could be a priest? It wasn't enough to love God, you had to be able to love the child of God in women like Ellen Brownlee; and this evening, right now, not only could she not do that, she lacked even the will to try.

"You can tell my mother she'll have to die without

my help. And if you've managed to save my mother's soul, my hat's off to you. For me, I'm not in the soul-saving business."

"Mrs. Brownlee, we don't know each other, and—"

"And we never will."

"There's a great deal I don't know about your mother. But you and she—"

"I'm not coming down there so she can relieve her conscience and die in peace."

Clichés were a kind of verbal shorthand people used when they did not want to think or feel.

"Think of it as something you might do for yourself. We've all got wreckage in our past, Ms. Brownlee, and once your mother is dead—"

"You're saying it's a use-it-or-lose-it thing? I'll take my chances, thanks." The phone clicked dead.

Chapter 16

At six-thirty that same evening Luigi's delivered two large deluxe, everything-on-them, double-cheese pizzas to the conference room at Cabot and Klinger. To make room for the feast on the scarred conference table inherited from the office's previous occupant, Allison pushed aside documents, laptops, water bottles, soda cans, and mugs half full of scummy coffee while David's administrative assistant, Geoff Woodworth, distributed paper plates and napkins with the flair of a blackjack dealer.

David hated pizza. It reminded him of being a student and always broke.

Gracie came into the room and closed the door behind her. Avoiding David's eyes, she snagged a plate and a wedge of pizza.

"He says no," she told the room in general, as she pulled out the chair at the end of the table farthest from David. "I quote, 'Fuck, no, no way.'"

"That Marshall," Geoff said, smirking. "Always so indecisive."

David said, "Did you tell him it's important?"

Gracie used her long silvery fingernails to pick the

green pepper off her pizza. "And he said the condo's not big enough for the two of us, forget a pregnant woman with attitude." Finally she looked at David, her almost smiling expression telling him she was glad to be off the hook. "You can't blame him for not wanting to give up his home office for Marsha Filmore."

"She's right," Geoff said, reaching over and putting the discarded peppers on his own pizza slice. "There's a limit, Boss."

"By which I take it you and Billy-Bob would not—"

"Billy Ray."

"You guys have that big house—"

"Abso-fuckin'-lutely N-O." Geoff rolled his eyes in horror.

David didn't bother asking Allison if she'd take in Marsha Filmore. Allison lived in a two-bedroom apartment with two other young paralegals, all of them just getting by. For the sake of show he tried to look put out; but he had known from the start how the play would go. Still, it never hurt to have the team feel a little guilty; that way they owed him.

"I'll talk to Dana."

Geoff whooped. "Can I watch?"

"Boss," Gracie said, her voice sinking, "you can't do that. Not after what she's been through."

People seemed to believe he had not suffered sufficiently during Bailey's absence because he had gone to work every day and most weekends, because while Dana fell apart he had remained one-hundred-percent functional. It was no way to get sympathy, but it was the only way he knew to behave in a crisis. Sophomore year of high school he played a whole season with a severely sprained knee. If he'd sat out, the season would have been a bust; as it was, even with a gimpy quarterback they'd won two thirds of their games, which wasn't great, but not a humiliation either. You hurt all over, and that's when you play your hardest. You play all four quarters. But that doesn't mean you don't suffer.

The conference-room door opened again, and the firm's other associate, Larry McFarland, came in and helped himself to pizza. The chair beside Allison groaned as he settled his big frame.

"You do it, Larry," Gracie said. "You take in Marsha Filmore."

McFarland didn't even bother to respond.

"If you don't, the Boss will."

"Jesus, David," McFarland said, his mouth already full of pizza, "you can't do that to Dana."

David pushed his pizza away. What he wanted was a steak.

"Run it by me again," Allison said. "Why are we rescuing Marsha Filmore?"

"Yeah," Geoff said. "She's the one who went and got herself pregnant."

"And now we know she's been there before," Gracie said. "It's all in Buddy's report."

Buddy Collins was the smartest and fastest investigator David knew. According to the report he submitted that afternoon, Frank and Marsha Filmore had lived across the border in the early nineties in Rosarito Beach, where many of the residents were snowbird retirees or Americans like the Filmores taking advantage of Mexico's favorable exchange rate. Filmore had commuted to work just inside the U.S. border while Marsha stayed home with their daughter, Shawna. According to Collins's report they had moved north after Shawna's death.

"She fell down a well, for chrissake," Geoff said. "She was down there three days before anyone thought to look. The guy who owned the well had been warned twice already to cover the top."

Allison asked, "Do you think the prosecution knows?"

"If they don't yet, they will," David said.

Mexican officials had found Shawna's death to be a tragic accident.

"What I'm wondering is, what's not in the Mexican report?" David said. He looked around the room. "Who's taking notes?"

"Me, Boss," Allison said.

"Okay, make a note to send Buddy back down there, talk to folks, see what he comes up with."

"It's years ago," Larry said.

"Yeah, but there's a big expat community in Rosarito. Once they get used to Mexico, a lot of 'em stay put."

"I'd like to give Marsha a little truth serum," Gracie said.

"That's my point." David hit the table with the palm of his hand. "That's why I wanted her to live with you guys. You could do the female bonding thing."

"Did you say bondage, Boss?"

Gracie said, "I don't think Dana's going to want to be Marsha's new best friend."

"Maybe not," David said, "but if she gets ready to share the secrets of her heart, I want our side there to listen, not someone Peluso plants in the local Starbucks."

Geoff said, "Can we move on to something else?"

David threw up his hands.

"It's about the hate mail."

Threatening and abusive letters arrived at the office two or three times a week. The police checked each for identifying marks, but it was hard to get clues from a sheet of ordinary paper and a message typed or written by hand or in cutout letters glued to the paper with the kind of glue stick found in stores and offices and schools everywhere. Lieutenant Gary didn't think there was necessarily a connection between the rock thrown through the Cabots' window and the messages addressed to the office. There were plenty of crazies to go around, he said. The most recent letter had called David a baby killer.

"It's so irrational," Gracie said. "What kind of jackass can't distinguish between a lawyer and his client?"

Marcus Klinger wanted David to hire a bodyguard for Dana and Bailey. He knew a woman, ex-Navy; David had been carrying her phone number around with him for two weeks.

Geoff said, "We'd all feel a lot better if we knew someone was watching your back, too."

"No," David said too quickly. He knew he sounded defensive. "We can't afford bodyguards. We're scraping bottom as it is."

Sometimes he awoke in the night shivering cold and saw the debt piling up like snow around a house, the storm of the century. Everything depended on winning this case. "I want Buddy back in Rosarito asking more questions." When Frank Filmore was a free man, the word would go out, and the big clients, the Court TV clients, would line up and take a number. They'd get out of debt, and Dana would relax and start being her old self again.

He looked at his team. He cared for every one of them. Loyal, hardworking: he could depend on them to give their best effort and then a little more.

"I'll be okay, guys. Trust me.".

It was after nine when the strategy session finished and the defense team filed out of the office.

David hailed Gracie, who was the last to leave.

"Can you stick around?"

"Sure, Boss. What's up?"

His eyes burned with fatigue. "What's your gut tell you about this case?"

"Are you kidding? He's guilty as Nixon."

David grinned. "But he's not a crook, right?"

"I'd say he was more a shit-eating pervert."

He had not asked Gracie to stay behind so he could hear his own thoughts affirmed. "The thing is," he said, "I keep thinking there's something we're missing here. That's why I want Marsha—"

"I told you, Boss," she looked wary, "Marshall says no, and when he—"

"I'm not talking about that. She'll stay at our place. Dana'll fuss at first, but she'll come around." David leaned back and kicked his feet up onto the conference table. Folding his hands behind his head, he said, "Let me talk this out, okay? I mean, if I'm going in the completely wrong direction, you'll tell me. Right?"

Gracie nodded.

"Okay. Here's Marsha Filmore. She's got a twenty thousand-dollar diamond ring and a five-thousand-dollar watch. She's eight months pregnant and living in a housekeeping suite in Mission Valley, and all she does all day is sleep and watch television. And cry."

"Only her eyes are never swollen. You notice that?"

"No, I hadn't, but you're absolutely right." He jotted a note on the yellow pad beside him. "She has no family on the West Coast, and apparently her friends have all deserted her. Not that she and Frank ever had much of a social life. The way she describes it—their life together—except for the Calhouns next door, they kept to themselves pretty much." He doodled a moment, drawing circles inside squares inside circles.

He asked, "You know what cognitive dissonance is, when your brain gets conflicting messages about something?"

"Like she's supposed to be a very smart and savvy businesswoman, but you'd never know it now. She can't even get to the doctor's office on time. All that expensive jewelry, and she dresses like a bag lady."

David said, "Married to a kid killer, that'd throw anyone off."

"Boss, it's more than that." Gracie leaned forward. "The way she talks about him, it's too weird. She thinks he's some kind of super-brain. The other day when I walked her to the elevator, she just suddenly stopped and told me how powerful he is. She talks like he's the Godfather and if I step out of line I better watch out. That's off, Boss. Plus, she says she loves this guy, but she hardly ever goes to see him. She says she cries, but we never see any sign of tears. And if you hadn't read between the lines, we'd never know about the first child. Shawna."

"You think she's complicit?"

Gracie shuddered. "You're creeping me out."

"Why? Doesn't perversion come in both sexes?"

"Yeah, but I see her for a victim, not a perp."

"Me too. But she knows more than she's saying. You agree with that?"

"Well, yeah, she's the wife. But so what? Neither of them's going to testify. And the case's got so much reasonable doubt, if I didn't know Frank Filmore personally, I'd never believe he did it."

"Maybe." Circles inside squares inside triangles inside circles. "We start getting complacent and I start to worry."

"Suppose we're wrong, David, and Marsha was part of it." Gracie narrowed her dark eyes when she was worried. "Do you want her staying at your house near Dana and Bailey?"

"That's no problem. Marsha's strange, but she's not a killer." David stood up. "And anyway, she won't be in our house. She'll have the apartment over the garage."

Chapter 17

He found Dana reading in bed when he got home. Her hair was loose and a little curly from a shower.

"I need to talk to you, David."

Trouble.

He leaned in and kissed her. "You smell like Johnson's baby powder."

"Bailey got carried away at bath time."

"That's a good sign, isn't it?"

"It's been a long day."

He knew she wanted him to ask what happened, but he had been listening to complaints all day. Enough.

He went into the closet, loosened his tie, and pulled it over his head, thinking how to tell Dana that Marsha Filmore was coming to live in the garage apartment. He used a shoehorn to remove his shoes, put trees in them, and laid them on the shelf of the closet. When he could afford it, he was going to have a pair of Italian shoes for every day and to hell with shoe trees. In his boxers and T-shirt he sat at the end of the bed. Dana reclined against a pile of pillows, a book on her lap, dressed for the night in a cream-colored night shirt patterned with sleeping bears. If she had the slightest interest in sex, she would have worn something else. Stress and fatigue had drawn lines in her cheeks. He felt a pang of remorse mixed with sorrow when he contemplated the extent to which he had failed her. He had not built a safe home for her to raise their daughter. It was his fault Dana no longer glowed with security and confidence. He almost didn't blame her for going off sex. Almost.

At Miami University, the prof in American History had asked her a question for which she wasn't prepared; and David, sitting one row behind her and two seats over, saw the bright rose blush of embarrassment rise in her cheeks. The sight called up a primal desire to punch out the prof. Instead, after class he caught up with her before she left the building, introduced himself. She didn't recognize his name, which knocked him back a little because it meant she didn't follow sports at all. He had never been attracted to a girl who didn't. Still, he asked her out for coffee. When he knew her better he realized how rare it was for her to be unprepared in class and that if she had answered the professor's question unhesitatingly, he might never have paid attention to her. There were plenty of pretty girls at Miami University, less prickly girls than Dana, girls who lived to serve a star quarterback. His life might have been more relaxed with one of them, but Dana was the only woman he had ever loved. He once told Gracie this. She said he was the sweetest white boy she knew.

Not now he wasn't.

He did not want to talk about Marsha Filmore or Bailey or anything else. His dearest wish was for Dana to strip off that dumb night shirt and give him the blow job of his life and send him off to sleep, a contented man. But there was no way that would happen; and if he didn't talk about Marsha, get it over with, he'd be awake all night.

He watched her face as he laid out his case. "Fixing up the garage apartment would only take us a weekend. Both of us working."

"You'd help? Really? I couldn't do it myself."

It ticked him off that she thought she had to say this. As if he never did anything to help. "We've got a problem with Marsha Filmore. Both Gracie and I believe she's got things to say that the team needs to know."

"Like what?"

"Jesus, Dana, if I knew, we wouldn't be having this conversation." He went into the bathroom and brushed his teeth ferociously. He could not hear what she was saying over the sound of the electric toothbrush, and he didn't care. He was so tired the soles of his feet hurt. At the end of the requisite two minutes he turned the brush off and wiped his mouth. He returned to the bedroom. Dana still sat with the book open, facedown beside her. It didn't look like she had moved.

"The other day, didn't you tell me the Filmores' little girl fell down a well?"

"That's the story."

"You don't sound like you believe it."

"Police said it was an accident." What he knew was that both Filmores had lied about having a daughter, and lies made David suspicious. His Uncle Ed had warned him he would hate the law because of the dishonesty. "Be a fireman," Ed told him. "When a house is in flames no one has time to lie."

As often practiced, the law was a dishonest profession in which one side—the accused—almost always lied, so the other side thought it had the right to do the same. To level the playing field. Cops lied to convict whomever they arrested. Jurors lied during voir dire about their prejudices, their pertinent experiences, to avoid duty or get on the panels they wanted. Witnesses lied for revenge or righteousness, or to protect themselves, to inflate their egos, to escape responsibility. Some judges took bribes or reached decisions by throwing a dart; David wished he were wrong, but why should they differ from the other players in the game? Defense attorneys knew prosecutors lied to muscle up weak cases, and prosecutors believed that defense attorneys did the same. It was here David's reluctant acceptance of the status quo hit snags. As he understood the role of the defense attorney, his only job was to make the prosecution prove its case within a reasonable doubt and to play by the rules while they did it. He deeply believed that without being called to the test in every trial, the state would take the law into its own hands as frequently as possible. There was no reason for a defense attorney to lie, because he was the only person in the system not required to prove or decide anything specific.

"Are you listening to me?" Dana touched his wrist. "I asked you if it would be safe having her here."

"Well of course it is. Do you honestly think I'd put you and Bailey in danger?"

"No. Not on purpose."

"Shit, Dana, give me some credit. She's harmless. Pitiful."

He sensed Dana's mind circling, stirring up the atmosphere in the bedroom. In such a mixing bowl he would never get to sleep. There were tablets in the bathroom cabinet, but he did not like to take them. When he thought of the vials of pills in his mother's bathroom and bedside table, he couldn't even take an aspirin without feeling weak.

"You've been mad at me since I came in the door," he said, taking the book from her hands. She folded her arms across her chest. "What happened today?"

"Nice of you to ask."

This was the way she fought, with the big chill and sarcasm and snotty back talk. She never yelled or threw things. It would be better if she did. It might help break through the wall between them.

She shoved her extra pillows onto the floor. "My grandmother called. She needs more money this month."

Imogene.

"That's what you wanted to talk to me about?"

"No."

"Did something happen today?" He sounded angry, but he wasn't. Not very. He was just sick of the tension between them and everything being so complicated. He had a sudden flying memory of himself at ten or eleven, riding his bike, no hands, down the hill behind his uncle's house. He wanted to feel that way again. He wanted to be happy and fearless to his toes.

He said, "Tell me what's up."

"Can you come home early tomorrow and watch Bailey? I hate to take her over there. She bangs on the piano and Grandma says it's okay but I can tell she doesn't mean it. . . . I know I'm being a bitch, David, but I get so tired. If it isn't Bailey, it's Grandma, and now it's Marsha Filmore moving in."

It was the closest he would ever get to an apology from Dana.

"Yeah," he said, "it's a bitch." He got into bed. "Did you call Lieutenant Gary?"

"I've told you, I don't want—"

"This isn't about you, Dana."

She sat up, hugging her bent knees and glaring at

him. "If you were really concerned about Bailey, you'd agree that the best thing for her is to be left alone. Why can't you just trust that I know what I'm doing with her?"

Sometimes she made him so angry his throat closed up.

"I'm convinced, David, completely and totally convinced, that she wasn't mistreated. I can't prove it, but I sense it; really deep down I know she's okay. But she was traumatized, and it'll take a long time for her to come around."

"And talk?"

"Of course she'll talk. David, she gets closer every day. She plays more, she has more enthusiasm. She had a great time at Bella Luna, and tonight she sprinkled powder all over the bathroom."

"Being a mute is not okay, Dana."

"Don't call her that." She threw back the bedcovers and stormed into the bathroom, not turning on lights. He heard the pop of a pill vial opening. Water ran, and a moment later she came back to bed.

"So. What about coming home to babysit? Can you do it, or shall I call Guadalupe?"

He used to enjoy being with Bailey, just the two of them. Though she was slow and her behavior unpredictable, happiness and affection for people and animals and life in general had bubbled up in her irrepressibly. He compared the new and old Bailey; and what he felt—the mash of anger, frustration, impatience, the compulsion to find and punish her abductor—made it hard to be alone with her.

"We could work something with Marsha where she could baby-sit once in a while. Could be a real plus for both of you." As soon as he spoke he regretted his words.

Her lips made a seam and almost disappeared inside

her mouth. For the first time that he could ever remember he thought she wasn't pretty, that he could do better. The disloyalty made him sick to his stomach. There was no one better for him than Dana, and he loved her with every neuron. He could not stand to think that their love for each other had gotten lost somewhere and that they would never be able to reassemble the scattered pieces of it. What kind of glue was there for a broken marriage?

Lately he had been thinking about marriage. How, despite the odds against success, no couple ever thinks its marriage won't work out. It's never in the playbook that giddy newlyweds will end up hurting each other just by breathing. And they can't imagine ahead how the loss of love will surprise them. It was like in a game, being taken down from behind, slammed into the turf and piled on. You feel your brain slosh around in your skull like an egg shaken in its shell, you lose sense of where and who you are, and your Osterized brain is asking, *Huh? How? What did I do wrong?*

"You're not paying attention."

"I am."

"I said I feel sorry for her, but no way do I want her baby-sitting."

She was really saying, *Abandon your clients and cases and forget about the payroll at the end of the month, and come home and watch* Lion King *for the tenth time with a seven-year-old who won't even talk to you.*

Allison would do it for him. He was her hero. He made the suggestion to Dana.

"Allison's a paralegal, David. A professional. You ask her to babysit and she'll quit on you. And I wouldn't blame her."

He laid his forearm over his eyes. They were talking

about Allison and babysitting when Dana hadn't yet given an okay to the Marsha deal, and her sleeping pill would kick in soon.

He was drawn and quartered by the demands made of him: as a lawyer, a husband, a father, a man who cared about doing the right thing by his client, his wife, his child. He wanted to say, *I love you, we love each other.* He wanted to ask, *Don't we? Don't we?*

"I'll come home," he said. "Four?"

Her eyes softened.

He said, "Promise me you'll think about Marsha."

It was how the game was played. You gave up a little yardage, but if you kept your eye on the goal, you got to the end zone anyway. It took a while and wore you out, and sometimes you wondered why you bothered, but you got there eventually.

Chapter 18

Dana knew she would eventually give in. And she knew that David also knew it. At breakfast she said Marsha Filmore could live over the garage until the case was over. She could have said it the night before and made it easy for both of them; but they did not dance that way at their house. Dana thought all marriages must have such patterns of feint and parry, dominance and submission, the unique choreography of the relationship.

She had not told David about the note left on her front seat. When he came home late and in a bad mood, thinking only of himself and his work, she had perversely kept silent, not wanting to share any more than the time of day with him. She wondered if she was being irrational, then decided not. There was nothing David could do about the note, and his mind was already crammed full. With a pinch of guilt she realized that knowing something he did not gave her an energizing sense of power.

In the afternoon she spent an hour trying to make a few notes about the Nerli Altarpiece but she did not get far. She liked thinking about her thesis more than writing it. Actually, lately, she wasn't much interested in thinking about it, either. Bailey pestered her, wanting to be held; and Moby barked at anything that moved on the street. Now, as she drove to her grandmother's house, she thought about families and wondered if, in the Middle Ages, husbands and wives had danced around each other as they did in the twenty-first century. Maybe Tanai Nerli had gone in his carriage to San Frediano to visit his daughter because his wife was driving him around the bend and halfway to the bughouse with complaints about the servants and demands for a larger, grander palazzo. Maybe he always escaped to his daughter's instead of staying home and fighting it out. And maybe the wife resented the daughter because of it. Or perhaps the art historians were all wrong and the woman in the background was Nerli's lover, not his daughter. In the painting Lippi had captured husband and wife kneeling in the foreground, gazing at one another devotedly. But if Dana knew how to paint smiles over her anger, it was likely the Nerlis also covered their grudges and resentments. Dana did not call this lying. Without masking, marriage would be impossible.

Or maybe it was her thinking that was cockeyed. Maybe most husbands and wives waltzed through marriage like Ginger and Fred. As usual, she could only guess at what normal was.

The North Park business district had been shabby for as long as she could remember. The big red and blue neon hand advertising VOICE OF THE SOUL PSYCHIC READINGS had occupied the same space since Dana scooped ice cream at the Baskin-Robbins down the street. There were a few restaurants with signs in their windows advertising DISCOUNTS FOR SENIORS, bars where Happy Hour stretched from two in the afternoon until nine or ten at night, some thrift shops, and a couple of storefronts where for a fee a person could borrow against the next month's government check. In her grandmother's neighborhood the houses were small frame Craftsmen built in the twenties or pseudo-Spanish bungalows, barely more than cottages. Some had been gentrified, a few had expensive additions, but most were old and worn out. The owners were probably senior citizens like Imogene, surviving on fixed incomes and paying in Prop Thirteen–protected taxes a fraction of what their golden property was worth.

A white Dodge van was parked in Imogene's driveway. It wasn't anything like the one that had run over Moby Doby, but, still, it was a van and it was white, and those two things were enough to encourage the voices of panic. For a few minutes Dana's imagination ran wild with "maybes" and "what ifs."

She drove around the block to find a parking place.

The bungalow where Dana had lived from the age of five until she went to college was not as rundown as those on either side of it. She and David had it painted every other year and paid for a once-a-month gardener to trim the grass and groom the pink hydrangea bushes under the windows. At the edge of the porch stairs Dana paused to check the bushes for whitefly.

Her grandmother's voice, still strong despite her eighty-four years, came from behind the screen door. "It's you. I didn't know for sure you were coming."

Dana drew her hands back covered with a sticky white powder. She brushed them together and a cloud of bugs, like tiny white dash marks, floated upward.

"You've got whiteflies."

"That man you send over, he's no good. Don't do anything but hack up my lawn with that noisy power mower."

"Hi, Grandma."

"Hi, yourself." She held open the screen. "Come in if you're coming."

Imogene's hair was the flat black color of India ink, and she wore it in a tightly turned and sprayed pageboy. She was tall, long-waisted, and not so much fat as large. "A big-boned gal," David said. As a girl Dana had been mortified by everything about her grandmother but especially by her baggy breasts swinging side to side under the outsized man's T-shirt she usually wore. Beneath Levi's rolled to midcalf, her legs were pale and blue-veined. Dana still hated the way her grandmother looked, still cringed with mortification at the sight of her ridiculous clothes, her painted mouth.

Imogene turned her cheek for Dana's dutiful kiss.

The kissing was new, and Dana did not like it. Up close, under a heavy dusting of rose-scented powder, her grandmother smelled stale and greasy, and although she claimed to have given up cigarettes, she smelled like smoke.

"I don't have long," Dana said.

"You never do."

"I brought you a check."

"It won't bounce, will it? That time last February, the bank wouldn't take it."

"I told you, Grandma, David had to borrow from our personal account to pay some of the office expenses."

"Maybe he shouldn't be in business if he can't pay his bills."

And maybe I should walk out of here and never come back. Dana slung her shoulder bag over the back of a chair and perched, glancing around at the familiar front-room furnishings. Her imagination cramped at the effort it took to see the child Imogene playing the baby grand piano that took up half the front room. She still played well, though her musical choices were peculiar: hymns and jazzy Broadway tunes. Dana dimly remembered being told that Imogene had once been a band singer, traveling across country in a bus, the only woman. Despite doubts about the truth of that story, Dana momentarily felt sorry for her grandmother's lost dreams, whatever they were. Then she remembered waxing the piano every week, and the sound of Imogene's voice sawing the air on Wednesday afternoons: "Elbow grease, Danita. Show some muscle."

"Why didn't you bring Bailey? I like that child. I'd like half a chance to know her."

"She irritates you."

"That's what you tell me, but I haven't noticed it myself."

"She's got a cold." It had always been easy to lie to Imogene. "Another time."

"Easy for you to say. You're not eighty-four years old." Imogene spoke of her aching hip, her stiff hands, her bad eyesight and constant indigestion. Dana tuned her out.

In the kitchen a drawer squeaked.

"Do you have company? I heard a drawer."

"Must be a ghost."

No more irritating woman walked the planet.

"We have to talk about money, Grandma."

"Two hundred's not so much." Imogene eased herself into her Lazy Boy recliner with its flattened cushions and threadbare arms. A blue towel lay across the headrest. "What happened to all the cash David got when he was a quarterback?"

"That was years ago." And David had never been a high-advance, big-paycheck athlete. Despite high school and college stardom, he had been chosen late in the draft; his only really big bonus came as the result of a Monday-night game against the Raiders when he went in after the half and threw two touchdown passes for an upset win. Commentators still talked about that game. For a while he'd been the team and the town's glory boy, but it had been a fluke performance, a lucky afternoon for David and the Chargers, nothing more.

"Maybe you shouldn't of bought that expensive Mission Hills house."

"This isn't about how we spend our money."

"I know Mission Hills, and I wouldn't want to live there if I couldn't afford to."

Heat rose up Dana's neck and spread out along her jawline. "Grandma, you've got to do better living on what you've got. You buy too many lottery tickets." She made no house payments. She did not drive a car. "We can't keep giving you extra."

Imogene had never given Dana anything extra. At fourteen Dana struck a deal with the owner of the ice cream shop. He paid her cash to scoop his thirty-six flavors through the dinner hour until ten, when business was always slow. She had time to study, and when she got home she stayed up half the night with her books and made the grades that got her a scholarship, first to Bishop's School and then to Miami of Ohio.

Dana said, "Since the start of the year—"

"You could work for the IRS, the way you count pennies."

"Seems like I learned from the Queen of Cheap."

"Don't start complaining."

Don't complain, because it does no good; don't complain, because, as Lexy had told her so often, it was all in the past now, and the past was just a story. It was Dana's choice to hold on to the story or let it go.

Let it go, let it go.

In the kitchen the radio blared and the voice of a

talk-show host sawed through the door between the rooms. As abruptly as it came on, it went off.

"Clock radio," Imogene said.

Dana would not give her grandmother the satisfaction of her curiosity. She put the check on the piano. "I can't stay, Grandma. David came home from work to watch Bailey."

"How is she?"

"She's fine."

"You bend the truth, bad as your mom."

Dana told Imogene about the bodysurfing and Bailey's gregarious behavior at Bella Luna.

"That's good news; you should be grinning ear to ear. How come you look like you're carrying a grand piano on your back? You've got something on your mind, Danita. Spit it out."

Conversations with Imogene were always this way. She knew more and better than Dana, no matter what the subject, what the issue.

"What happened?"

"Oh, there was a note."

"Another one."

"Different. Not threatening this time. Just someone wanting attention."

"What did it say?"

Dana told her. *Don't be afraid. I love you both.*

"Gives me gooseflesh." Imogene rubbed the tops of her arms. "What's the cop think?"

"I haven't told him yet."

"Why not?"

"There hasn't been time."

"Bullshit. For something like this, there's always time." Splaying her hands on the arms of the recliner, Imogene levered herself onto her feet. She winced and rubbed the small of her back. "Danita, what do you know that you're not telling?"

"If I knew something, don't you think I'd tell Lieutenant Gary?"

"That's what I'm wondering."

Dana jerked the door open and stepped onto the porch. "I don't have time to stand here and discuss this. David has to go back to the office." She could not wait to get away.

"If you were to ask me, he's wasting his time defending that slimy s.o.b. Everyone knows he did it. He's gonna get the gas for sure." She tugged her denim pants down at the crotch. "Probably done plenty else, from the smarmy looks of him."

"His wife's going to live over our garage." Dana knew this would outrage Imogene. "We're going to fix the place up this weekend."

Gracie had called that morning to say that if Dana agreed, they should make a party of it. All Dana had to do was provide the beer. She had been looking forward to a whole day with David to herself and a task to keep them busy. Long firelit conversations and dawdly dinners had never been their style. But with a project and occupation for their hands and bodies, they never ran out of conversation. She had almost declined Gracie's offer, but they rarely had company anymore, so she said it was a great idea, and now she was looking forward to it.

Imogene said, "You don't want to let that little angel girl around her."

"It's the husband who's on trial."

"Even so."

"She's pregnant and the press is hounding her and she can't even go to the supermarket without being accosted. Her doctor says if she gets more upset it's bad for—"

"That little Bailey, she's a special one; you don't want to take any chances."

It was an insult that Imogene felt she had to say that. As if Dana did not adore her daughter.

"You watch out for her. Bad things happen fast."

Easy to give advice and lecture now. What about the haunted house? And Imogene had been a block away playing mah-jongg when Dana was eight and three junior high school boys chased her down the alley behind the house, shoved her to the ground, and tried to pull down her underpants. Mr. Valdez, the electrician who lived three doors from Imogene, came out his back door waving a .38 revolver. The boys ran off laughing and stumbling over themselves. The chivalrous old man had helped her to her feet, averted his eyes from her torn clothes, and walked her home.

From the kitchen, a cupboard door slammed, and a tap ran and then shut off.

"You *do* have company! Whose van is that?" As Dana opened the screen door and stepped onto the porch, a slightly disgusting possibility occurred to her. "Grandma, have you got a boyfriend?"

Something sly crawled into her grandmother's expression. "More like family."

"We don't have any family."

"Oh no? What about your mother?"

Chapter 19

You're a sick woman, Dana thought as she hurried up the sidewalk toward her car. She gripped the steering wheel until her hands hurt. The old bitch had only mentioned her mother to get a rise out of her. That was Imogene's way, to goad and tease until she got some reaction. And Dana never learned. For a crazy moment she had actually believed her mother was in the kitchen. She had felt excited.

On impulse, she made a screeching U-turn and drove back around the corner, passing the bungalow. There was a parking space across the street now. She pulled into it and turned off the ignition.

Drumming her fingernails on the steering wheel, she stared at the van in the driveway and tried to see her drug-addled mother behind its wheel. How could Dana have been so stupid when she knew perfectly well the meaning of *I don't want you, gone forever,* and *never coming back.* Nevertheless, she got out of the 4Runner and walked back across the street and peered in the van's front passenger window. A yellow plastic rose rode in a plastic bud vase on the dash.

So much for the boyfriend theory.

And the interior was pristine.

So much for the mother theory, too.

Dana opened the side gate and closed it softly behind her. Dry leaves from the avocado tree in the next yard crumbled and crunched underfoot like bags of corn chips as she tiptoed along the cracked and buckled cement path that ran beside the house to the screened-in laundry room at the back. Something heavy like tennis shoes bounced around in the drum of the dryer. Her heart felt the same way.

A movement in the kitchen caught her eye—a man had walked into her field of vision and opened the refrigerator. He wore his gray hair in a long, ragged pony tail and was so thin and tall he had to bend like a paperclip to look in the refrigerator. He pulled out two bottles of beer, holding them by the necks in one hand. As he turned to leave the kitchen, he stopped and peered at the window. Dana froze. He touched the top of his head and then patted the breast pocket of his denim shirt while he continued to stare long enough for her to see that he had a narrow, sharp-boned face like a martyred saint's. At the sound of Imogene's voice he turned from the window and walked out of Dana's sight.

She dropped to a crouch, breathing hard and shaking. What luck he appeared to be half blind. As she hurried back down the path and out onto the driveway she heard Imogene laugh and then the notes of "Blue Room." After several measures, a jazzy violin joined in with the piano. Dana dashed across the street and into her car. She locked the door and sat, hearing the music in her head.

A man, duets: suddenly her grandmother's life held worlds of mystery she could not guess at. She felt the pinch of guilt and dismissed it. Imogene had been at the heart of all her youthful misery, and Dana was not going to start feeling sentimental about her now.

The feast Dana brought home from the Real Food deli did nothing to mollify David's bad temper.

"How long has she been sucking her thumb?" he asked, jerking his head toward Bailey while he twisted a corkscrew into a bottle of Chardonnay. "I told her to stop, but it's like she's deaf now. On top of everything else."

"Later, David."

Since Bailey's return David had begun to talk about her in her presence, as if she were either deaf or invisible.

Dana emptied clear plastic containers of crab cakes, marinated green beans, and grilled vegetables onto a large serving plate and set the kitchen counter for the three of them. Bailey tracked her steps with one finger hooked through a belt loop on Dana's Levi's, her thumb jammed in her mouth. She seemed to have lost ground since her outgoing day at Bella Luna.

Dana handed David two chilled wineglasses, settled Bailey on a stool at the counter, and sat down herself. A large swallow of wine, followed quickly by another, and she began to relax. They ate in silence until Dana said, "My grandmother had a guest today. Very sneaky. She said it was my mother."

David looked up, appalled. "The bitch."

"Who? Grandma or my mother?"

"Both."

Dana smiled. It was good to have someone on her side. She put ketchup on Bailey's crab cake to make it more appealing. Sheepishly she confessed how she had sneaked around the house and narrowly missed being seen. David thought it was funny and said he'd hire her as an investigator. Bailey stopped eating and watched them.

"So who was it?" He poured more wine.

"A man. A violinist like that Hungarian—"

"Menhuin?"

"No. The jazz guy. We have a CD."

"Django Reinhart."

"Yeah, him. When I left they were playing "Blue Room." She hummed a few bars of the old song. "Can you believe it?"

"She's a weird old coot."

A moment later Dana said, "There was a white van in her driveway. I guess it was Django's."

"There are a million white vans." He swallowed the rest of his wine. "They're all over town. You don't mean you suspect Imogene?"

It was almost like he was trying to misinterpret.

She wanted him to understand the pressure she was under; but she did not want to tell him. Better for him to realize it himself and speak the reassuring words of comfort. They were just platitudes if she had to prompt him.

After the meal they were alone for a few minutes.

"Look," Dana said, "about the thumb-sucking, let her do it. It must be comforting."

"It's going to ruin her teeth. We'll pay thousands of dollars for braces."

"I sucked my thumb until I was seventeen and went away to college and met you."

"You did? You never told me that before."

"It never came up."

"What about germs?"

"Just let her be, David. She needs time, is all."

She told him Bailey had been enthusiastic and responsive during their visit to the Humane Society shelter that morning. "I almost let her choose a kitten. Sometimes kids with voluntary mutism get started talking again if they have an animal."

"She can talk to Moby. Cats make me sneeze." He swallowed his wine as if drinking were an act of aggression.

"You might at least think about it."

"Why?"

"You act like you don't want her to get better."

"I want her to see a shrink."

"Now you're on Gary's side? I thought we agreed to let her get well on her own."

"That was almost a month ago."

Dana thought about how good it would feel to throw her glass across the room.

David said, "There's a sick bastard out there; he had our daughter. . . . If I didn't know better, I'd think you didn't want him brought to justice."

Maybe she would sweep her arm across the counter— send dishes, glasses, and all flying.

David stared into his glass as he swirled the last of his wine. "I want to kill him. I don't get how you can not care."

"I do care; you know I do."

"Then explain to me—"

"I've done everything a specialist would do. I've had her draw pictures, I gave her special dolls to play with. I examined her, David. I touched her and she didn't cringe."

"Maybe she got used to it."

She hated him.

"I'm sorry, Dana. That was an awful thing to say."

She had been planning to tell him that Bailey could bodysurf, that she had enjoyed herself at Bella Luna, and that this definitively proved she was getting better. Now she couldn't even make herself speak to him. She was like a closed oyster at the bottom of the sea, the pearl growing inside her black and deformed.

"We fight all the time, Dana. It didn't used to be like this. You're always mad at me for something. Mostly I don't know what the hell I've done."

It wasn't fair that he accuse her of anger when she felt *his* anger as if it had hands to pin her shoulders back and pull her hair.

"Just let Gary's people . . ." The skin around his mouth was white. "I know you had a bad experience when you were a kid, but it won't happen to Bailey."

"You guarantee that, do you?"

"Gary says you can watch the whole interview through a mirror. If you don't like what you see, you can run in screaming." He ran his hands through his thick hair. "Just do it, Dana. Just fucking call the cops and set it up."

Dana stared at him. "You know what I'd like?" She stood and started banging the china and cutlery into the dishwasher. "Just once in a while I'd like to have a conversation that doesn't involve me doing something I don't want to."

As she spoke, he was walking out the back door.

Predictably, as soon as he was gone she regretted her anger and would have liked to run behind the car, catch hold of the fender, and drag it to a stop so she could tell him that she loved him and hated what was happening between them.

Instead she went to the phone and called Lieutenant Gary. She was surprised when the operator put her through to him.

"Don't you ever go home?"

"Occasionally." She heard the squeak of his desk chair. "What's up, Mrs. Cabot?"

Dana cleared her throat. All at once she realized that it had been two days since she took Bailey to the beach. Gary would think it peculiar she had not called him immediately. And it was peculiar. She could not really explain why she had delayed. Or why she wanted to slam the phone down right now.

"Has something happened?"

"Yes." She told him everything. As she spoke she ended every sentence with "and" so she would be forced to continue, so she would not stop until the full story of the day was told.

When she finished he asked, "What did the note say?"

She told him.

"Why didn't you come right to the station with it?"

She couldn't think of anything to say except the truth. "I don't know."

More silence. "Right. Well, how soon can you get the note to me—the rock, too? You want me to send someone over?"

Suddenly light-headed, she leaned against the kitchen counter. "I don't have it."

"What do you mean?"

Icy perspiration beaded the back of her neck.

"What the hell do you expect me to do if you don't have the note?"

It had felt like filth in her hand. How could he expect her to hold on to it one moment longer than she had to?

She heard his chair squeak again and then a slamming sound as if he had kicked his desk. Eventually he spoke to her.

"You sure there even was a note, Mrs. Cabot?"

"Why would I lie?"

"That's a really good question, and I don't know the answer." He had an edgy, sarcastic laugh. "Like I also don't know why you wouldn't call me first thing and bring over the evidence."

"I'm telling you the truth." She had been rash, throwing the note away, and she regretted it. She wasn't used to feeling stupid and irresponsible. She had spent her whole life proving to everyone that she was just the opposite. She wanted him to understand.

"This whole thing—I'm not myself. Since Bailey disappeared it's like my life has fallen apart and I can't seem to put it together." She was crying for the first time in many years, more years than she could number for certain. Even when Bailey vanished, her eyes had burned but stayed dry. Now she could not stop herself. "I know I'm acting crazy. I know it's not normal, but I can't help it. I know what I should have done, but the note, it was like . . . shit. In my hand. I felt so dirty from touching—"

"Okay, okay. It's done, we can't change history."

"I'd never lie about something like this. You believe me, don't you?"

"I just wish I could see that note."

"I'm not a liar, Lieutenant Gary. I swear to you."

"Yeah, yeah. I believe you." He sounded very tired. "You just got to promise me if anything else shows up you won't toss it."

"I do promise," she said. "I do."

Chapter 20

A struggling congregation like St. Tom's could not afford to pay an assistant priest, so it depended on retired clergy to fill in or take over as needed. Lexy's assistant was old Father Bartholomew, a retired priest from the Channel Islands, beloved by the congregation and so blind now he said the Eucharist by memory, frequently jumbling the order of things. Lexy could not leave St. Tom's in his loving, unsteady hands. In January the retired dean of the cathedral was coming to take over for a month, and she had already bought a ticket to Hawaii. Until then an early-morning walk on Pacific Beach with Dana felt like a mini-holiday.

Before seven A.M. neither wind nor surf disturbed the chill mist that lay close to the water and sand in a silvery froth. Unless the animal-control cops drove their Jeeps down to the water's edge, they would see neither Moby Doby joyously breaking the city leash law nor Bailey chasing the birds with him.

That morning, as always, Dana was a good listener. She let Lexy ramble on about her work, and she didn't judge.

"It's not that it's a hard job. I don't care if it's hard and the hours are long. It's the work I love, the work I chose. But there are times . . ." It was difficult to say aloud what she hardly permitted herself to think. "I wonder what made me think I'd be a good priest."

"Oh, Lexy . . ."

"No, listen, this is what I'm talking about. Yesterday I stopped in Target on the way home and saw Beth Gordon with Jason and I had to turn my back on them. I went out of my way to avoid them. That woman . . . How many times can I say thank you for what she does at St. Tom's? And the kid . . ."

"He was great when Bailey was gone."

"It gave him something to do. Better than robbing banks." She choked on the words. "Do you hear the way I talk? I'm supposed to love him as Christ would love him. I'm supposed to see him as a child of God, but I'd be happy if I never had to look at his pimply face again."

"You're a priest, Lexy. Not a saint."

"I know that. But I believe—" She stopped and stared out toward the horizon. On a foggy morning, the world seemed mysteriously small and empty. Without visual distraction, Lexy's inadequacies multiplied and crowded in on all sides, trapping her in a tense, tight world. "I know I don't have to be a saint, but I'm a Christian because of Christ, and I think the most important thing I'm asked to do is see His face in every person I meet. That means deadheads like Jason. I promised to do that when I became a priest. It's the kind of job where the harder you work at it, the more you realize how inadequate you are. So much of the time I'm just going through the motions, acting as if I'm a real priest. You wouldn't believe how dishonest I feel." Disgusted, she kicked the toe of her Nike into the damp sand. "If you could listen in on my thoughts you'd know I'm not worthy to be a priest."

"Name me one person anywhere who's really, really good."

"What about the Dalai Lama?"

"Don't count on it. Jesus was the only perfect person, Lexy. And sometimes I have my doubts about Him."

It was good to laugh and change the subject. Dana turned the conversation to a movie she wanted to see and for a while they talked about movies and television. It was what Dana called *airhead conversation* and perfect for the moment. When their talk became personal again, Dana told the story of her visit with Imogene. She tried to make it an amusing anecdote, but the effort did not come off.

Lexy had learned that people rarely came right out with what was bothering them. Even at AA meetings most speakers talked circles around their troubles before getting to what was on their minds. She had been trained to nod and listen and wait for the truth.

Dana said, "It freaks me out to think my grandmother might have this rich personal life and I know diddly about it." She stopped to watch Bailey drawing scrawls in the wet sand with a stick of driftwood. Lexy saw how avidly Dana observed her daughter, almost as if she were expecting her to write a message. "What if I've been wrong about my grandmother? What does that say about me?"

They walked on. "What if she's really . . . an okay person?"

"Didn't you tell me David likes her?"

"Oh, yeah, he thinks she's funny and eccentric, but, then, she didn't raise him. And did I tell you? The latest? He's conned me into letting Marsha Filmore move into the apartment over the garage, and Grandma says I'm an idiot and I shouldn't let her near Bailey. What do you think?"

Pausing between question and response was something else Lexy had been trained to do.

Bailey came back into sight, kicking the spindrift as she ran in and out of the shallows and then up the hard sand, her arms out at her sides, wheeling and careening after the gulls.

I think Dana's right. She's getting better on her own.

"Maybe I'm just paranoid."

Lexy said, "You're not paranoid."

Lexy did not say what she most deeply felt, that Dana should worry less, stop trying to manage life down to the last detail. Unlikely as it almost always seemed, God was in his Heaven and all was right with the world. Seen from God's eyes, even Bailey's abduction made sense.

Now was not the time to open that philosophical door. Dana had just gotten over being mad at God.

"And I haven't told David about the note in the car. I know I should, but these days I just don't feel like telling him anything."

Dana stopped at the edge of the water and looked at Lexy with an expression of fierce pain in her eyes. "I love David, but something's changed between us." Behind her the horizon was scarved in fog. "It's my fault, too. I know it is, but even so he does nothing to help the situation. He works all the time. And when he's home he's thinking about work. That horrible case. I don't think he really sees me anymore."

"What about you? Do you see him?"

Dana started to answer but stopped, and Lexy wondered what she wasn't saying.

We all have secrets.

"Shit, I don't know what I see."

It seemed to Lexy that in marriage, daring to look at the other with clear and open eyes was an act of faith.

What happened when what you saw displeased or disgusted or disappointed you? Of all the demands set down by God, Lexy thought the requirement to forgive and love others as ourselves was the most challenging.

Dana said, "I don't know why I'm telling you this. I'm not even sure I care anymore."

Lexy put her arm around her shoulder. "Oh, you care, Dana, you care big time."

Despite its unhappy outcome, Lexy did not regret her marriage to William Parker Trent III. Because of her time with Billy she knew something of what it took to make marriage work, of the great effort required to sustain love and respect over a stretch of decades.

When Lexy walked out on William Parker Trent III before they'd been married a year, it had been with a sense of personal failure that only deepened with time. Their mutual friends had expressed astonishment and asked how it could happen to such beautiful people with successful careers and so much in common: sailing and riding and gourmet cooking, cocaine and wine— lots of wine and martinis and champagne whenever possible. The *New York Times Magazine* had featured the kitchen in their Amagansett house the same month Lexy walked out, taking with her only what filled one suitcase small enough to lodge in an overhead compartment. She had left Billy Trent, their friends, her appointment book, and shoots scheduled months in advance to move into the St. Ann retreat house in Warrenton, Virginia. She had remained there for seven months, leaving only to attend AA meetings in town. Years later, when she sought permission to pursue ordination, her bishop asked her why she had chosen to end her marriage without trying to make it work. She gave him the only answer she had ever managed to come up with. She had thought Billy Trent was her great love. It took less than six months to realize he was just a life-style.

But Dana and David had more than a lifestyle.

"There's something good and strong and very special between you and David. You can't neglect it, and you can't give up on it."

"Easy for you to say."

"It takes work, Dana. I don't have to tell you that. Suppose you were growing a plant, a tree, and it cost you a lot of money, and it's very rare, and you did all your landscaping around it." It was the best metaphor Lexy could come manage in the middle of the beach on a foggy morning. "You wouldn't give up if it didn't thrive. You'd take care of it, wouldn't you? You'd help it through the bad time."

Dana laughed. "Bad metaphor. If we were really talking about a tree David would lend me a hand occasionally. I thought the modern marriage was a partnership. How come I've got to do all the heavy lifting while he does nothing?"

"Living with you isn't nothing." Dana could be prickly and hypersensitive. She wanted things her own way, and she wanted life organized according to her master plan. She did not like surprises.

Dana said dryly, "Maybe I should pay David a reward for just sticking around."

A few yards ahead of them Bailey had stopped running and stood waiting for them to catch up. Her overalls were wet to the knees and covered with sand. Dana sighed and seemed to sag.

"If you knew how tired I get. . . . All my life, Lexy, I've done what I had to so I'd get what I wanted. I keep waiting for someone to say, 'Relax, you've made it; here's your reward.'"

"You don't really believe life works that way."

"Then why have I tried so hard for so long? Why have I always done the right thing? Always." Dana paused, and in the silence Lexy imagined she heard the murmur of another conversation, one they would never have.

"You think I'm a monster?"

"Am I the Dalai Lama?"

"When I look ahead . . ."

"Well, there's your first mistake. Focus on today, this day." Lexy took the leash from Dana, called Moby Doby to her, and hooked the lead on his collar. "Take it from an old alcoholic, Dana. You can move through the deepest ca-ca if you do it one step at a time."

Lexy had appointments scheduled until midafternoon. At three a couple brimming with good looks and hope came in for premarital counseling. Lexy said to them what she had wanted to tell Dana. God, knowing that his children would be lonely without partners, blessed and encouraged all loving unions: friendship, parents and children, lover and lover, husband and wife.

She told the couple, "The thing you must never forget is that a marriage is a fragile organism, and it takes more than love to keep it alive. It requires forgiveness and trust and forbearance. Lots of forbearance."

She wished she'd said that to Dana.

The monthly meeting of St. Tom's vestry was held in the undercroft and was always a potluck to which Lexy was expected to contribute only her smiling, upbeat self. When everyone was seated and their plastic plates were heavy with Konnie's Mexican casserole and Beth's green salad, Lexy blessed the food, the vestry, and the work it did, and the meeting began. There were the usual matters of money and mission to discuss. Someone asked Lexy if she could schedule noontime Masses during Advent, and she said she would, though she had no idea how she'd manage. Beth reported on plans for the upcoming Day of the Dead, All Saints' Day celebration. The building committee reported on the estimated cost of wheelchair ramps. By the time Lexy returned to her office it was after nine, but she worked on a grant proposal until almost eleven, when the figures on the spreadsheet became a blur. She made herself a cup of drip coffee and dialed Micah's number, barely hoping he would pick up. When he did, she was momentarily tongue-tied.

"You answered. Hi. It's me."

"Yo, Me. It's eleven o'clock at night. Why aren't you in bed with someone?"

He laughed, and she guessed that he was stoned. Micah was not a laugher by nature.

"How are you?" she asked.

"How are *you?*"

"Oh. Working. Same old."

"You need to get a life."

"That's what Dana says."

"How is Dana?"

"I think she's hit one of those bumpy spots."

He laughed again, and she wondered why.

"You sure you're okay?" she asked as she wondered *Are you stoned? Depressed? You sound depressed.* Or: *Are you taking your meds? You must take your medicine, Micah.*

I'm not depressed. Of course I'm taking them. Or: *They make me sleepy.* Or: *I'm too young to abandon my libido.*

"I thought maybe the black dog had you," she added.

"Actually I'm feeling pretty good," he said.

"How 'bout I come over tomorrow after work, take you to dinner? Sound good?"

"Thing is, I won't be here. I've got this gallery in LA interested in my Florentine scenes. I want to see you, but—"

"Crap."

"Reverend Mother!"

"You want me to believe you?"

"Hey, you're not the only busy person in this family."

"You're selling?"

"How many times do I have to tell you, Alexandra, it's not about selling." He added with mocking pretentiousness, "It's about the art, darling."

"I can't help it if I'm my mother's daughter."

"Omigod, wash your mouth out with soap."

Lexy's grip on the phone relaxed. "So *are* you selling?"

"Enough." Neither spoke for a moment. "How's business with you? Saving lots of souls?"

"I'd like to have a go at yours."

"Yeah, well, you can pray at my funeral."

"You're sure you're okay?"

"Lex, give it a break, will you? You know the way I am, up one day, down the next. Tonight I'm cool."

"You're stoned."

"Shit, what a nag."

"I think about you all the time."

"Well, now, that's your first mistake."

"Love's never a waste of time, Micah."

He snorted. "Oh, yeah? What about Mr. William Parker Trent the Third?"

"I learned a lot from my time with Billy."

"And I learned a lot from Edie Parkhurst in the back of her grandmother's Rambler."

He was pushing her away. She was wise to all his tricks.

"Anyway," he said, "you didn't answer my question. Why aren't you in bed with someone? What happened to that guy you were dating last year? What was his name?"

"Isaac."

"And?"

"I haven't seen him."

"Why not? You liked him, you told me you did."

For a few months Isaac Slotkin had made her laugh and feel desirable. He was fun to go to movies with and baseball games; from the first they had talked like old friends. He wanted more than friendship, but she had neither time nor energy to complicate her life with sex. That's what she told herself and mostly believed. Dana said the collar was protection. If so, the protection was not from the world but from herself.

"Like all women, you're a heartbreaker, Lexy."

"I'm not. Why would you say that?"

"You married Billy and then you left him, and now there's this guy Isaac."

"Billy's getting along fine. He sent me an e-mail to tell me he's getting married again." Why was her brother talking about love and heartbreak?

"Micah, are you seeing someone?"

"No."

She waited.

"I was, but it's over."

Her heart sank. She had been his protector forever. His truest friend. "Tell me who she is. I'll bust her chops."

"That would be an interesting scene."

"Does it help if I say it takes time to get over someone? But it'll happen, Micah. Time'll pass and you'll stop hurting so much."

"No. I won't. Love is for a lifetime. It's old-fashioned, but that's what I believe."

Love and marriage, it was all she'd talked and thought about that day.

Micah said, "Go find yourself a nice man, Lexy. A guy who turns you on and makes you laugh. And promise me you'll be nice to him. Cross your heart and hope to die."

"Micah, I can't stand it when you hurt. Tell me what's going on with you. Is it this woman?"

"I need to know someone loves you, Alexandra."

Chapter 21

Saturday morning. *Early* Saturday morning. Bailey was pulling the blankets off the bed and tickling Dana's toes. She groaned and turned her head to read the clock. Small hands on her ankles tugged.

"Wait a minute, wait a minute." Dana sat up and, catching her daughter in her arms, she turned her onto her back and blew into the hollow of her neck. "What's happening here? Is it Christmas? Is it Easter?"

Bailey squirmed off the bed and pulled Dana to the window overlooking the side yard and garage. Larry McFarland was lumbering up the stairs to the apartment with a long aluminum ladder stuck under his arm, threatening to unbalance him. Three steps behind, Gracie carried a gallon paint can in each hand. Behind her came Allison, looking like Santa, with a pair of huge plastic bags from Home Depot hanging over her shoulders.

David called from downstairs, "Rise and shine, Number One." From the kitchen came the sound of the Wynton Marsalis CD Dana had given him on his birthday.

This is lovely, she thought. *This is how it's meant to be.*

Afterward she would remember what she wore that day—Levi's and a Miami University T-shirt that had faded to pink—the breakfast of eggs and sausage David made for the work crew, the sound of Wynton's willowy clarinet. Most of all she would remember how much fun they all had fixing up the garage apartment so Marsha Filmore could move into their lives.

The apartment was only one room and a bath, but the previous owners of the house had partitioned off a section to create a kitchen nook with a small refrigerator and microwave, a space comfortable for one person temporarily. The paintwork was straightforward, no crown moldings or eight-inch baseboards; and David and the team had the holes puttied and everything painted twice by midafternoon. Geoff rented a carpet cleaner, and the job was done by the time David put the steaks on the grill. Throughout the day Bailey had watched and sometimes helped. Once, hearing her laugh, David looked at Dana, his face alight with happiness, and she felt the old lightness, the familiar carbonated lift his smile prompted in her. They stepped toward each other and kissed, ignoring everyone around them.

Afterward, she would remember the kiss.

Dana and Geoff set out plates and cutlery and kept an eye on David's filets while the crew cleaned up. The sun had dipped below the eucalyptus in the canyon behind the house, and the deck was in shade. Dana brought out a pile of sweaters and shawls. Across the yard Bailey swept the stairs to the apartment.

"Be careful," Dana said and then to Geoff, "I wish those stairs had a banister."

"Quit worrying so much." Geoff opened a plastic

container of Greek olives and shot one into his mouth. "She seems way better. What do the cops say?"

"About what?"

He stopped folding paper napkins and looked at her over the top of his glasses.

"I don't talk to them. She's been through enough." The muscles of her jaw tightened as she prepared for Geoff's response.

"I'm with you," he said.

"You are?"

"Well, sure. The way I see it, she's here, she's healthy, and obviously she's not depressed." He tapped his temple where his red hair had begun to turn gold and gray. "Believe me, I know from depressed."

The meal was like old times with a gang of friends and plenty of good food and beer. Dana and David shared the wicker love seat, and she was conscious of their bodies touching at thigh and hip and shoulder.

They talked about the hate mail that arrived at the office two or three times a week. Some letters were typed, some printed out in pencil, and some bore messages written in cutout letters stuck to paper.

I have to tell him eventually. Why not now, in a crowd.

"I got a note the other day." She did not look at David.

He asked, "Why didn't you tell me?"

"You've been so busy. I spoke to Gary."

The team looked from Dana to David and back to Dana.

"There wasn't much he could do." She drew a deep breath. "I'd thrown it away."

No one said anything. Then Geoff cried, "Right on, sister! Garbage in, garbage out."

"What were you thinking?" David asked.

"I wasn't thinking, David."

"Give her a break, Boss," Gracie said. "She was in shock."

Geoff said, "I'd 'a done the same thing, Dana."

David did not seem to have heard anyone. "That was evidence. There might have been fingerprints."

"Look, I'm sorry I did it, but it's done and—"

"What about that message?" Geoff shuddered. "*I love you both?* Is that bizarre? Omigod."

"You might want to rethink what we were talking about," Larry said to David.

"Rethink what?" Dana asked.

David answered, "Dana, do you want a bodyguard? Larry knows a woman, an ex-Navy type."

"What a crazy idea." For one thing, she knew the firm could not afford a personal guard for Bailey and her; for another, she did not want David to think she was afraid. She wasn't, exactly. Whoever had written the note had taken Bailey—Gary said this was so—and returned her strong and healthy, traumatized but undamaged. If he had wanted to hurt her—or Dana—he would have acted by now.

Allison said, "We're going to trial in a few weeks. Once the case is finished, the mail'll stop."

David laced his fingers together and twirled his thumbs, looking from Dana to the members of the defense team as if weighing whether to debate, concede, or negotiate. His colleagues had taken her side, and she sensed that he felt in some way betrayed. She saw the anger and the effort it took to conceal it. As Dana's good mood faltered, she made a quick decision. There was nothing she could do about the lost evidence, so, to pacify him, rather than argue, she would agree to the bodyguard if he insisted. But he surprised her by changing the subject. The conversation turned to Frank Filmore, to trial strategy, and to Marsha Filmore.

"How long do you think it'll take for the press to find her here?" Allison asked.

"The press?" She had been tricked. "You didn't tell me there'd be reporters."

"Uh oh," Geoff said, standing up. "Time to do the dishes."

"Stay where you are." Dana stood up. "You guys have done enough." It was a relief to escape into the house. If she had to talk to David right then, or even look at him, she would get mean; and mad as she was, she did not want to embarrass him in front of the team.

None of them would have any peace after the cameras arrived.

As Dana collected the dishes, Gracie said, "I hate to ruin the party, but I think we'd better get her before she calls from some street corner."

"She's coming today?" Blindsided again. "But the paint won't even be dry."

"She says she doesn't care about the paint smell," Larry said. "She just wants out of that housekeeping motel in El Cajon."

Dana hipped the door into the kitchen, put the dishes on the counter, and sat down at the breakfast bar. Geoff and Gracie followed her, letting the door slam behind them.

"I can't believe David didn't tell you she's coming tonight." Geoff laid his hand on her shoulder.

"We all assumed you knew." Gracie sat beside Dana. "Here's what we'll do. For tonight we'll get her a hotel."

"No." Dana would not be the one to make David break his word. "You told her she could come, so go get her." She looked up in time to see Gracie and Geoff exchange a glance. "What?"

"You listen to me," Geoff said. "If you don't want that woman here, you just say so. This has not been a good year for you, and, personally, if you're asking my opinion, which I know you're not, but I'm going to give it to you anyway—"

"The boss can be a bully," Gracie said.

Dana instantly and automatically rushed to his defense.

"Who are you, anyway? Laura Bush?" Geoff said as he pulled out the stool beside her. "Gracie's right."

They meant to be supportive, but their concern cut into her like a trap.

"We all know when David wants something, he gets it."

"God, all the times he's got me to work overtime when I didn't want to." Geoff rolled his eyes.

Gracie said, "None of us thought it was fair to ask you to have Marsha in the apartment in the first place. We all argued against it."

Annoyed as Dana was, it still hurt to hear David criticized by his friends.

At the sink she began scraping fat from the steaks into a plastic dish to sweeten Moby's dinner. Through the kitchen windows she watched David in conversation with Larry McFarland. He tilted his head back and drank the last of his Corona, and the movement was so familiar, her eyes stung in memory of the college boy she fell in love with. He would be deeply wounded if he knew Geoff and Gracie had called him a bully. He took charge, called the plays; he was the quarterback.

"You don't really know him," she said and snapped a top on the plastic dish. "He didn't bully me. He and I, we're a team. This is something I want to do to help the case. I honestly don't care if she moves in today or next week. I was just caught off guard."

Gracie looked at Geoff. "You're sure?"

"Absolutely."

"Okay," Gracie said. "In that case, I'll go get her."

"Me too," Geoff said.

They wanted to end the conversation in the kitchen and continue it in the car between themselves. For a while, as she imagined what they might be saying, Dana indulged in a fit of peevishness that stirred the sparks of her resentment and annoyance until she was angry again, not just with David now, with all of them. She was wiping the granite counters when Bailey pranced into the kitchen with each of the fingers of her right hand stuck into beer bottles.

"That's dirty," Dana snapped. "Put them in the recycling and go wash your hands."

Bailey shook her head and grinned at Dana from between huge fingers.

Dana felt her face redden and her pulse quicken. "Do as you're told, Bay." She tried to swallow back the anger. It wasn't Bailey's fault. It was David who was driving her crazy.

Bailey grinned and waggled her fingers in Dana's face.

"Dammit to hell—"

Bailey jerked back her hand and slammed it down against the granite counter. Three bottles shattered, and shards of glass flew onto the counter and floor. Bailey saw blood dripping from her hand and began to scream. David raced through the back door and scooped her into his arms at the same time he grabbed for a dish towel and wrapped it around her hand.

Dana stood frozen, staring at them, then fled upstairs.

Chapter 22

Dana opened her eyes when the gray light of morning began to fill the bedroom. She stared at the open-beamed ceiling, feeling nothing, her mind a blank. Suddenly she remembered the night before, and as the guilt rushed in, it flattened her, squeezing air from her lungs as if she had awakened in a two-dimensional world. Beside her David turned fitfully, taking half the bedcovers with him. She would never get back to sleep. She might as well go for a run. When she came back she would apologize to David and agree with whatever he said or suggested.

Who was she, anyway? Lately she hardly recognized herself. Organized, sensible, goal-oriented, and successful: that's who she was. But it certainly had not been sensible to throw away the note and say nothing about it. Whoever was sending notes had taken Bailey from them. It could happen again, and maybe this time he wouldn't bring her back.

Dana's strange behavior had come from the shock of the kidnapping and return; it must be a kind of post-traumatic stress. This made excellent sense. She had other symptoms: she couldn't concentrate anymore, her mind was a sieve, she slept poorly, and her relationship with David wasn't good. She had suffered a massive emotional trauma. When she thought about it that way, it was a miracle she wasn't in a rubber room.

She walked softly down the hall, stopping at Bailey's open door to look in. She lay on her back with her arms flung out. Dana saw the bulky white bandage on her hand and her throat closed. She had reacted to the scene with the beer bottles as thoughtlessly as Imogene once might have. Swearing to make it up to her husband and child, she went downstairs, her bare feet sticking to the hardwood floors. Moby came in from the living room and put his wet nose under her hand to get her attention. After giving him a biscuit, she walked to the sink and splashed water on her face.

On the front steps she sat down to lace her running shoes. The air was cool and damp as she stretched out her hamstrings and quads on the brick front steps. From the next street she heard the regular thump of the Sunday paper being tossed from a car onto driveways and porches. A dog barked a halfhearted protest. In the park across the street the details of the trees and shrubs had begun to emerge gradually, like visitors from another world. A figure stood at the foot of a white-barked eucalyptus fifty meters into the park. She thought she recognized Micah's insouciant slouch, and a thrill ran through her, followed by dread like a heavy coat on a hot day. She glanced up at the bedroom window to make sure the light was off, then jogged across the street and into the park.

Micah straightened as she approached. He wore Levi's and a leather jacket over a T-shirt.

"What are you doing here?"

Once she had thought him attractively boyish, but the half-light revealed his face to be more gaunt than she recalled and etched with fatigue. She did not remember the deep lines bracketing his mouth or the pleat of skin between his eyes.

"I have nothing to give you. How many times do I have to say it? Why do you keep pestering me?"

"Pestering?"

He had last contacted her months ago, but seeing him concealed in the shadows of the park, spying on her house, she felt as if he had been tormenting her constantly and for a long time. It occurred to her that in a sense he had been, though not intentionally. Since Italy thoughts of him had never been far beneath the surface of her mind. She had been reminded of him by Lexy, by a winning flash in the eyes of a stranger, by the sight of someone with a boyish grin or tall, slender body like his.

"Just tell me why you're here. What do you want from me?"

"You know."

"You're wrong. I don't know. I thought we'd talked this through. I thought you understood me."

"I couldn't sleep and I couldn't stop thinking about you. . . ."

"You're off your meds, aren't you?"

He laughed. "You and my sister, you act like everything's a pharmaceutical problem. I don't need medicine."

"Don't you want to be happy?"

"I want to be alive. You make me feel alive. Not pills."

"It's not fair to lay that on me. I don't want that responsibility."

"You said you loved me."

"But I didn't mean it the way you thought I did."

"Why do you lie to me? You loved me, I know it."

"Micah, the police patrol this park at night. You're not supposed to be here after sundown."

"That's not what bothers you."

She despised his satisfied air of knowing her better than she knew herself.

He said, "You always follow the rules."

"That's not the point. This isn't about me. It's about you leaving me alone. I know I hurt you, and if I could undo what happened, I would. But since I can't—"

"You wouldn't change a thing. You say you would, but I know you better than you know yourself."

"This is an insane conversation."

"Don't say that." He grabbed her hand and held it pressed between his palms.

"You're hurting me."

"Not as much as you've hurt me."

"Oh, God, Micah, I'm sorry. Why can't you just believe me when I say there can't be anything between us? Let it go, let *me* go for God's sake."

He dropped her hand. "If you were mine I wouldn't let you run at night."

"Don't change the subject."

"He doesn't deserve you. He leaves you alone. He stays away most nights."

"He works."

"If you were mine I'd never let you out of my sight."

"That's it," she said, backing away. "I'm done. I'm going for my run now, and if you're not gone when I get back, I'm calling the police. I will do it, Micah, I promise you. I'm going to say you're stalking me."

He touched her shoulder and she flinched. As he ran his fingertips down her upper arm, she thought of a sculptor stroking the clay beneath his hands, warming it into life.

"You're so strong, Dana. You look delicate, but you're not. You're tough. I always forget that about you."

Move, she thought. *Run.* She didn't know why she was

still standing there, mesmerized by his hands caressing her shoulders and up her neck into her hair.

"If you came to Mexico sometimes no one would have to know except us. And I'd be satisfied with that, Dana. It's not much, but I'd be okay, I wouldn't ask for more than four or five times a month. I'd be able to work then. See, that's the deal, I can't work now. It's like I'm flat all the time, but just knowing I'd see you would give me something to hope for."

It was pointless to argue. She had nothing to say to him that she hadn't said before. Micah was a creature of whim and emotion, a man inured to logical arguments, one who reveled in the life of his senses.

Hopelessly, she covered her face with her hands.

He pulled them away, and his large dark blue eyes peered into her face. In the heat of his gaze what was hardened against him melted and spilled. Sensing this, he put his arms around her, and she did not resist but took a deep breath and, letting it out, came to rest against the familiar lines of his angular body.

He was hard against her, and without thought her hips moved toward him. His arms tightened around her. She saw the future. Saw herself lying on the damp grass within view of the house and yet as lost as if she were both blind and deaf, abandoned in a dark land beyond rescue.

She jerked away and stumbled backward, regaining her balance against the trunk of the eucalyptus. "I can't be your hope, don't make me your hope. You have to let me go."

"Never. As long as I live—"

The crisp lemon scent of the tree sharpened her senses.

"You need help. Not hope. You need to go back on your meds and see a doctor, talk to someone. Not me," she whispered. "Not me."

Chapter 23

As Dana retreated from the park and crossed the street she sensed him watching her, hoping she would weaken, turn back and return to him. She tried not to run or reveal in any way how frightened she was. He might call out, and she was not sure what the sound of his voice might do to her.

As she came around the corner of the garage she saw Marsha Filmore sitting on the top of the steps to the apartment, smoking a cigarette. She wore a huge sweat-shirt and black leggings. Even pregnant, she looked thin, with skinny legs and arms and shoulders rounded like a dowager's. In contrast, her stomach bulged as enormously as if an exercise ball had been stuck to the front of her.

Dana stood in the shadows, watching and waiting for her body to stop shaking. Marsha lit a fresh cigarette off the burning stub of the first. Dana felt a flash of outrage on behalf of the fetus but then saw the script of despair on Marsha Filmore's face and her disapproval became pity. It was not Marsha's fault Frank Filmore was a monster. And in the old days plenty of women smoked during pregnancy, and their children mostly turned out fine. Dana's own mother had used tobacco and only God knew what else.

She opened the gate to the yard and said good morning. Then, "I'm just making coffee. Would you like a cup?" Any distraction would help break the spell of Micah.

As she measured grounds into a filter Dana realized she was beginning something David had known she would not be able to resist. He never said he wanted her to pump this woman for information. He wouldn't dare. But to Dana his motive was clear.

Since when was Dana supposed to do David's work for him? Didn't he pay an investigator to dig up the dirt? Resentment distracted her further and burned like chronic indigestion. It seemed like she was always resentful of something these days.

Through one of the large kitchen windows Dana watched as Marsha settled onto the redwood chaise, tilted her head back, and closed her eyes. Dana imagined Marsha had once loved Frank Filmore and perhaps had held on to that love as long as she could, but now it was gone, yet she was stuck with him. That seemed like a pretty good reason for smoking. Or maybe she loved him in spite of what he was. Maybe she couldn't help loving him.

Having filled the kettle, Dana had begun slicing strawberries for Bailey's breakfast when David came downstairs. Although it was Sunday, he was dressed for work in chinos and a cotton sweater. His eyes were bruised with fatigue.

"Did you run?" he asked.

"It was chilly. Very fallish."

"Uh huh."

"You're going to work?"

"Uh huh."

Dana ticked her head toward the deck. "And leaving me alone with her?"

"I'll be back around three-thirty. The game's at four."

"You're going because you're mad at me?"

His expression said she had just asked a question too profoundly stupid to be acknowledged.

A sharp retort was on her lips, but she remembered her vow to be agreeable and forced a smile instead. "I don't know what happened to me last night." She hated making apologies. "I just lost it." She wondered how long he had stayed up drinking with Larry and the others. Once the sleeping pill took effect, Dana had slept through the night without waking. "First there was the stuff about the press and her moving right in, and then . . ." She shrugged and hoped he understood.

"It doesn't matter." Translation: he was pissed.

"David, please. Don't be mean." She whispered so that Marsha would not hear her through the open back door.

Bailey wandered into the kitchen wearing only her underpants and a pair of bunny slippers.

"Look at her hand," David said. Gloved in bandage and gauze it was twice its normal size.

"It wasn't my fault. She hit the bottles against the sink,"

"Why'd you make a big—"

"Lower your voice, David. We can talk later."

"—deal of it? When you were a kid didn't you ever put beer bottles on your fingers?"

Imogene drank beer from cans.

"Why can't you try just a little harder, Dana? I know it's not easy, but what the hell else do you do?" He shook his head. "I'm sorry, I didn't mean that."

But of course he had. Her job description was simple: wife, mother, and team player. And right now she was failing in all three.

He looked as if he wanted to say something else, but instead he lifted his shoulders and smiled a little—sheepishly, she thought. A smile she had once found irresistible. A man who smiled that way, she could forgive him almost anything and for a long time. Not forever, but for a long time.

"The game's at four," he said.

At four o'clock the house would be full of David's buddies and some of their wives, women Dana knew only from Sundays in the fall. Beer, California sushi, chips and salsa; someone would bring lasagna or pizza or nachos. Football food.

"Did you forget it's our Sunday to host? I wrote you a note." He gestured toward the refrigerator, where Dana saw the pink Post-it note. It had been there ten days at least, and she had stopped seeing it.

On the deck he paused to lay his hand on Marsha's shoulder and say something. Words of consolation and encouragement, Dana supposed. He was good at that when he wanted to be.

She wondered if Micah still stood in the park watching the house and how many times had he done it before tonight. She could look out the living room window, but she really did not want to know. Feeling the way she did right now, she could not trust herself.

"Shit," she said, aiming the word at life in general.

Bailey tugged on the sash of Dana's dressing gown. "What?"

Bailey patted her lips with her index finger and shook her tangled head. Beautiful silent angel.

"I'm sorry," Dana said. "That was a bad word." She

lifted Bailey into her arms and kissed her bandaged fingers one by one.

Bad wife. Bad mommy.

Eventually Dana carried the coffee to the deck. "Sorry I took so long." She laid the tray on the table. Marsha had stubbed out her cigarettes in a pot of geraniums. Dana handed her an ashtray.

Bad mommy. Bad wife. Great hostess.

"I never sleep anymore," Marsha said. "And there wasn't any coffee in the apartment."

Dana wondered if she imagined criticism. Had Marsha been expecting a full larder? Ten-dollar-a-pound coffee and deli packs from Real Food?

"I hate to go out," Marsha said. "People look at me."

Common ground at last.

"It was the same for me when Bailey was gone. After the first article in *People*."

"Ghouls," Marsha said. "Where is your little girl?"

"Eating breakfast. She's nervous around strangers."

"Ha! Me too."

Dana flinched as a hummingbird whirred by her ear. It hovered, piercing the blossoms of the leggy pink buddleia that grew in a pot at the edge of the deck. Down the street someone was using a leaf blower, and there were children in the park playing soccer. It was a normal Sunday for everyone but the Cabot family. It would take the fingers of both hands to enumerate how off-kilter their individual and communal lives had become.

"I saw you," Marsha said, looking at Dana over the rim of her coffee cup, "in the park."

Dana swallowed sand.

"It doesn't matter, you know." Marsha regarded her steadily. "Who you meet, who you talk to, it's none of my business. I won't tell your husband."

Dana's cheeks reddened as much with anger as embarrassment. "You can tell him what you like. A lot of people around here run." Dana's voice did not want to cooperate. "Early runners. We know each other."

Marsha smiled and took another sip of coffee. "You want to be careful, out on the streets so early."

Dana stared. Who was this woman to tell her anything? She blurted, "You shouldn't be smoking."

Marsha looked surprised and then dismissive and amused. "Considering everything, cigarettes are the least this little girl's got to worry about."

"It's a girl?"

"Yeah. Poor little cunt."

Fingers and toes tingling, Dana stood up. She took Marsha's cup from her even though she hadn't finished it. "I'm going shopping. I'll buy you groceries. Leave the list on the tray."

She walked into the kitchen and locked the door behind her.

Chapter 24

On Sunday Lexy taught an adult Bible class following the ten-thirty service and afterward enjoyed a three-mile run on the beach. She stopped by El Cholo for carryout and now lay on the couch in her gray sweats, the remains of a beef burrito on a plate on the floor beside her. There was no question she had earned this day of rest, but it was the same on Sunday as on the other six days of the week—when she stopped moving, doing, acting, and working, she felt the disapproving eyes of God upon her. Or were they her mother's eyes? She couldn't always tell the difference.

She should have worked through the God and mother thing in seminary, where she had been given countless opportunities to lay bare her neuroses. But it was such an embarrassing cliché to admit she suffered from the neurotic equivalent of the common cold, a sense of never being good or worthy enough. She did not want anyone to know about the anger that lay at the heart of her childhood.

The white walls of Lexy's apartment were bare except for a Swanson print of the Tower of Babel that she had told Dana was a portrait of her mind when "the committee" took over her thinking. Her furniture, a cherry red couch and easy chairs and a footstool the size of a Volkswagen, was classic Ikea. No fancy pillows, not a knickknack in sight. Her one indulgence was the flowers she bought weekly from a wholesaler and arranged in a blue Mexican bowl on the plank coffee table.

She clicked up the television volume, hoping to drown out the committee carping in her head, though she knew there was really only one effective way to silence the racket. It was the alcoholic's aspirin, the all-purpose remedy for every ill: a meeting, a meeting, a meeting. Take thirty meetings in thirty days, ninety in ninety days; no committee could survive that. The nagging never went away completely, however. It waited just below her consciousness, ready to erupt when provoked. The current rant had begun with Micah's call the previous week. Her intuition that something was wrong had segued into guilt for not having spoken to her mother in more than ten days.

Several of the committee members in her head had her mother's weather-worn face and spoke with her flat western drawl, the accent of wide skies over empty, arid land. *What makes you think you can be a priest? You—a cocaine addict, an alcoholic who slept with half the eligible men in New York before settling down for less than a year with William Whats-his-name. Plus you neglect your brother and you're lazy and self-centered and vain as a mare in heat.*

She did not think her mother had ever been consciously cruel, but as Billy once said, she was a ropy old pioneer broad. She had her own way of thinking and never considered there might be another, equally valid point of view. She was neither stupid nor uninformed; nevertheless, she believed alcoholism and depression were defects of character and will, conditions that stank of carelessness and, worst of all, an absence of self-discipline.

Lexy was grateful to alcoholism. It had brought her to her knees, to surrender. It had bent her toward God in a way that nothing else could have. In meetings she heard variations of her own story told by teenaged crackheads, suburban matrons, bums and businessmen. The wonder of it knocked her over, lifted her up, and then dropped her to her knees. And on her knees she had found her faith.

God accepts us all, Lexy thought. *Why can't you, Ma? Why couldn't Dad?* He had died not speaking to either Lexy or Micah. Lexy blamed her mother for this. As far as she knew, she had never spoken up for either of them, never defended their right to be themselves.

This is what Dana and I have in common, she thought. *Neither of us had a mother worth a pot of peas.*

Chapter 25

An arrangement had been made with Miss Judy at Phillips Academy for Bailey to visit school during playtime. Reluctantly Lieutenant Gary had said it would be safe if the visits were unscheduled. The important thing, he had repeated half a dozen times, was not to establish any activity patterns a kidnapper could rely upon. Bailey loved her school outings. Her silent eagerness to be part of the wider world both gratified and encouraged Dana.

On the Monday morning after her meeting with Micah, Dana delivered Bailey to school and then looked in on Rochelle at Arts and Letters. She was helping a customer choose a birthday book, so Dana went into the stockroom and began unpacking boxes of books from a distributor. These were popular novels whose titles Dana recognized.

Rochelle stood at the stockroom door. "I intend to deep-discount those. Perhaps the vision of a woman committing economic hari kari will bring a few more customers in off the street."

"Business bad?"

"Of course, darling. When is it otherwise? But I sold

that beautiful Giotto book yesterday, and this month's rent is paid. Who am I to fret?"

Dana always felt a pang when one of the magnificent coffee-table books of stunning reproductions left the shop. She thought of the upstairs loft as her own private library.

"Do you have time to help me shelve this week?"

"If I can bring Bailey."

"But of course. A child who doesn't speak is a blessing to the world." She flipped her hand. "Just teasing. Not to worry." She sailed back to the front of the shop trailing chiffon scarves in shades of blue and green.

Dana was folding down a box for recycling when Rochelle came into the back room again. "I've been meaning to ask how your thesis is coming. You know you can take home any book you need. You've only to jot a note."

"Thanks." Dana dropped the flattened box into the recycling bin. "I've got a ways to go."

"Well, darling, what's holding you up now that Bailey's back? I adore having you here, but really."

"Bailey keeps me busy."

"Garbage, garbage, garbage. I raised four children. I know whereof I speak."

"I'm not as organized as you, Rochelle."

"Sit down and listen to me, Dana." She patted the box beside her. "I want you to take advantage of the books while you can. I don't know how much longer I'm going to be able to keep this place afloat. I adore Arts and Letters, you know that, but it's terribly difficult to sell books these days, and I'm not sure I want to be bothered anymore."

"You'd sell?"

"In an instant. Though I've no idea who'd buy the place."

"I'd buy it. I'd love to own a bookstore."

"Indeed? What about 'The Significance of Visual Subtext in Italian Renaissance Art'?"

Once Dana had enjoyed thinking and talking about her thesis, but the life had gone out of it. She told herself she did not know why. "It's hard, Rochelle."

"My God, darling, what isn't?"

While Dana and Bailey were out, the mail had been dropped through the old-fashioned slot in the middle of the Cabots' front door and lay scattered on the entry tiles. As Dana stooped to gather the envelopes, flyers, and catalogs, she noticed one long white envelope in particular. The address on the outside was printed in individual letters cut from magazines.

No stamp.

Someone had watched and waited until she and Bailey were away from home, then stepped onto their porch and slipped the envelope through the mail slot. Her intestines knotted, and automatically she looked around for Bailey and saw her headed upstairs, stretching her small legs to take the stairs two at a time.

Safe.

Dana slumped onto the bottom stair. She did not have to open the envelope to know what kind of message lay inside. She smelled the hostility coming off it as if the writer had poison on his fingers. She also knew she had reached the limit of her patience. If she had to, she would take Bailey away from San Diego, hide with her in some gray and anonymous eastern city until the Filmore trial was over and the police had caught her daughter's kidnapper. Maybe it was a crazy man working on his own, maybe a whole gang—women as well as men—waging a hammer-of-God vendetta against defense attorneys. The threat to Bailey and David, to the family, was as real as the air in Dana's lungs and the sweat on her skin.

She would have to begin working more closely with the police and dragging Bailey—willing or not, happy or not—to shrinks and therapists and anyone who had a chance of getting her to talk about what happened during the three and a half months she was gone. Until then the notes, the threats, the constant abrasion of anxiety would continue. It was so simple, really. Coopcrate with Lieutenant Gary, love David and Bailey. Why did she insist on complicating it?

She called Gary, and he came over immediately.

Chapter 26

She showed the detective the envelope, still lying on the tiles. Putting on gloves, he carefully slit the seal. A photo of David and Bailey taken at the time she was returned had been glued to a sheet of white paper and a noose drawn around David's neck in black marker.

Dana ran to the kitchen sink and vomited acid. She splashed water on her face, dried it with a paper towel, then gagged again. As she turned, Gary was at the counter in the kitchen putting the envelope and paper into a plastic evidence bag. He slipped it into the inside pocket of his sport coat.

"Well, it doesn't look like Bailey's their target anymore," he said. "I'll get someone over here to check for prints around the mail slot." He rubbed his eyes and dragged his hand down his face and across his mouth. "It's a long shot. There's not much I—"

"You can talk to Bailey, ask her questions. You can talk to her now, here."

He looked surprised.

Bailey grumped and dragged her feet when Dana told her to turn off *Sesame Street* and come into the

kitchen. She refused to sit in her own chair. She strad-
dled Dana's lap with her back to the officer.

"What happened to her hand?" he asked.

"Cut herself."

"Serious?"

"No."

He looked at the back of Bailey's head. "Just a couple of questions."

Dana watched his body language relax. She wondered if he had children of his own and thought it
strange that she had never asked.

His voice held a smile as he asked, "Bailey, when
you went away—"

Bailey pressed her forehead into Dana's collarbone
and clapped her hands over her ears.

Dana tried to pry those little hands away, but her
daughter was surprisingly strong. Over Bailey's head
she looked at Gary, feeling helpless and vindicated at
the same time.

"It's okay," he said, and mouthed the words, *She's
listening*.

He said, "When you went away, Bailey, did you go
in a car with a lady?"

Bailey shook her head.

"Were you in the car a long time?"

No response.

"Did you sleep in the car?"

Nothing.

"Did you have good things to eat while you were
away?"

"What's the point of a question like that?" Dana
asked.

The detective's head dropped forward, and he stared
at the counter for so long the silence became uncom-

fortable. Dana wondered if she should apologize for interrupting him, or if there was something he expected her to do.

He shifted forward on the chair. "Look, Bailey, your mother told me that when you were going to school you learned all about policemen and firemen and the kind of work they do."

For the first time Bailey turned her head to look at him.

"I'm a policeman. It's my job to find people that do bad things."

"You were stolen away from me," Dana said, holding Bailey's heart-shaped face between her hands. "Stealing a little girl away from her mommy and daddy is just about the most bad thing anyone can do."

"That's right," Gary said. "But policemen can't work alone. They need helpers. That's why I'm asking you these questions, Bailey. I need you to be my helper."

"Bay?"

She had fallen asleep.

As Dana walked the detective to the door she told him about taking Bailey to the beach and her new courage in the water. In the foyer, she sat on the bottom stair, pushing aside the pile of unopened mail, as she told him what she had realized about herself a few hours earlier. "Normally I'm a cooperative person. You might not believe that because you've never seen me actually *be* helpful, but it's true."

"What happened to you isn't something you get over fast. Maybe it stays with you the rest of your life. I don't know. Tell you the truth, I never worked a kidnapping where the child was returned."

She felt a surge of pity for him. "I've been hard on you. I'm sorry."

He nodded, looking at her with narrowed, assessing eyes.

"And you know, it's still crazy around here. Marsha Filmore's living with us now."

"In your house?"

"God, no. There's an apartment over the garage."

He shook his head, obviously perplexed.

"Marsha didn't do anything." Dana folded her arms across her chest. "She's a victim. Why should she suffer because she has lousy taste in husbands?"

"You're a strange woman, Mrs. Cabot." He stepped around the mail and opened the front door. "Every time you see a white van you panic, but you destroy a piece of potentially important evidence and 'forget' to tell me things, and then you let the wife of a child killer come and live with you."

"There's a presumption of innocence, in case you've forgotten."

"Actually, I haven't forgotten," he said. "I've been presuming you're innocent for months now."

"Me? Of course—"

"My chief keeps saying I'm naive. Am I?"

Dana swallowed what felt like a marble.

"I mean, is it true, you're acting weird because you're still kind of in shock? Or are you covering for someone?"

He leaned toward her.

"Do you know who kidnapped Bailey?"

David called to say he would be working late. Dana and Bailey drove to Big Bad Cat for hamburgers and milkshakes. On the ten-minute drive home Bailey fell asleep, and when Dana carried her upstairs to bed she did not waken. Dana unlaced her shoes and eased off her pink-and-white striped overalls. For one night she could sleep in her underwear.

As she knelt beside Bailey's bed watching her settle into deep sleep, Dana replayed the conversation with Gary. She would call his superior tomorrow and complain. She wanted him demoted, fired for the crime of insulting her. At the least he deserved a reprimand. But she knew it would never happen. Gary and his superior thought she was lying to protect someone. In a little while she would call Lexy and say, "Can you believe what jerks they are?"

More than offended, Dana was hurt by the policeman's suspicions. She thought of the person who had kidnapped Bailey and of the picture with the noose carefully drawn around David's neck. Gary must think she was a monster to protect such a person. Her stomach turned in disgust. She closed her eyes and rested her forehead on Bailey's mattress, letting the room spin around her.

She wouldn't call Gary's boss. He had hurt and offended her, but when she made herself replay the last few weeks she could not blame him for misinterpreting her behavior.

Later she poured a glass of wine, intending to take it upstairs; but she felt too edgy to sleep or settle down to watch television—simultaneously wrung out and wired. She walked around the house, turning on all the lights, checking the locks on the windows and doors downstairs, pulling the blinds and drapes. The house felt airless as a sealed box.

She put on a sweater and went outside to sit on the deck. No sooner had she done so than she realized Marsha was sitting up on the stairs. Without invitation she came down and sat beside Dana.

"He always come home late?"

"He's got a lot of work."

"Means you and the little girl are alone a lot. You lock your doors?"

Dana asked, "Did you talk to the police?"

Marsha blew smoke out the corner of her mouth and shook her head. "Must have been him knocked on the door, but I didn't answer. I don't have to talk to cops unless I want to."

"This wasn't about you. He wanted to know if you saw anyone at the house. Maybe making a delivery?"

Marsha stubbed her cigarette out in an empty tuna can. "Someone in a white van stopped by. Put something through your mail slot."

Dana felt a huge relief. She was not paranoid. A white van had been following her and Bailey. "A man or a woman?"

"Guy. Why? What's happened?"

"We got hate mail today."

"Because of Frank, I s'pose."

"Would you be able to recognize the guy from the van?"

"Maybe."

Dana went back into the house and called Gary. She left a message on his voice mail. "It was a white van," she said, not bothering to identify herself or hide the gloating in her voice. "Marsha Filmore saw it, and she might be able to identify the man who came to the door. She said she'd go down to the station, but you'll have to send a car for her."

She wanted to tell David, so she rang his office, but the answering machine was on there, too. She hung up, gave Moby his nighttime biscuits, and turned off the kitchen lights. As she crossed the foyer to go upstairs, she saw the pile of mail she had left on the floor. She picked it up, sat on the bottom stair, and went through the usual advertising flyers from grocers and drugstores, catalogs, bills—a couple she had deliberately let slip the month before. There were three manila envelopes, two of them official-looking and addressed to David.

The third stopped her breath.

She recognized Micah's bold, square printing on the bulky envelope. She stood up and walked into the living room. She turned on a lamp beside the couch and sat down, curling her feet beneath her. As she turned the envelope over and over, her fingertips left damp smudges. Finally she shoved her first finger under the flap, tore it open, and tipped the contents out.

The striped sash to Bailey's pink and lime dotted Swiss dress dropped onto her lap. It was the dress she had been wearing the day she disappeared.

Chapter 27

She could not move off the couch. There were things she should be doing, important calls to make, but she was stuck in place.

The sash had come with a note.

Forgive me, Dana, for taking her. Without you I am a monster.

Where her stomach should have been there was a crater, a vast cavity as if she had been hit by a meteor. One thing she knew: Micah would not have hurt Bailey.

She'll be okay, she'll make it. Thank You, God.

Moby inched his black nose under her hands and gazed up at her with questioning concern.

Loving me has made him a monster. She wrapped her arms around the dog's neck and sobbed until he squeaked and squirmed and pulled away from her. He lay down at her feet, resting his head on his neat front paws, his pointed ears pricked attentively.

I have to do something. . . .

But she could not focus, could not carry any thoughts through to the end. Except these:

Micah had taught Bailey to bodysurf.

He had been kind to her.

He would not have molested her, because he only took her to hurt Dana.

Thank You, God.

The synapses connecting her brain and her muscles had shorted out. She looped the pink and green sash around her neck like a scarf and absently rubbed the nubby fabric back and forth against her lips. She touched the dotted Swiss to her cheek and felt the fuzzy dots, no bigger than ants. She held it to her nose and tried to inhale something of Bailey, something of Micah. Her daughter's kidnapper.

A spark of rage caught fire in her chest.

Call someone. Gary.

She remembered the expression on Gary's face when he virtually accused her of protecting Bailey's kidnapper. Learning about Micah would confirm his worst suspicions.

David.

The details of the scandal would be a gala for the press.

She shoved the note and sash in her pocket and walked into the kitchen, turned on the tap, and, leaning forward, let the cool water soak her hair as it ran across the back of her neck.

In David's hierarchy of values, loyalty ranked above all others. Dana had never doubted his fidelity although she knew he must have had countless opportunities. Women loved power, and even back in college David had it. But it wasn't in him to cheat. Everyone who knew David knew he could be trusted. He would not understand that in the language of her week with Micah there had been no word for loyalty. In Florence nothing was real, everything was fantasy.

Micah would be arrested and tried for kidnapping. The affair would come out, and David would probably leave her, and the turmoil of it all would destroy Bailey.

She dried her hair and neck with a dish towel, then knelt to mop up the mess she'd made on the tiles.

The way out of her situation was obvious. The answer to her dilemma was silence. She would act as if the note and the sash had never come in the mail. She sat back on her heels. For that to work she had to make sure Micah never came near her family again. Micah. Now when she said his name in her mind, she felt bugeyed with rage. Incendiary. She wanted to stand before him and let him feel the heat of it. She would tell him to get out of San Diego and never come back. If he came near her or anyone in her family again, she would go to Lieutenant Gary.

This time she would not destroy the evidence. She would hide the note and the sash in one of her shoe boxes as insurance.

If you ever come back, if you breathe a word of any part of this, I will go to the police. I swear it on my daughter's life.

Dana went outside and across the deck, up the stairs to the garage apartment. She knocked on the door.

"It's me, Marsha. Let me in." She heard sounds from inside, and the door opened. Marsha Filmore wore a black nightgown with spaghetti straps. She held a bottle of scarlet fingernail polish in her hand.

"I was doing my toes."

"Look, I don't have a lot of time to explain, but an emergency's come up and I have to go out. David's working late, and it would really help me if you could babysit."

Marsha laughed.

"What's funny?"

"You. Asking me to take care of your little girl."

If Dana had been able to think of an alternative, if Guadalupe hadn't been miles away in Tijuana, if she could have called Lexy without making her curious—

"Can you do it?"

"Sure, sure. Just give me a second to change my clothes."

Months before, when he had surprised Dana at Arts and Letters in the middle of the night, Micah had told her he lived on the second floor of the old apartment house on the corner of Fourth and Spruce. She nearly ran the light at Washington and Goldfinch, went up University and down Fourth into the Hillcrest District, darting through another intersection on the corner of Fourth and Robinson, swerving around pedestrians in the crosswalk. Driving fast suited her anger and fed it. She knew herself, the way her mind worked. If she did not get to Micah fast, doubt would worm its way into her thoughts and she would begin to second-guess the deception she was setting in motion.

She parked in front of Micah's building and looked up to the windows on the second story left, where all the lights were on. Either no one was home in the other apartments or the tenants were sleeping. She did not know what she would do if Micah wasn't at home. Beside the front door there were mailboxes, and his name was on number four. She tried the knob, and the door swung open.

Luck, she told herself. A sign that she was meant to follow through with this.

The apartment house had the sour detergent-and-cabbage smell of too many tenants cooking meals and washing clothes over a span of too many years. The maroon carpet on the stairs had worn to the wood in the middle of each tread, and the handrail had a metallic shine where the paint was gone. Two apartments opened onto the second-floor landing. Beside one door stood a plastic potted plant and a life-sized ceramic cat with a mouse in its mouth.

Micah definitely did not live there.

Dana knocked on the other door and stepped back, surprised, when it, too, opened to her touch.

Another sign.

She stood on the threshold and called his name. She stepped inside. "Micah?"

Next door a dog yapped.

"Micah, it's Dana. You left your door open."

It was an old-fashioned, railroad-style apartment. The front door opened into a tiny anteroom, which opened into an old kitchen floored with swirls of yellow, orange, and blue linoleum. A sash window over the sink was open, and from the sill a yellow cat with a bell around its neck observed her.

"Micah?"

She looked into the living room.

Was it too late to turn around and go home? Perhaps pack a bag for herself and move to some far desert town, change her name, and find hard work, brain-numbing work? Eventually the desert sun would burn the memories out of her.

In Micah's palazzo in Florence there had been paintings and pictures everywhere. Between the back of the couch and the wall, canvases had been filed on their sides, tacked to temporary wooden frames. There were paintings in the bathroom and on the back of the front door. The main room had been a montage of color and images. Nothing matched, but everything in the space seemed to belong there. She remembered waking in Micah's bed, the smell of turpentine and oil paint, and across the room Micah in the doorway with cups of syrupy Italian chocolate in his hands and a bag of pastries between his teeth like a dog. She remembered the feel of the sheets and the river-smelling air coming in the window over her head.

She remembered everything.

In the bare-walled and shabbily furnished living room on Spruce Street he lay lengthwise on the floor, and his feet were bare, the soles pink, as if he had just bathed. His head was turned to one side so that what Dana saw was his ruddy cheek and the way his hair curled around his ears and the golden glow of his earring. From where she stood, paralyzed, he looked almost perfect.

His other cheek lay in the blood that had pooled around the bullet hole in his head and soaked into the worn wooden floor.

She did not scream; her throat had sealed shut.

She looked at his feet again, at the vulnerability of their tender pinkness. Waves of despair and shame and grief hit so hard they seemed to have velocity. She dropped to her knees, took hold of his ankles, and rested her cheek against his instep. She remembered that she had loved Micah. Not forever, not even for a long time, but for a few days, and as intensely as she had ever loved anyone.

The dog was yapping again. She heard footsteps.

Dana turned around and looked into Lexy's eyes.

Chapter 28

An ambulance had taken Micah's body. The police arrived and asked questions impossible to answer honestly.

"Why would he want to kill himself?"

Lexy replied, "He's always talked about it. Since he was a teenager." Not an answer, barely an explanation lost in tears and confusion. The policeman led her to the couch and told her to sit. Dana saw how he stood over her, his body language a mix of protection and frustration.

Lexy had come through the door into the apartment, and there was no time for Dana to explain anything. Lexy's grief rushed out of her, filled the moment, and left no space for questions or explanations to form. It was Dana who called 911.

"Why were you here, Mrs. Cabot?" Though the officer, Robert Oliphant, was younger than Gary by a decade, he had the same tone of voice that implied he had seen everything and could not be fooled or surprised or shocked. "How'd you get in? D'you have a key?"

"The door was open."

"How do you know the victim?"

Dana looked at Lexy. "His sister's my best friend."

Dana could not tell if Lexy was paying attention to the questions. She sat on the edge of Micah's saggy oatmeal-colored couch, staring down at the ancient parquet. Dana did not try to comfort her. There was no way to break through the wall suddenly between them. She did not want to try, because an army of questions lay in wait on the other side.

She had to get home quickly, send Marsha Filmore back to her apartment, and get into bed before David came home.

Now, in panic mode, her priorities were clear. Answer Oliphant's questions quickly and decisively. Look him straight in the eye and give him no reason to suspect she was being anything but true-blue honest.

"He's my friend's brother." She added in a softer voice, "He asked me to come over because he had a picture he wanted to give me."

Lexy looked up, her face flushed and tearstained. "Which picture?"

"I don't know. One of the Florence sketches, I think. He always said he was going to give me one."

Oliphant rubbed his chin. "Seems peculiar, him calling you and then killing himself. And it's pretty late at night. He didn't say anything that might have let you know . . ."

"Nothing."

"When did he call you?"

Dana was not sure, but she thought the police might be able to check the phone records. So she said, "He didn't call. I ran into him on the street. I was buying bread." As she held her breath, she thought of what Imogene had told her, that she was a liar like her mother. She knew this to be true, because while she strung the lies together she was perfectly calm. It wasn't even a challenge to meet Oliphant's gaze. She read in his expression that he believed her. She was free to go.

"We'll call you if there's anything comes up. You'll have to make a formal statement."

"Of course," she said. "You know I'll help in any way I can."

She picked up her purse and walked over to the couch where Lexy huddled, watching her. She sat beside her friend and wrapped her arms around her. In her arms, Lexy felt bony and cold.

"I've got to get home to Bay. I'll come by your place tomorrow."

"I'll be at work."

"No one expects you—"

"You didn't see him on the street." Lexy's neon green eyes stared at Dana. She added, softly, "Why did you lie?"

It had been a snap to mislead Oliphant, but Lexy was her friend and priest and knew her better than anyone except David.

"Why did you come here? How did you even know where he lives?"

"A picture—"

"You're lying."

"Is there a problem?" Oliphant asked from across the room, where he was talking to a man taking photographs of the apartment and blood splatters.

"We're both upset," Dana said, as if anyone in the room needed to be told.

Oliphant turned back to the photographer.

"Dana, for the love of God, my brother's dead. If you know why, you have to tell me."

Dana stood up.

"You *know,*" Lexy whispered, wide-eyed. "You know."

* * *

I know. I know.

Dana heard David's car in the driveway and pretended to be asleep. Sometimes she pretended so convincingly— her eyes closed, each breath deep and even—that she woke in the morning having slept the night through. But method acting would not work tonight. She would not sleep, had no right to sleep.

She had known Micah was unstable, but he was so full of life when they were together that if someone had suggested he would one day put a bullet in his brain she would have said it was impossible. Now, too late, she remembered what Lexy had told her years before. Micah's depressive disease had been severe. Twice he had been hospitalized, once for violent behavior. In high school he had often talked about suicide. He never stayed long on his medication, claiming it dulled the edge of his creativity. He'd never had a sustained relationship with a woman.

She remembered all this now. When she met Micah and fell tumbling into his dream of love and let it seal around them and make a closed world impervious to reality and subject only to the laws of passion and impulse, the Micah she knew every day had been so vital that he drove out everything Lexy had told her.

And when his dreamworld no longer suited her, she had hacked her way out of it and come home to safe San Diego.

On the dreary flight from Italy she had sworn to expunge Micah from her thoughts. If she could do that, she would be safe. David would never know she had been unfaithful, and for her, too, it would eventually seem that the affair never happened. The details would fade, as details always did.

She cringed as she recalled how confident she had

been that she could erase what was inconvenient to re-member.

Imogene had called her willful, as if it were a flaw in her personality. Until now Dana had seen it as strength. In her efforts to forget Micah and pretend their affair never happened, she had been more successful than even she would have believed possible. When she didn't talk about Micah, Lexy had assumed they didn't get along and left it at that, though she was perplexed. She told David that Micah was a nice guy, but kind of peculiar. David said what did she expect? He was an artist.

Micah had sent passionate letters, and at first she thought it would not hurt to read them; but his threats and pleas and fervid declarations only made her miserable and more aware of how narrowly she had avoided a ruinous mistake and more determined to obliterate him and Florence from her memory.

No wonder she didn't want to work on her thesis.

She had burned his last two letters in the barbeque, unopened. She had willed herself to forget everything about Micah.

Now, lying in bed, she kept hearing Lexy's words. *You know. You know.*

She had been careless and cruel, and, yes, she did know why Micah shot himself, but she would never tell Lexy, because then David would have to know.

The man asleep beside her was capable of the most intense and complicated legal thinking, and his compassion ran broad and deep. But his thoughts about loyalty and honor were as black-and-white as those of a knight in medieval times.

She slipped out of bed and into her running clothes. Outside, she sat on the edge of the deck and laced up her Nikes. After midnight in the middle of the week the streets were silent except for the occasional yip of a coyote and the yowls of a pair of cats facing off under a parked car. She felt safe in Mission Hills at any hour of the day, but she avoided the unlighted park and ran along the sidewalk to the end of Miranda Street, where she turned up toward the lights of Fort Stockton Boulevard. All along the way, like spectators at a race, blue and black trash cans were lined up at the curb for emptying the next morning.

She let herself into Arts and Letters, locking the door behind her. As she did, the air went out of her. The lump she had been carrying between her breastbone and her ribs since she'd opened the mail that afternoon suddenly gave way. Her legs wouldn't hold her up. She leaned against the door and slid to the floor. A sound issued from her mouth, a low, sustained cry like a woman in difficult labor.

Micah would probably be alive if not for her, and Bailey would not have gone missing. Lexy would not be suffering.

She had slashed through the lives of everyone she loved.

Chapter 29

"What's up, Boss?"

Gracie stood in the door of David's office, leaning one leather-skirted hip against the doorjamb. Beatdown exhausted he might be, but the sight of her made him smile. David wondered how long he had to work with a woman, respect her as a colleague and love her as a friend, before he'd finally stop noticing her breasts and hips and the way her skirt rode halfway up her thigh when she crossed her legs.

She said, "You look like someone stepped on your face."

"You're a real confidence builder." He knew how he looked. He had gotten home after midnight, his thoughts in turbo drive, slept badly, and not at all after he heard Dana leave for her run just before dawn.

Gracie sagged against the door. "Oh, God, am I tired. Tell me again why I wanted to be an attorney. My husband is still in bed, I haven't been to the gym in three days, and I haven't eaten anything since—"

"I fed you lunch yesterday."

"Half a vegetarian sub. BFD."

At the credenza she poured coffee from the pot David

made for himself. She settled into the wing chair, slipped out of her stiletto heels, and tucked her feet under her. He had seen Gracie in cutoffs, her face scrubbed, and her hair knotted and clumpy, and she was still sexy. Born that way, he thought.

"How late were you here last night?"

"Quarter to one."

"Shit, David, you got less life than me."

"I went to see Frank yesterday," he said. "I wish I didn't . . ."

"Hate him?"

"No, no, I don't hate him." At least he hoped he didn't. "But I always feel like I need a shower afterwards."

Gracie laughed. "Oh, Boss, welcome to the world of women. There are so many men out there make me feel dirty just breathing the same air. Frank's worse than most, though. It's a matter of degree."

"Do I make you—"

She laughed again. "When you look me up and down—and you do, you know you do—it's like you're still that twenty-year-old quarterback, Mister Squeaky-Clean."

David wondered if he should be insulted.

"The thing about Frank is, even when he's washed his hands there's still shit under his nails." She took a sip of coffee, looked over her shoulder at the closed door, and leaned forward. "Personally, I wouldn't mind if we lost this one."

"Peluso doesn't have a case."

"Yeah, but I've been thinking about that. If he plays it right he doesn't need one. The better I know our Frank the more sure I am the jury's gonna get one look at—"

"Allison says he's good-looking."

"I worry about that girl."

Gracie was a good friend, a trusted colleague. David could say what he really thought.

"So what's it mean? If we get him off and he goes and does the same thing again?"

"Can't think about that. It's the way the system's set up, Boss."

He knew the mantra like his own name: *Better that a guilty man go free than an innocent man be punished.* David believed this the same way he believed a good man took care of his family and played all four quarters.

He turned his swivel chair to face the window. Cabot and Klinger had their offices in an older building without air-conditioning. On the fifth floor they kept the windows open most of the year, and this morning the breeze off the water was sharp with the changing season. He thought wistfully of the rain that lay a month or so in the future.

"Can I ask you a personal question, David?"

He turned his chair. "Be my guest."

"How's it going with you and Dana?"

She had caught him off guard, which he didn't like. "We're great. We're always great."

She eyed him over the rim of her cup.

"Do you know something I don't?" he asked.

"It's none of my business, David. I'll back off."

"I don't want you to back off. I want to know why you asked the question."

"I've known you two since Charger days."

He felt a pressure in his chest, the kind that could only be relieved by a heavy sigh. He held it back and then let go. It felt good to let go. "It's obvious?"

"To me," Gracie said. "First year, my girlfriends and me used to say you and Dana were Super Couple. You seemed perfect for each other."

David had believed that what he and Dana had at twenty could only get sweeter and stronger with time.

"If you want to talk . . ." Gracie said.

His inability to put his finger on anything specifically wrong embarrassed him. He told Gracie something Daniel Boone was supposed to have said, how he'd never been lost but he'd been bewildered a time or two.

They sat in silence, and the quiet was companionable. David could not remember the last time he and Dana had been as comfortable together as he and Gracie were now.

"Maybe there's something you aren't seeing. You get tunnel vision when you're on a case."

He heard what Gracie said, and because he respected her opinion he made a space in his mind for seeing. But nothing came, and as easily as the space had opened, it closed.

"Allison asked me the other day how come you guys don't have more kids."

"What'd you tell her?"

"None of her business."

"We stopped after Bailey because of money." They had planned to have a second child when they could afford it, but that changed when they learned Bailey would probably require expensive special schools and care for the rest of her life. He explained this to Gracie, adding, "Dana blames herself."

"She'd take responsibility for the Holocaust if she thought that'd explain her mother leaving her."

"It's worse now than it used to be. The guilt, I mean."

Gracie swallowed the last of her coffee, put her shoes on, and stood up. "You guys need to talk." She flipped her jacket over her shoulder. "I gotta meet with Geoff to work out the questions for jury selection."

As David watched her cross the office, he thought

about sex. Between Dana and him it had become a matter of routine and occasional lust. No surprises, no blood-rushing thrills. He knew she sometimes pretended to be asleep when he came in late.

The night before he had been reluctant to go home, even though it was after midnight when he left the office. He thought of stopping at Dobson's for a nightcap, and his spirits had sunk deeper in anticipation of the people he would see there. The crowd would be the heavy drinkers, the men and women with nowhere special to go, desperate to hook up.

When he pulled into the garage he had seen Marsha Filmore sitting on the top step with a blanket around her shoulders. Already she seemed like a fixture in their lives.

She raised her wineglass. "Want some?"

Across the yard and deck, upstairs, the bedroom light had been off and the blinds closed. A little wine might help him sleep. He sat on the stairs, using the garage wall as a backrest. She handed him a glass of burgundy with a rich woody bouquet.

"This bottle cost fifteen bucks when we bought it," she said, watching him sip. "It's worth over a hundred now. Frank could sure buy wine. I told him he should open a wine and cheese place."

David tried to imagine Frank Filmore behind a counter, taking orders and cleaning up other's messes.

Marsha blew smoke up from the corner of her mouth, away from David. "So, Counselor, what's going on in the big wide world?"

He shrugged. "Saw your husband today."

She nodded.

"He says you haven't been to see him in a while."

It was her turn to shrug. "I'd have to call a cab. The driver might tell the press where I am."

"I'll drive you." Or he could get Dana to do it.

"Maybe." She reached behind her for the wine bottle and refilled her glass. "So whaddya think? You gonna get him off?"

He had thought then of her unborn child swimming in burgundy, breathing Virginia's finest.

"There's always room for surprises, Marsha."

She snickered. "Can't pin you down, huh?"

"Like I said—"

"What happens if they find him not guilty?"

"He goes free."

"If we move to Idaho he won't have to register or something?"

"Why should he? He won't have a record."

"And if he changed his name there'd be no way to connect him with any of this?"

"Not easily." He had held the wine in his mouth a moment, letting it burr his taste buds as he tried to picture Frank Filmore among the cowboys and survivalists of Idaho.

"Frank wants to live somewhere we can support ourselves off the land. He's studying up on it. Frank can do anything once he makes up his mind," she said. "Did you know his IQ's over one hundred and fifty? That makes him a genius. He says he can make the time we've been in San Diego like it never happened."

Not even Frank Filmore could do that. Dealing with the justice system was like walking a hazing line. A man might come through the experience, but he was bruised and lumpy with scar tissue afterward.

Across the street in the park, a late-night dog walker whistled to his animal. The dog yapped, and the high, light notes of female laughter floated on the damp night air.

"If I had the guts," Marsha said, "I'd throw myself down these stairs. It'd be easy."

He stared at her.

"Frank'd probably sue you for not having a railing. It'd be a tort, right? How much could he get?"

"Why would you want to do that?"

"Maybe I don't want to live in the country. Idaho, that's the boonies."

"Then don't."

David recalled her tolerant smile. "If Frank wants to go to Idaho, we go."

"Marsha, you don't have to stay married to him."

"I know that. No one's forcing me."

"But you were just talking about killing yourself. You make it sound like you have no choice in any of this."

"Choice isn't all it's cracked up to be."

Talking to Marsha Filmore made his head spin.

David watched her empty the bottle into her glass. The diamond on her left hand flashed in the porch light, and he thought about the bargains married couples made to get along.

She said, "You don't have to understand this or agree, but I think we ought to get something straight between us. I like Frank being in charge. Mostly, life works better that way. He says it's the same as the military: if there weren't any generals the whole thing'd fall apart."

"A marriage isn't the army."

"Frank's boss in our house, and if he wants to go to Idaho, I'll pack the bags and go."

He had offered Marsha the garage apartment hoping to learn more about her husband. If he pointed out all the contradictions in what she'd said she would probably clam up.

"It won't be easy with a baby, making such a big change."

"Oh, she'll behave. She'll learn the rules." She squinted at him. "Why are you smiling?"

"I guess it was the idea of a baby learning rules."

"You think it can't be done?"

"Not with a baby."

"Frank says you have to let them know who's in charge from the git-go, soon as they're born."

David thought of a baby being "trained" by Frank and Marsha Filmore and a sick revulsion filled him. He suddenly longed to see Bailey sleeping safely in her bed and to smell the sweet damp spot behind her ears.

He watched Marsha drain her wineglass.

"What if she doesn't learn the rules?" he asked.

"She'd be better off dead."

Sitting in his office hours later he still heard the way she said it. Not as an overstatement or a sick joke but like a statement of fact.

Later, he had lain in bed, his hands shaking, the back of his neck and shoulders rigid. He hadn't bothered to brush his teeth, just dropped his clothes on the floor and got under the covers. Dana slept on her side with her back to him. She had not moved since he came into the room.

"Dana," he whispered, fitting his body into the curve of her back. "You 'wake?"

Her breathing was regular and deep.

"I need to talk to you." He laid his hand on the curve of her hip. *Let me hear your voice in my head, not hers.* "Wake up and talk to me, Dana. Please."

He remembered her sigh and how she stirred just enough to put a little space between them. His hand had slipped from her hip, and then he was asleep.

Chapter 30

The next morning David came into the kitchen and saw exactly what Dana wanted him to see: a sunny room, at his place on the counter a cup of coffee, a glass of juice, and that day's edition of the *San Diego Union Tribune*. Bailey smiled when he kissed her and went back to that morning's fascination, picking blueberries out of her pancakes and pyramiding them beside her plate like cannonballs.

"Hungry?" Dana asked brightly.

"Always."

She heard the scrape of the stool on the Mexican tiles and the rustle of the paper being unfolded.

The pancakes did not burn despite the sugary blueberries, and the syrup came out of the microwave at the perfect temperature. Moby barked at the garbage man, and Bailey jumped off her stool and ran to the living room to wave at him from the big window. Dana moved around the kitchen like an ordinary human being.

She put a short stack of pancakes on his plate.

"How 'bout a little sour cream?"

As she opened the refrigerator she felt him looking at the back of her head.

"What's this all about?" he asked.

"It's not like I've never cooked breakfast before."

"Out with it, Number One."

She leaned her hip against the stove and stared down at her bare feet. She thought about making up something, but she was tired from her sleepless night, and after yesterday she thought another lie might break her back.

"You were awake?" he asked.

She nodded.

"How come you didn't talk to me?"

Inadvertently a sheepish smile pinched the corner of her mouth, and immediately she saw confusion cloud his eyes. He was always surprised when people dealt with him unfairly. She thought of the boy parceled off to his uncle in Texas because his mother couldn't cope without pills. Once he told Dana that though he loved his uncle and aunt, a part of him used to wonder what terrible wrong he had done that his three older siblings had not. There was an innocence in David that she treasured, but it made him vulnerable, even to her.

He pushed his plate aside and dragged his hand across his face. "I needed you."

"You'd been drinking. With Marsha."

"She was on the steps."

"She's always on the steps."

"Is that why you're mad at me?"

She sat at the counter and rested her head in her hands. "I'm not mad at you," she said, glad to be able to tell the truth. "Not even a little bit."

His voice softened as he touched the inside of her wrist with his fingertip. "Then why?"

"Did Marsha tell you she baby-sat?"

"Marsha? You said you'd never—"

"Lexy needed me." She couldn't go an hour without lying. "Her brother shot himself."

"Oh, Jesus, poor Lexy." He pushed his plate away. "And you, you knew him. You said he was kind of weird, but you spent time with him, he showed you around. Honey, I'm so sorry."

His straightforward sympathy screwed her guilt in tighter and deeper. Her stomach contracted. She moved away, just a little. Perhaps he would not notice. "I just needed to be . . . alone, I guess. After you fell asleep I went for a run."

"You could have woken me up; we could have talked."

Once upon a time that was what they did when one of them was troubled. Dana wondered when they had stopped and why and might it be possible to turn back time in just this small way.

"I wish you wouldn't run at night."

"It's safe enough. Isn't that why we moved to Mission Hills?"

The subject changed. The morning went on.

As David was leaving for the office, he paused by the back door. "I almost forgot. Last night I told Marsha you'd take her to see Frank today."

She looked at him. "Today? Oh, David, I can't. Not today."

David put his arms around her. "Look, honey, I know you liked Lexy's brother—what was his name? Michael?—but I really need you to do this for me. If you sit around you'll just feel miserable."

"She can wait—"

"Dana, why can't you for once just say okay?" His smile never reached his eyes. "Just try it: 'Sure, David, happy to help out.'"

"I don't even want Bailey in the car with Marsha Filmore."

"Yeah, but you let her babysit last night." He sighed and patted his mouth with his tightened fist. She almost heard him counting down his temper. "Whatever happened to the Number One I could go to, no matter what?"

She wasn't a wide receiver; she was his wife, his lying and adulterous wife. She looked away, sensing that if he looked into her eyes he would see the truth there.

"I don't get what's happening to us, Dana. I feel like I barely know you anymore. I mean . . . are you in the game or not?"

She closed her eyes and whispered, "In."

"Then start acting like it, okay?"

A moment later she heard the garage door groan as it went up and the car backing down the driveway to the street. All at once it seemed that if he went away angry it would be like the moment when the razored edge of a steel trap slammed down on an animal. There would be no going back. The wound would never heal. The death would be a slow agony. She ran out to the driveway and grabbed hold of the half-open window on his side.

He shifted into Neutral.

"David, I'll take her, of course I'll take her. I'll do it this afternoon. But after this case is done, promise me you won't take any more like it. You could stick to personal injury and torts and stuff. It's this case that's got me acting so weird."

He shook his head. "Don't blame the case, Dana, though it's a pisser, I'll grant you. What's going wrong with us is more than that." He twisted the plain gold band he wore on his left ring finger. "The thing about you and me, Dana, was the way we used to work together. Only now we don't. Now we can barely have a conversation without one of us going off." He stared at her.

"It's my fault."

"Did I say that? Didn't I precisely say 'us'?"

"But you meant me."

David shifted into Reverse. "I got a big day ahead of me. If you won't take Marsha—"

"You weren't listening to me. You never listen to me. I said I'd do it."

He closed his eyes and then opened them. "Why couldn't you just say that in the first place? Why did we have to go through all this crap first?"

San Diego Central Jail is a multistory sandstone-colored monolith that occupies most of a block near the courts. Dana dropped Marsha at the visitors' entrance and drove to Seaport Village, where she and Bailey browsed the tourist shops, ate ice cream, and watched the boats in San Diego Harbor. Though the sun was bright, the weather had begun to change. The wind had shifted and carried a bite of the north in its current now. Dana and Bailey, dressed in cotton slacks and long-sleeved T-shirts, were cold by the time they returned to the jail two hours later and found Marsha pacing the sidewalk, smoking. Driving home, Marsha leaned her forehead against the passenger-side window, leaving an oily smudge on the glass.

Dana parked the car in the driveway "You're shivering," she said to Marsha. "You need a heavier coat."

"It's in storage."

The woman looked so beaten down Dana felt sympathy for her. "I'll get it out of storage for you."

"It's a mink. Full-length."

"In San Diego?"

"Frank gave it to me." She looked at Dana as if to size up her reaction to this. "I have a fox jacket, too. He gave it to me for my birthday last year."

"Generous."

"He always gives expensive gifts." She showed Dana her Rolex in case she needed convincing.

"Unless you'd rather get it yourself. . . ." Dana wished she hadn't volunteered.

Marsha's eyes narrowed. "Why're you being so nice all of a sudden?"

"You're having a hard time."

"I don't want your pity."

"I don't pity you." It was hard to say exactly what she did feel. She disliked Marsha Filmore, yet at the same time she felt an inexplicit kinship with her. She was strangely reluctant to break the connection and send her back into isolation. She asked, "Why did you go to see him?"

"You husband said I should."

"He can be persuasive."

"He's okay, your husband. Better'n most."

"If I were you, if . . . Frank were my husband, I'd never go near him." She carried so many lies around with her these days that she had a powerful longing to speak her true mind. "You should file for divorce."

"He's my husband."

"But you don't want to see him."

"I never said that."

"You said David told you—"

"I didn't want to call a taxi, have the TV people follow after me."

Dana's face turned hot with embarrassment. "I'm sorry. I misunderstood."

"And, by the way, I never told your husband about babysitting. I could of said something last night, but I figured . . ."

In the backseat Bailey fussed and kicked.

"Is that the only sound she makes? Does she ever talk?"

"Not since she was taken."

"Bet you'd like to see that guy hanging by the balls."

"No." Dana rested her head on the steering wheel, exhausted. "Not really."

She got out of the car and went around to open the door behind Marsha. Bailey fiddled with the lock on her seat belt. Dana's hands shook as she pressed the button and opened it for her. Bailey grizzled and beat on the arms of the seat with her fists.

Marsha said, "How do you stand the noise? It'd freak me out. That Lolly, she was a fusser, too, believe me." She followed Dana into the backyard. "We could hear her all the way inside our house, yelling and crying and whining. It was hard for Frank especially. One thing about that high IQ he's got, he needs quiet to think. Did you know his IQ is over one hundred and fifty? The mind of a genius, it's sensitive. He couldn't think with Lolly making a racket."

Dana looked pointedly at Marsha's belly.

"Yeah, I know. But like I told your husband, I'm going to train this baby. She won't make a peep unless I want her to."

Chapter 31

The morning after Micah's suicide Lexy did not get up in time to see the sun rise. She lay in bed with her eyes shut, playing a game from her childhood. So long as she kept her eyes closed, nothing that had happened the day before was real. The game hadn't worked well when she was eight, and it was useless now. Scenes from the night before pressed down on her eyelids until they burned.

Since seminary her morning ritual had been a comforting discipline. The words of Morning Prayer and the day's Collect and lessons calmed the waters of her mind in all weather. But on the first day of a world without her brother, Lexy could not pray. The gears of faith did not engage. She sat in her easy chair by the window and thought about life without faith, spinning out of control into a place where nothing mattered. Not God. Not sobriety.

Call someone. Go to a meeting.

She got to work late. With laypeople reading the Morning Office, she told herself there was no reason to be prompt. The members of the stewardship committee filled up the chairs in the waiting room, eyes on the clock as she came in fifteen minutes late for their appointment. That was the kind of day it was.

She had only glanced in the mirror when she left home and must have looked a wreck. The head of the committee asked her if she felt okay.

"I had a bad night." She wasn't ready yet to talk about Micah. "You have to be nice to me today. No surprises."

The committee smiled and chuckled, reassured.

After the meeting she sat in her chair with her feet on the windowsill and waited for the phone to ring. Maybe it was true that Micah had told Dana to come by for one of his Florence pictures, but she didn't believe they had met on the street. It was too unlikely. Lexy knew Dana had trouble with the truth. This had never been an impediment to their friendship, but Lexy had known her to lie to protect herself and those she cared for, to simplify, to dismiss the truth when it was inconvenient.

Lexy called Alana, Dorothy Wilkerson's nurse. At the sound of her calm, kind voice, she told her about Micah.

"I grieve for you, Lexy. A brother is a precious thing."

"He was on antidepressants. Stopped taking them."

"Oh dear," Alana said. "You blame yourself?"

"Of course I do. I should have tried harder—"

Alana cleared her throat. "May I speak honestly, Lexy?"

Why not? Be my guest. Lexy gave silent assent.

"It was your brother's choice, made between him and God. Beyond that, we can know nothing."

Lexy was crying, and Alana kindly changed the subject.

"Her Ladyship has been asking for you. Half the

time she thinks she's done something wrong, the rest she says you don't deserve what she pays you."

It was possible to laugh and cry at the same time.

"What about pain?"

"You know she's not a complainer. Stoic or stubborn, I don't know which. There's pain in those old joints, of course. And her legs are swollen big. But mostly she just lies there, hasn't opened her eyes in two days. She said to me this morning, 'Ellen left me. Lexy left me too.' I told her you're coming back. . . ."

Lexy dreaded sitting at Dorothy Wilkerson's bedside in the company of her present thoughts. On fashion shoots there was always confusion and contradictory directions, and she could go from morning until day's end without concentrating on anything more pressing than a visit to the bathroom. And then Billy would arrive and whisk her away in his black Mercedes. First home for a bath and a few drinks, then to dinner with a noisy crowd, most of whom would not know a serious thought if it handed them a calling card. In her old life it was possible to go for a week without thinking about much of anything.

On her desk she kept a photo of Micah with a mostly empty beach in the background. He had sent it from Mexico back in July. He stood beside a fruit stand piled high with mangoes and papayas blushing like schoolgirls. His dark hair curled untidily around his shirt collar; his eyes, the windows to his soul, were hidden behind wraparound sunglasses.

For the rest of Lexy's day, nothing went right.

The evening meeting with the church school committee stretched a tedious thirty-seven minutes beyond its allotted hour. Lloyd Beecham, chair of the adult learning subcommittee, was saying that what St. Tom's needed was a book group. "For lovers of fine books . . ."

Lovers of fine books. Lexy doodled the words in the margin of her notebook.

Lovers of fine books.

Lovers.

In a blink she understood.

She stood and excused herself to the committee, claiming an emergency. She ignored the curious faces as she walked to her closet, got her purse and jacket, and left without further explanation. Overhead the sky was a deep navy blue against which the scudding clouds were startlingly white. A sliver of moon hid in the branches of an oak. Lexy closed her eyes and took a long, deep breath of air. Across the street the palm trees in the sidewalk strip in front of the nursery bent and rustled. She held her hand before her, astonished by how calm she suddenly felt.

From the street Dana's house was dark, but when Lexy walked around the back, the lighted kitchen looked welcoming. She saw Dana at the counter with a magazine open in front of her. As Lexy stepped onto the deck, Moby rushed out of the shadows and barked ferociously until he recognized her; then he wagged his stubby tail and butted his nose against her thigh.

Dana said through the screen, "I've been expecting you." She opened the door, and Lexy stepped inside. She had been in Dana's kitchen dozens of times, but this night she felt like a stranger.

She walked past Dana into the living room and sat in one of the padded chairs set off to the side of the fireplace. She knew how she looked: prim and unnatural with her knees pressed together and her hands folded around the strap of her handbag. Dana sat across the room on the couch. She had never regained the weight lost during Bailey's absence. Her cheekbones and small chin had an unfamiliar sharpness, and she was pale as the wind. Dana was a careful and tidy woman. Lexy had never seen her when her hair wasn't smooth and shiny. Except for during Bailey's absence, she could number the times before this when she had seen her without lipstick and blush.

"Where's Bay?"

"Bed."

"David?"

"At work."

"Tell me," Lexy said. "I need to know. Everything."

"It's too . . . complicated. You deserve an explanation, I know that. But when I tell you . . ."

"I knew there was something strange when you came back and didn't talk about him. Before you went, I would have bet anything you'd really like each other."

Dana nodded. "We did."

"You could have told me," Lexy said. "I wouldn't have condemned you. You're married, but these things happen. I know that."

A deep blue-green cashmere throw lay across the arm of the couch. Dana pulled it across her legs. "It didn't end well between us. He wanted me to stay, and when I wouldn't—I couldn't, Lexy, you see that, I know you do. But not him. He became very angry and . . . hostile. I was afraid of him."

"You knew what he was like. I told you about the mood swings—"

"Yes, yes, but once I met him, I forgot about everything except him."

"But it must have been obvious he wasn't—"

"Like other people?" Dana's expression held a strange bright glow. "Lexy, I loved that he was so different. Not like any man I'd ever met. It was like I'd been climbing a ladder all my life, one foot in front of the other, never looking down, terrified that if I so much as paused, I'd fall off. And then I met Micah and he showed me there was a trapeze, and he said to grab it. He told me all I had to do was step off the ladder and I'd fly. And I did."

Lexy saw that Dana wanted to be understood and forgiven.

"I flew so high I barely breathed."

But Lexy did not want to understand. The white collar tightened around her throat.

"And he was always happy when we were together, Lexy. He told me he didn't get depressed anymore. I believed him."

"Because you wanted to. Because it suited your purposes."

"It was like I wasn't myself anymore. I know that's not a good reason, but it's the only way I can explain it. Not just to you, Lexy. To me, too."

Lexy didn't care if Dana believed her own words. They were just an excuse. "You broke my brother. You broke his spirit, the stuff that held him together."

"But I didn't know. I didn't mean to. Yes, it was a dangerous affair, but I was the person with something to lose. I thought if anyone got hurt it would be me."

Lexy ran her finger between her collar and throat. "I trusted you with him. If I thought you might seduce—"

Dana jerked back. "I didn't seduce him."

"You took one look at that beautiful face and thought you'd have a fling, one week, and you'd toss off all the traces, do anything you pleased and then go home and back to being the quarterback's wife, 'the team player.'" Dana recoiled from her sarcasm, and Lexy felt a jolt of satisfaction. Land a good punch and it's like whiskey straight from the bottle.

"And you know what, Dana? I believe you when you say you couldn't help yourself." Out of her anger she felt an old cruelty rising, a cruelty she'd believed vanquished by prayer and sobriety.

"Does David know?"

Dana looked surprised. "Of course not. I won't tell him for the same reason I wouldn't stay with Micah. I love him, and I love Bailey—"

"That's why you fucked my brother? Because you love Bailey and David? How stupid of me. Now it all makes perfect sense."

Lexy took off her collar and folded her hands around it as she held her purse.

"So who've you got in your sights now? Why not Beth Gordon's grandson? Or you could pick up a boy at the beach—"

"Micah wasn't a boy. He was a man, and he made choices, and I was one of his choices, and now that you know, I'm glad."

She did not look glad; she looked trapped and battered.

"We both loved him, Lexy. But neither of us could have helped him."

"My brother is dead and it's your fault. You can't make that go away with words. You're going to have to live with it the rest of your life."

"There are things you don't know, Lexy."

"What I'm going to do is walk out of your house, and we're not going to be friends anymore." Lexy's voice broke. "You know, in the church hardly anyone tells me the whole truth about things unless they're making a confession. Mostly people want me to like them; they want the priest to be their friend, like it gives them some cachet. So they say what they think I want to hear, or they try to impress me with how saintly they are. I thought you were different. I thought you were a *real* friend."

Lexy walked to the front door and stood there. "You can't wrap yourself up in a lie like it's that little green blanket and expect to stay warm and cozy for the rest of your life. This is all going to catch up to you, Dana. You better make sure you tell David the truth, because if you don't, someone else will."

Lexy opened the door, and Dana batted it shut with the palm of her hand. "Don't threaten me," she said.

Lexy's laugh scoured her throat. If she didn't get out of Dana's house she would be sick.

"If I have to face the truth, Lexy, then so do you."

"What are you talking about?"

"Micah killed himself because he couldn't live with what he'd done. He killed himself because he couldn't live with his guilt. He kidnapped Bailey. I have a note to prove it."

Chapter 32

Dana stumbled upstairs and swallowed two sleeping pills. She did not have to pretend sleep when David got home after another late night. But just after four the next morning the sound of sprinklers going on in the park awoke her. She heard Lexy's terrible words in her head, and she knew she would not sleep again. She slipped out of bed and into her running clothes. In the cold, gray dawn a heavy fog lay over everything. As she crossed the deck and lawn she looked up and saw the flickering white light of the television in the apartment window. She felt, reluctantly, a bond with Marsha as she imagined her sleepless as well, lighting cigarette after cigarette and thinking only God knew what terrible thoughts.

Could they be more dreadful than her own? Not unless Marsha Filmore was sitting before a mirror, seeing herself as she truly was for the first time.

Lexy had held the mirror up to Dana.

Fog blanketed the streets and homes of Mission Hills, ghostly vines of it twisting through the trees in the park and drawing scarves of gray across the faces

of the houses along Miranda Street and Arboles and
Felicita. Near the corner of Arboles and Descanso she
ran past a house with all the windows alight, a man in
the driveway loading suitcases into a minivan. He turned
his head as Dana ran by and lifted his arm in a friendly
gesture. She did the same. A normal family, going on a
trip.

All her life she had wanted the safety and assurance
of a normal life. How could she have guessed there
was a corner of her that did not want these things at all,
that craved risk and sensation.

In her thoughts the fog parted, and she glimpsed her
future. If David never learned about Micah, and if Dana
could forget Micah and Florence, and if Bailey talked
again, and if she never spoke the name of the man who
had kidnapped her daughter . . . Dana had tried to create a safe and predictable life for herself, but now here
she was, the days and weeks ahead littered with contin-
gencies, the hours held in place by "ifs."

Turning down Ramona, she cut up through an alley
toward the lights of Fort Stockton. The footing was insecure there, a mixture of gravel and broken pavement,
and she slowed her pace. Then a dog barked suddenly
and loudly from behind a redwood fence, jolting her
nerves. Before she recovered from the surprise, something leapt out from behind a pile of garbage cans, startling her afresh. There was a screech and a cackle, and
a female face loomed so close she could see the lined,
leathery skin, the pale, watery eyes, and smell the reek
of urine and sour wine.

Jumping back, she tripped and fell. As she scrambled to her feet, the woman hung over her, snorting and
laughing from the black cave of her mouth. Dana
thrashed out with her arms, touched the woman's filthy

clothes, and recoiled. Gaining her feet, she sprinted toward the lights of the boulevard.

She needed light; she needed people. At that hour the only place open in the neighborhood was the Jack in the Box on Washington Street. Speeding up, she moved out into the broad street and ran from streetlight to streetlight, counting her breaths and flexing her hands to dispel the tension in her arms.

One word had flashed through her mind when the woman jumped out at her. *Mother.* Her mother might have ended up like that derelict. She had certainly been on her way to that destiny the night she left Dana shivering on Imogene's porch.

Dana welcomed the sterile fluorescence of the Jack in the Box. She ordered a cup of coffee and a sweet roll from the sleepy-looking Hispanic girl whose fate it was to be taking orders in the middle of the night, paid with the five-dollar bill she kept in her shoe, and took her order to a corner table facing the wide street. Like bizarre golden-eyed fish, the headlights of the predawn traffic emerged from the fog and vanished in flashes of piercing crimson. At the stoplight a sedan screeched to a halt. The woman driving banged the heel of her hand on the steering wheel.

Any angry woman anywhere might be Dana's mother.

What did Lexy know, finally, of what it meant to be Dana? *Tell David,* she had said. But Lexy had not been abandoned like a stray dog, just another consequence of her mother's mistakes. Lexy had not spent her life waiting to be found again, and she would never understand that it was this that bound her to David. He had found her. *Tell David,* Lexy had said with the certainty of one who has read the rules but never played the game.

Dana got home just before five. She showered in the downstairs bathroom so as not to wake David. Afterward, she returned to their bed, clean and warm, smelling of flower fields. David turned over and put his arms around her, nuzzling her neck where the hair was still damp. She kissed his ear, his neck, and the hollow of his throat where his pulse leapt. He was her quarterback and hero. It was he who had found her, and if God would only let her escape disaster one more time, she would never hurt him, never give him reason to wonder why, or if, he loved her.

He drew her to him, and they made love with their eyes closed, wrapped in the musky warmth of halfsleep. Vision seemed an inferior sense to smell and touch. With her hands she explored the familiar territory of his body, the landmarks: a break in his collarbone that had healed poorly, the long, powerful thigh muscles, and the ridge of an appendix scar on his flat belly. She drew him deep inside her, wanting nothing more than to dissolve the boundaries between them and merge into one indissoluble being.

After they made love they lay in each other's arms, talking sleepily.

David ran his palm along the curve of her hip. "I was thinking about what you said the other day about not taking any more cases like this one." Although David had other clients, they both knew he meant the Filmore case.

"You shouldn't listen to a crazy woman."

"Not so crazy. It's a head thing. This kind of case, it's different than a regular murder, because it's a kid. And the repercussions . . ." He stroked her hair back from her forehead. "I can't stand that Bailey got taken because of me. It doesn't matter if it all works out and she's okay. I'll never forgive myself for putting her in harm's way."

Dana put her fingertips on his mouth. He kissed them, and she changed the subject.

"We need a vacation. We need to put all this behind us."

"How's Hawaii sound?"

"I was talking to this woman at church, Nova Harris? She lives in that big house on Paloma?" Dana propped herself on one elbow. "She and her husband went to Fiji, and she said it was fabulous. No huge crowds, great service, and gorgeous beaches."

"Isn't that where they have cannibals?"

"Idiot. You're thinking of Papua, New Guinea, and there aren't even cannibals there anymore. Fiji's on the way to Australia."

David closed his eyes, smiling. "What about Alaska? We could fly into one of those fishing camps—"

She punched his shoulder. "Grizzlies, with fangs!"

He chuckled and nuzzled her neck. "But think of the fish and the firelight."

"Think of me *cooking* the fish." Laughing, she got out of bed and in one swing pulled the covers off the bed.

Later, when they were sharing the electric toothbrush and the vanity mirror, Dana caught the scent of cigarette smoke and stepped to the bedroom window. She pulled the blinds back, letting in the morning sun.

"She's out there, on the steps, with a blanket around her."

David stood behind Dana, his arms wrapped around her waist. Already the warmth and intimacy had begun to dissipate. Reality was back, making a space between them.

"I told her I'd get her mink coat out of storage."

"She's one peculiar female. I just can't get a read on her."

"Oh, I can," Dana said, sighing. "She's hiding something."

Trust me. I have a sixth sense for deceit.

Chapter 33

Dorothy Wilkerson looked tiny and peaceful in her high, old-fashioned bed. Pretty. In a room downstairs Lexy had seen a picture of her on her wedding day; and now, as she slept, and the lines and wrinkles relaxed, the girl emerged from the face of the old woman. Lexy thought of the dreams and ambitions and disappointments of Dorothy Wilkerson's long life; and when occasionally a pulse jumped in her eyelid and she groaned or murmured something too softly for Lexy to make out the words, she wondered what thoughts and memories streamed through her sleeping mind. One hundred and two years was a long time to live.

Someone had brought in branches of lavender and arranged them in a tall glass vase. Set before the window, which was open just a crack, their fragrance filled the room. From the other side of the door the radio played softly. Lexy recognized Mahler's transcendent Planet Suite.

She wanted to know Micah's thoughts in the moments before he shot himself. Had it even occurred to him to write her a note of good-bye, she who loved him most, his Irish twin? She snuffed the uncomfortable feeling of anger toward him. He had been too sick at heart to serve her needs. Lexy hoped he regretted stealing Bailey and had prayed to be forgiven. Maybe he was just glad he'd made Dana suffer.

There was meanness in him, too.

Lexy held her prayer book on her lap unopened, though the need to offer up her anger and pain was a raw second skin burning beneath the surface.

For many years prayer had been a joy and a continuing conversation Lexy could pick up at any time. In the car, and while she cooked or cleaned, she talked aloud to God. She lost herself to God in meditation. At night she knelt beside her bed like a child and offered up the wins and losses of her day. Some seminarians had spoken of doubt and being blocked in prayer, but it had never happened to Lexy until now.

Estranged from God and Dana, she had never felt lonelier. Not only could she not pray, she now had no one to talk to. No more coffee-saturated conversations with Dana at Bella Luna. No more midnight phone calls and trips to Nordstrom for shoes with three-inch heels. Where would she go after church on Super Bowl Sunday? Who would make her a Christmas stocking and leave it on the front seat of her car to find after Midnight Mass?

Mass.

We confess that we have sinned against You in thought, word and deed, by what we have done and by what we have left undone. We have not loved You with our whole heart; we have not loved our neighbors as ourselves; we are heartily sorry and humbly repent. . . .

Loving God meant loving Dana, and Lexy could not do that. *We are heartily sorry and humbly repent. . . .*

She did not repent. Not a word, not a thought.

Dorothy Wilkerson stirred and moaned. Lexy wondered if she dreamed of visitors in plumed hats. Or was she thinking of her daughter, chewing over the old argument that had divided them.

Maybe I'll regret all this when I'm old. God, standing at the gate of Heaven, might turn Lexy away because she had not loved Dana as she loved herself, as her ministry called her to love all the fallen and broken of the world.

I should forgive her.

Never.

I should atone for the pleasure I took in being cruel.

Dorothy moaned and muttered in her sleep.

We are heartily sorry for these our misdoings. The burden of them is intolerable.

Lexy remembered the day of her ordination, the end of a long and difficult journey of self-examination and questioning by others as she sought to understand her call.

The bishop had asked her, *Will you endeavor so to minister the Word of God and the sacraments of the New Covenant, that the reconciling love of Christ may be known and received? . . . Will you undertake to be a faithful pastor to all whom you are called to serve? . . .*

She had answered yes to these questions and more. Yes without qualification. Yes with enthusiastic confidence. She should have said, "Yes, I will keep my vows until my best friend kills my brother by loving him." Then she would turn her back on her promises and love herself and her rage first, God and His Son second, Dana last.

She bent forward and laid her head on her knees, borne down by the weight of what she knew now that she had not known when she entered Dorothy Wilkerson's bedroom. She still believed in God; it would be easier to lose her faith in oxygen than in God. But she could not follow God's law.

I can't be a priest anymore.

Chapter 34

As soon as David left for work on Saturday morning, Guadalupe arrived from Tijuana.

Dana could not spend another day cooped up with just her guilt and Bailey for company. She stopped first at the Filmores' storage unit, to which Marsha had given her the key the day before. As she opened the door, a wave of warm air smelling of stale cigarettes engulfed her and a dim interior light switched on automatically, revealing a long, narrow space filled from floor to ceiling with plastic storage bins, cardboard boxes, and dark, oppressive-looking Victorian furniture. Standing at a right angle to the door was an armoire almost eight feet tall made of some dark red wood like mahogany and embellished all over with carved fruit and vegetables and the heads of birds and fish. The mirrors on the doors were etched with pastoral shepherding scenes. Dana could not decide if the piece was very beautiful and unusual or a nineteenth-century monstrosity. She opened one of its doors and inhaled a whoosh of tobacco and perspiration smell so strong she turned her head aside and took a step back, almost stumbling on a stack of books. Then she reached in and slipped the sable-colored, full-length mink coat off a wooden hanger.

Without thinking, she put her arms into it, and pulled the shawl-collar up around her neck and laid her cheek against the lush, silky fur. In the pocket her hand touched a piece of paper. She pulled it out and looked at it. It was a receipt, and Dana recognized the date immediately.

Chapter 35

Two hours later David knocked on Marsha Filmore's door. She opened it wearing jeans, a black T-shirt, her fur coat, and no shoes. "Come on in, Counselor."

The bed was unmade, and the overheated air smelled of cooked coffee, tobacco smoke, and microwaved meals. A black bra hung on the knob of the bathroom door.

David eyed a half-full glass of wine sitting in a moist ring on the table.

"Care to join me?"

"We have to talk, Marsha."

"Sit down, then. Talk."

Her skin was the color of oatmeal, with raspberries of pink on the cheeks, and her thin, straight hair lay flat and uncombed against her head. David remembered one of Filmore's offhand remarks during an early interview, something about his wife being plain but serviceable.

Without preamble David told her about Dana's discovery of the garage receipt. Listening, she sat still, her head cocked slightly to one side.

"And?"

"Marsha, don't pretend you don't get it. The receipt

says you got a loaner car from the garage on the day Lolly Calhoun disappeared. A two-thousand Honda Accord. Have you told anyone you took the car to the garage?"

"Of course not."

The window by the table looked over the side yard and deck and right into David and Dana's kitchen. It was not a stretch to imagine Marsha Filmore sitting at her table night after night, drinking and smoking and watching his family. With the windows open she could probably hear them talking. His jaw began to ache.

"Let's start at the beginning. How did you pay to have your car fixed?"

"Cash, of course. We always pay in cash because we don't want anyone poking around in our business. They can find out all sorts of things about you if you use cards to pay."

Moby sauntered out his pet door and across the deck. He still limped a little from where he'd been hit by the white van. He walked to the edge of the deck and thoughtfully looked down at the grass. Like a swimmer testing the water, he gingerly lowered one paw and then another, his hind end following after.

"If the jury finds out about Shawna—"

"She has nothing to do with this. You should just forget about her."

"I can try to keep her off the record, but Peluso's going to do what he can to make sure it gets out. I wouldn't be surprised if the press gets wind of it about the time impanelling starts."

"But she's . . . irrelevant."

"Really?" David said. "Are you sure of that?"

Marsha stared out the window.

"Tell me what happened."

She pulled a handful of lank hair around in front of

her face and looked at it. "It was a long time ago. I'm not sure I remember exactly."

"Try. Tell me about Shawna."

Marsha dropped her hair and stared at the butcher-block tabletop. "She was never right. From the beginning she didn't smile and gurgle like other babies, and when she got older she never could just ask for something, she made this mealy little baby sound. She was almost four years old, but she just stood there with her arms out and whining to be picked up or carried or given something. Frank didn't believe in holding her; he said it'd spoil her, but sometimes I did when he wasn't there." She looked at David. "I mean, what was I supposed to do? If I picked her up, she got quiet, but then I didn't have enough time for Frank, and that upset him, so we got this maid named Tina, and she was okay, I thought, only Frank didn't like her because she spoiled Shawna, and she was nosy, too, always poking around in our business, so we had to fire her. Shawna cried for days. Even when Frank spanked her she wouldn't be quiet."

David rubbed his jaw, just below the earlobe.

"And then one day . . . she was gone, and I got frantic, so did Frank, and after two or three days the police found her in that well and she was dead. . . ." Marsha stared into the bottom of her wineglass. "Afterwards he told me what he did, and he helped me understand why it was . . . not so bad. Better for Shawna, actually."

If she knew what she said was monstrous, it did not show on her face. David loosened his tie and undid the top button of his shirt.

Marsha said, "Have you ever studied population management? Frank has, and he says the world just doesn't have room for children who aren't strong. Tough. There's a finite amount of resources to go around." She lit a cigarette, shaking out the match with a flick of her wrist. "In the beginning, before he explained it to me, I was upset and said I'd go to the police. He said the police in Rosarito were no good, and if he told them I did it, they'd believe him."

"You're afraid of Frank."

He watched her throat move when she swallowed.

"Has he threatened you, Marsha?"

"We're going to Idaho to live. Get a fresh start."

David remembered his first impression that Marsha Filmore was like two women in one body: the competent bookkeeper who could run the office of a major drugstore chain, and a woman in thrall to a husband who'd driven the gumption out of her. A bully bearing mink and diamonds could buy a lot of acquiescence.

David said, "Let's go back over what happened the day Lolly disappeared."

"What do you want me to say?" Her face brightened suddenly, and her hands dropped to the mound of her stomach. "She's kicking." She smiled for an instant, then just as quickly seemed to collapse in on herself. David expected her to cry, but she didn't.

"Frank said I was too old to have another baby, and he doesn't think I'm a good mother, anyway, because of Shawna. He was angry when I told him I was pregnant. Now he acts like he's happy, but I thought he'd kill me when I showed him the test result. It's the only time he ever hit me." She stubbed out her cigarette. "The trouble with me is I don't have a really strong mind. Not like Frank. He says when they were handing out character, I stood in the line for waffles." She covered her mouth with her hand and giggled. "It's true. I don't know what I want half the time. Sometimes I wish I'd never conceived this baby, and I think if she were to die I wouldn't care a bit. Other times I can't wait to see her and hold her. I have fantasies about what she'll be like when she grows up. Like maybe she can be a dancer; I always wanted to be one." Her shoulders dropped, and, angrily, she swept her wineglass off the table and onto the carpet. "What do I know? There probably aren't any ballet teachers in Idaho. Frank says I'm a wimp and I haven't got backbone and that's why he has to be in charge. Sometimes I think he's right; sometimes . . ." She raked her hands through her hair. "Have you ever been where you don't know anything for sure? These days everything's just mush in my head."

David realized he had been holding his breath.

"I don't think you're a wimp, Marsha. I think you've been under huge pressure."

"Really?" As if this had not occurred to her.

"Tell me the story of Lolly, Marsha. Maybe I can help you sort things out."

She shook her head.

"You don't have to be afraid. He won't hurt you."

"You don't know. Frank looks like an ordinary man, but he's not."

"Where did you change cars?"

She sighed and laid her hands flat on the table before her. "He called me. Then I drove over to Ralph's parking lot, the one underground. We switched there. He told me he needed my help. He said there'd been an accident."

"Did you ask him what kind?"

"He just said some trouble with Lolly but he was going to fix it. He told me not to worry because worrying would make my baby sick and maybe retarded."

In the Miranda Street Park a couple spread what looked like an old chenille bedspread on the grass. Even at a distance the girl's hair was so blond it looked like sunlight. The breeze kept making a mess of it, and she kept smoothing it back. He remembered fall in Ohio, the roar of the Miami fans, and the crisp cut of the air against the back of his throat when he took a deep breath and ran out onto the field. He wanted to be young again, with nothing more complicated on his mind than the black-and-white of a football game and whether he'd get laid afterward. A loathing for the work he did and the people he did it with rose within him. He felt Frank Filmore's evil suffocating him.

"You're sweating," she said. "Frank hardly ever does, but his face was all shiny when we changed cars, and he was excited in a way I didn't like; he spooked me. Plus I could smell the chloroform." She smiled at David. "It has a nice smell."

"Did you see Lolly?"

"No. He said she was in the trunk. In a plastic bag. Frank's very fastidious."

"Did he tell you she was dead?"

"She wasn't."

"He told you she was alive?"

"He said so. Yes."

"And you believed him."

She looked surprised. "Of course I did. What happened was an accident. He only meant to frighten her so she'd learn her lesson and stop whining." A tear slipped down her cheek. "What was I supposed to do? If I called the police and something happened so he didn't go to prison, he'd come after me. Frank can be very mean. I suppose he's got all of you charmed, but if you knew him . . ."

"I'm not charmed."

"He said your partner, the black woman, she was hitting on him. The blonde, too."

"He's lying, Marsha."

"No. He can tell about people. Sometimes he knows things they don't know about themselves."

"There's nothing personal in any of our relationships with your husband, believe me."

"Don't underestimate Frank, Mr. Cabot."

He watched Dana come out of the house and crouch to pet Moby. As she did, she looked up at the apartment window, and David sent her a telepathic message to look away, to go inside and lock the door. The evil he felt around him was strong enough to hurt them all.

Marsha asked him if he was finished with questions.

"Did he tell you what he did?"

"When Sandra went into the house he went in through the alley gate and grabbed Lolly and made her breathe chloroform. He said it worked fast on such a little kid, and she didn't make a fuss at all. Shawna did. She bit his hand. He told me if she hadn't done that, he would have only hung her over the side of the well to give her a good scare. He only meant to teach her a lesson. Same with Lolly."

David nodded, not trusting himself to make a comment.

"Then he took her in the garden shed and double-bagged her in two of those big green garden bags, only not tight, because he didn't want her to die. That's what he said. He was going to take her somewhere and leave her. He said the Calhouns didn't know how to discipline her, and what she needed was the scare of her life."

This made no sense at all. The girl had been three years old. "What about afterward? She'd be able to identify him."

Marsha looked at him, blinking.

"Anyway," she said, "it was when he got to the mountain and he undid the bag and she started screaming. . . .

The thing people don't understand about Frank is how sensitive he is. He can't take a lot of noise. That's another reason why we're going to move to Idaho."

When Frank's hotshot lawyer gets him off.

"What did he do?"

"Got upset, I guess. Bashed her head."

He stood up. "Mind if I open the door?"

"It's cold," Marsha said.

He opened it anyway.

"Why did you get pregnant again? If he can't stand the whining, how will this baby be any different?"

"Oh, she will be. Frank's taught me about discipline." She lowered her eyes. "In a way, you see, it was my fault Shawna was such a bad little girl. If I'd been a better mother—"

David walked onto the landing at the top of the stairs and took a deep breath.

She said, "You're not going to tell him what I said, are you?"

"No."

"And promise you won't tell Mr. Peluso."

Through the window David saw Dana's back. He didn't need to see her face. Every line and the curve of each feature were familiar to him, imprinted on his heart and mind forever. All that he loved and believed in was in the house across the yard.

"I'm Frank's lawyer, Marsha. Your secrets are safe with me."

Chapter 36

David came into the house, and Dana saw at once that he was deeply troubled.

"Tell me," she said, resting her palms against his chest.

Without looking at her he moved away.

"You'll feel better . . ."

"And you'll feel worse, so just don't ask me again." He went upstairs, and she heard the shower running. When he came back downstairs his hair lay damp across his forehead. He had changed his shirt and put on a new tie.

"It's after four. Do you have to go back?"

"I don't know when I'll be home."

"David—"

"I need to work, Dana." At the back door he stopped, came back, and held her. "I'm sorry I snapped. It's the case. . . ." His body vibrated with tension.

"Come home early, then. Let's go to the movies. Why not, huh? It's Saturday." She recalled their sweet early morning together, the hope she had felt that despite everything their love for each other could be salvaged.

"Guadalupe can stay with Bay. Let's eat at the Cat and see something mindless."

"We can't keep paying a babysitter—"

"This is for us, David." She pressed her index finger to his lips. "Now isn't the time to economize."

He pulled back, abruptly angry. "If I lose this trial no one's going to hire me."

"You're exaggerating. Of course—"

"Not the clients we need. You know, Dana, it takes money to live the way we do."

She did not remind him that it was she who paid the bills and stroked their creditors with minimum payments.

"Babysitters all the time, housekeeper, private school. And you don't work—"

She would not be drawn into an argument and away from what mattered. "Tell me what Marsha said to you. You don't have to carry this by yourself."

He bent his head and rested his forehead against hers.

"Mind meld," she whispered. It was an old joke between them.

"You're right. A movie'd be good. Great. And dinner at the Cat."

They ate in silence, listening to oldies chosen by the disk jockey seated in a glass booth over the bar.

"Hear that?" she asked. "'A Whiter Shade of Pale.'" It had been her mother's favorite song. "And The Doors. Oh, God, she played 'Riders of the Storm' until I was dreaming the lyrics."

David nodded vaguely. Obviously his thoughts were somewhere else. *With Marsha Filmore,* Dana thought, and wondered what had transpired between them that morning. At another time in their lives she would have nagged a little, and eventually he would have told her. But she had her own secrets. What Dana wanted was happy talk—conversation, not interrogation.

"What kind of music did your folks listen to?"

"My mom and the judge—I don't think they listened to anything much, but my uncle liked Patsy Cline and Merle Haggard, all that country stuff." David looked up when a man paused beside their table.

Dana recognized a local television reporter and saw the camera.

"Mel Gorson, Channel Seven News."

David groaned.

"I went by your house, and your maid told me you were here."

"Our house is off limits, Mr. Gorson." Dana spoke as sweetly as possible, but it was hard to be pleasant when she remembered the days following Bailey's kidnapping and Gorson and the other reporters' persistent questions. None of them had cared that Dana was dying inside. "My husband will be happy to talk to you at the office on Monday."

Gorson ignored her. "I knocked on the door of the apartment, but no one answered. Marsha Filmore's staying with you, isn't she? What do you think she does in her spare time? Can you tell me why you decided to have her live with you?"

"She doesn't live *with* us," Dana said.

"My wife's right." The tone of David's voice brought her to the edge of her chair. "I'll talk to you on Monday."

"Just three questions. Thirty seconds each." Gorson had a wide, white, television smile. "Your food'll still be warm."

"I. Said. No."

Dana put her hand on her husband's forearm and felt his pulse jump.

Gorson said, "I'm sure you agree it looks kind of strange, her living at your place."

David stood up, knocking back his chair. He towered over the reporter. From the corner of the room Dana saw the manager come across the dining room fast. Diners around them had paused in their meals and conversations to watch the scene. A red light flashed on the video camera.

"David, stop." She walked around to his side of the table and stood beside him. "Why not answer a couple of questions?" She squeezed his hand.

Was it true that Marsha Filmore was living with them? Why was she living there? And, finally, "Mrs. Cabot, don't you worry about your little girl, living with the wife of a killer?"

It seemed to Dana that all her life she had been smiling when she felt like screaming, smiling to make people like her, to look normal. Her face ached with the memory of false smiles, but she forced another for Mel Gorson. "First of all, it is not a crime to have terrible taste in husbands. If it were, your wife would probably be in jail." She laughed and patted Gorson's wrist lightly, as if to say she did not mean it. "Second, this city has dealt very harshly with Marsha Filmore. The press has made her a pariah. I'd just remind your viewers that this woman has not been accused of anything. And as for Frank Filmore, in the United States we have something called the presumption of innocence. He will be guilty only when and if a jury decides he is."

Later, as they waited in the dark theater for the feature to begin, David took up her hand and kissed the palm. "You were great, Number One. Saved my bacon."

"It felt like the old days." Standing beside him after good games and bad.

"Yeah." He smiled at her. "Those were happy days."

"They'll come again."

David laughed curtly. "You mean Frank Filmore isn't going to be around for the rest of our lives?"

The theater lights went down. Dana pressed her lips to his ear. "Promise we'll be happy again."

St. Tom's had a bronze plaque on its oak door declaring the church a San Diego historical site. It had been one of the earliest of the mission churches, built in the late nineteenth century from redwood cut in northern California and carried by coastal barge to San Diego. The fifteen stained-glass windows depicting the lives of the saints had come around the Cape in boxes packed with sawdust, each box filled with hundreds of pieces of colored glass precisely designed and cut and labeled for assembly in San Diego. The floors were of intricate oak parquetry, and the ironwork had come from Mexico in a wagon someone had tried to hold up but been outrun by. Everything in St. Tom's had a sense of history about it, a story to go with it.

The next morning, when Dana and David stood for the processional, St. Tom's was three quarters full. She knew the names and histories of most of the people standing around her; others were nameless, yet later they would "exchange the peace," hand to hand, a company of believers.

Dana felt connected to God when she was in St. Tom's waiting for the service to start, and even more so when she and the people around her recited the Episcopal liturgy in unison. At such times it came to her that whatever God was or was not, the presence of the congregation proved God was powerful enough to bring together people of all varieties in a common declaration of love and belief. That alone was astonishing.

In the moment before opening prayers, she knelt and vowed not to lie or bend the truth anymore, to be loving to David, more patient with Bailey. She would have to figure out what to do about her thesis, but she did not expect God to help her with that. She begged forgiveness for her sins and strength to follow through on her promises. If God would just preserve her family . . .

Jason Gordon was St. Tom's crucifer that morning. He carried a cross of cypress cut more than three hundred years before in the Holy Land. The figure on it wore robes and a crown and was called Christ Victorious. Dana dipped her head as it passed. Next the choir and then Father Bartholomew, his grizzled old head high, a smile tickling the corners of his mouth. Last, Dana knew without looking, was Lexy. She did not turn her head; she never did. In church Lexy was the High Priest, not her best friend—and now, not her ex-best friend.

Before church Dana had expected that everyone would be talking about Micah's death and planning ways to make this time easier on Lexy. When no one said anything, she surmised that Lexy had decided to keep the news to herself for the time being. The massed condolences of St. Tom's would be hard to bear. She thought about Micah lying in his own blood; she remembered how it felt to love him.

"Why're you crying?" David handed her his clean handkerchief. "You never cry."

She made herself think of Micah stealing Bailey from her home, terrifying her. She stopped crying.

During the "prayers for the people," the Sunday school director, Laura, eased into the pew beside Dana and whispered, "Bailey needs you."

Dana heard Bailey's screams before she opened the kindergarten door and saw her standing in the middle of the room with her arms pressed rigidly against her side, hands in fists. The other children huddled against the walls gawking, one or two looking ready to scream themselves.

"What happened?"

The director shook her head. "As far as I can tell, she just started, no reason."

"Baby, baby," Dana soothed as Bailey fell into her arms, hot and sweaty and coiled with tension. "Never mind, Bay, Mommy's here. Nothing's going to happen."

Laura said, "Last week I thought she was improving."

"She is, every day." She kissed Bailey's forehead. "But some days are better than others."

"Sounds like a description of normal life, doesn't it?"

Laura left them alone, and Dana settled into the soft cushions of the storybook chair with Bailey nestled beside her. She glanced at her watch and saw there were twenty minutes until the end of the service. They would stay put.

Later, Beth Gordon's voice broke into Dana's thoughts. "You two make a beautiful picture. I wish I had my camera."

Jason stood beside her, still robed as the crucifer. "I got one of those disposables in the van." He brushed the top of Bailey's head with his hand. "Hi, there, Bailey."

"Jason, you're huge." Dana got a crick in her neck looking up at him. "You must have grown since last week."

"Nothing fits him, of course." Beth smiled at her grandson with such unabashed devotion Dana thought it must embarrass the boy. "Run get that camera, will you?" As he took off Beth said, "We'll put you two on the front page of next month's newsletter."

After church David went to work, and Bailey napped on the couch with her favorite blue and white blanket, her thumb in her mouth. Dana walked around the house, unable to settle down to anything. She turned on the television to check the score, saw the Chargers were losing, and turned it off. She took meat from the freezer for dinner, peeled potatoes and put them in a bowl of cold water. She sat down, tried to read a magazine, stood up, sat down again. She called David and hung up before he answered. Called him again and told him the score of the game. He had the radio on in his office. She stood at the sink and looked at the garage apartment. Something about the church's newsletter gnawed at a corner of her mind.

She walked into the entryway and sat on the lower step, where she had been letting the mail accumulate in a basket. Sorting through the junk flyers and one-time-only offers, the ads for contractors and cut-rate dentists, she tossed them into a pile to be recycled later and made a separate pile of catalogs and another of periodicals like the *New Yorker* and *Better Homes and Gardens*. The front page of that month's church newsletter had a picture of Lexy and the landscape gardener St. Tom's had hired to rehabilitate the garden in front of the offices.

Dana stared at the picture a long while. As she did, a thread of perspiration slipped from her hairline down her cheek.

The week after Bailey came home, the church had printed a special one-page bulletin. Dana knew that if she looked she would be able to find it somewhere in the house. Not that she needed to see it to remember. It was a sheet of ordinary print stock with one word written across the top in bold block letters: FOUND. Below this was a picture of David with Bailey in his arms. This was the picture that had come through the mail slot in a manila envelope with a noose drawn around David's neck, the picture Jason had taken. She remembered Beth saying he was making copies of the bulletin at the copy shop where he worked. He would deliver them in his friend Bender's van.

Dana reached for the phone and called Lieutenant Gary.

Chapter 37

David tried to work, but even when he turned off the Charger game he could not wrestle his thoughts into order. Finally he capped his pen and turned his chair toward the window. Through breaks in Little Italy's skyline of partially constructed buildings, the San Diego harbor was the color of blueberries and dotted with white sails. When he moved to San Diego he had imagined sailing on the bay, even though he did not know a jib from a spinnaker. Sailing, like tennis, and afternoons at the beach, and a Spanish colonial home, was part of the dream life he and Dana had envisioned.

A client like Frank Filmore had never been part of his dream.

He had begun the practice of law with high ideals and believing that every individual deserved the best defense. He remembered once telling his brother, a corporate attorney in Wheeling, that when he paid attention to the circumstances of a client's life he could not say that anyone was all bad or all wrong. In his practice he had dealt with sociopaths and lowlifes he didn't want within five miles of his family, but in all of them he had tried to discover at least one redeeming quality—a sense of humor, an admirable resilience, something that would enable him to put his full effort into their defense.

He had a framed sign in his office: YOUR DEFENSE ATTORNEY, LIBERTY'S LAST DEFENSE.

He hated to admit how naive he had been when he imagined himself a hipper, thinner, and much better dressed Clarence Darrow defending the powerless.

Frank Filmore was far from powerless. He had enough money to buy himself any five-star attorney in the country. By contrast, Darrow's constituency—the desperate men and women crowded into downtown holding cells— were lucky to get the services of an underpaid, overworked, and minimally qualified ninety-day wonder.

David thought of the bills piled up in the basket by the stairs, of the debts the firm incurred just by turning on the lights every day. He and Dana had talked about a trip to Fiji when they couldn't even afford a weekend in Las Vegas.

He needed Frank Filmore to pay the bills.

David flashed on a mental image of Shawna Filmore at the bottom of a well. He blinked and it was Bailey's elfin face he saw staring up at him from the green water. A sick nausea arose in him. He did not want to defend Frank Filmore for any amount of money. He wanted to throw him in jail and make him fight with the rats for bread and water. But if he went to the presiding judge and said he hated the s.o.b., the judge would chuck him out of chambers.

Liking your client was not a requirement of a good defense.

He could hand the job over to Gracie and Larry, but the judge would object to that, too. More to the point, it didn't matter who took the case; David knew what he knew. Filmore had killed two children and would prob-ably kill a third.

He opened his middle drawer, took out the Owens Garage receipt, and spread it smoothly on his desktop. This was the evidence that would take Filmore down, but there was nothing David could do with it that did not compromise his ethics. He might as well toss it away.

He tipped his chair as far back as it would go and tried to relax; he counted his breaths and imagined his mind with branches like a tree and roots that spread wide and deep. Eventually, gratefully, he slipped into a drifting state of half-sleep.

The ringing of the phone woke him. No one called him on the back line except Dana. He didn't want to talk to her until he'd done something with the information Marsha had given him the day before.

Just after three he sat forward and stood up. He gathered his jacket and briefcase, locked the office, walked downtown to the jail, and asked to see his client. After a short wait a guard escorted Filmore into the interview room. He looked healthy and fit; every black hair was slicked back and perfectly in place.

"What's up?" he asked in his phony accent. "Has the prosecutor finally figured out I didn't do it?"

"No," David said. "I've figured out you did."

Frank cocked his head to one side.

"And if I know, by the time we go to trial next month, Peluso will, too."

"I'm innocent. There's no way they can prove I did it."

David wanted to point out that the two claims were not necessarily connected.

"I took my car to be serviced the other day." It was the kind of statement it would be easy to disprove if

Filmore decided he wanted to sue David for ineffective assistance of counsel. "And guess what? You and I have the same mechanic, Floyd Owens over on Washington Street."

"So?" Filmore's right eyebrow twitched.

David leaned forward, resting his elbows on the table between them. "If Floyd's talking to me about loaner cars, it's only a matter of time until he talks to the cops."

David was spinning Filmore. Though it might happen that way, the odds were against it, because ordinary law-abiding citizens were notoriously reluctant to get involved in high-profile cases.

"And you want me to be worried about this?" Filmore asked the question with the slightly ironic, British inflection that made David want to pop him.

"What I want is for you to plead out while you still can. I think Peluso'll settle for life if I can burn the deal before the police find out about Floyd Owens."

Frank looked amused. "Your lack of confidence astounds me. I really expected better of you. I'm going to walk out of here. The prosecution's got no case, and I've got the hardest working lawyer in town."

"Did you hear what I said, Frank? He hasn't got a case now, but he will by the time we go to trial."

"I think I'll take my chances." He rubbed his eyebrow with the side of his thumb. "I'm feeling rather lucky these days."

"I wouldn't if I were you. I can smell the gas on this one."

Filmore sat back, scowling.

David said, "Here's what you need to know. Peluso is an ambitious man, and he wants to be mayor. After that, who knows, I wouldn't be surprised if he dreams of being governor one of these days. And you're his ticket. He won't rest, and neither will the police, until they find evidence that links you to the crime conclusively." David paused a moment to let his words sink in. "But you've got more to worry about than that. Even if Peluso ends up going forward with a nothing case, I still don't like the odds.

"It's the nature of the crime, Frank. Most people when they hear about a child being killed, tied up in a plastic bag and dumped over a hill, they react from their gut. There's pretty much no one in the city doesn't want to see you go down."

David paused again to let his words register. Filmore was vain and arrogant, but he was also smart. David counted on his intelligence to cut through his ego.

"In a case like this Peluso doesn't need much to get a conviction, because there's no way to impanel an honest-to-God neutral jury. Jurors are supposed to assume you're innocent until proven guilty, but they don't. Jurors think because the cops arrested you and the judge refused you bail you *must* be guilty."

David counted five breaths. When he spoke he sounded like a man deeply grieved to bring up a painful topic. "They know about Shawna."

"But you're going to keep that out of the trial, right? It's irrelevant or prejudicial or something. And even if you can't, subpoena the records. Get someone to translate for you. The Mexican cops said it was an accident."

"Mexican cops don't have a lot of credibility in San Diego." David rubbed his jaw. The joint below his ear ached with tension. "You see how it looks? A lousy case, but—"

"I didn't kill her." No English accent now.

David said, "The way this city feels, I could put God Almighty on the stand to vouch for you and it probably wouldn't help. The jury is going to want to convict you, Frank. And when Peluso talks to Floyd Owens, he'll send the cops to go over that other car with a microscope." David shrugged. "Once they come up with DNA evidence there won't be much I can do for you."

"My wife had the car. The police'll arrest her."

"She was at work all day. Dozens of witnesses."

Frank chewed his thumbnail, and sweat popped out on his forehead. David remembered Marsha saying her husband never perspired.

"Now I get it." Filmore's eyes narrowed. "*She* told you. You probably never heard of Floyd Owens before the bitch opened her mouth. But she paid cash; we always pay cash. There's no credit card receipt, so there's no way the cops'll find out. All I've got to do is sit tight."

"Maybe."

Filmore sat straighter. "I want to testify." He smiled and ran his hand back over his temples. "I'll make a good impression. They won't want to convict me once I tell my side of the story."

"Sorry, Frank, I can't let you do that."

"What do you mean? Who the fuck's paying you?"

"I can't let you go on the stand because I know you'll lie. As an officer of the court and your attorney, it's my responsibility to see you don't perjure yourself."

"I'll toss you out." He slammed his fist onto the metal tabletop. "Defend myself."

And if it could happen that way I would bless your name and walk out of this jail a free man. But the judge is a hardnose. He'll never let it happen.

Filmore's eyes lighted. "That's what you want. To get off this case."

David tried to look aggrieved.

"I'm paying you a lot of money. Every time you

come here you've got your hand out. I paid for you to defend me, and that's what you're going to do."

"And that's what I'm doing. I'm telling you how to keep from tasting gas. I'm giving you the scoop on your chances. As your lawyer, I advise you to take a plea. If you can get one. We're talking life and death here. You want to roll the dice?"

David was worn out when he left the jail fifteen minutes later and drove his car across Mission Valley and up the hill to the parking lot opposite the Church of the Madeleine. He rolled all the windows down and let the cool westerly wind rush through the car. The Madeleine Hill was one of the highest points in the city. From his car he looked down on the park surrounding Mission Bay, where jet skiers in wet suits bucked on the choppy water. Slightly south, the Point Loma peninsula extended into the Pacific like a thumb, dividing Mission Bay from the harbor and skyscraping profile of the city. He could see the naval hangars on Coronado Island, the sweeping curve of the bridge, and even farther south an occasional beam of late-afternoon sunlight flashing off the hazy outline of the Tijuana hills.

He felt like a complete shit.

And yet as he waited for Les Peluso to join him, he knew he was doing what he had to in order to live with himself. Long ago his uncle had told him that a man could betray anyone in the world and probably get away with it. He just couldn't betray himself, because he could never walk away from that. David knew that if he went ahead with the trial and got Frank off, he would betray all that was strongest and best in himself.

The Madeleine was Peluso's church. He'd know where to come.

Forty minutes later the prosecutor pulled into the lot and parked his little black Boxster alongside David's Honda. He laughed as he got in beside David.

"This is real cloak-and-dagger stuff, man. Feels like TV."

"Great view, huh? Once I saw the constellation come in from up here. Huge motherfucker. If the church had to pay taxes on this property it'd be out of business in a minute."

Peluso's wide mouth grinned. "And this is why you've brought me up here? To discuss the church's tax-exempt status?"

"My guy wants to plead."

"No kidding."

"Take his plea. Give him life forever. Let's get this thing done with."

Peluso chuckled. "I seem to remember I warned you you'd be sorry you left the good guys."

"Point of view, Les, point of view."

Peluso rested his elbow on the open window. "Why don't you go to the judge, get him to take you off the case?"

"Wecker the Wanker? I'd have to be dying of a contagious disease."

"You were headed for the top in the DA's office. If you'd given it a little time . . ." Peluso shook his head. "You ever miss football?"

"August to January, but never on Monday mornings."

"You weren't that great, but you were better than the idiot they got now. When I think what management paid for him . . ."

"Quit stalling. Do we have a deal?"

"Well, the thing is . . ."

"You want the case to go to trial so you can look good. The Sword of the People and all that."

Peluso pretended to be shocked.

"I'm offering you a guy we both know stinks. I'm saving you time, and I'm saving the city maybe a million bucks. You'll get your camera time."

Peluso shook his head. "A case like this, David, I think the people need to see the trial, see justice in action.

"When the crime is really horrible, a nightmare scenario, a plea doesn't satisfy the people's indignation. They need to see justice done. It helps them believe in the system."

"I don't need a civics lesson."

"And you'll excuse me if I'm just a little suspicious. How come you're copping a plea now, not a couple of months ago, when I might have taken it?" Peluso chewed his lower lip and watched out the window. "It's all over the news that Marsha Filmore's living at your place, which makes me think maybe she knows something. I'm thinking I should send the cops over there to chat with her. She might be more forthcoming now."

"Another way of thinking is that if you lose this case, you won't be able to get elected dogcatcher."

"You've got a point there." Peluso chewed his lip some more. "Let me think about it. I'll be in touch."

Chapter 38

David did not sleep well that night, and consequently neither did Dana, who lay awake feeling the bed shift each time he turned. Around two he got up and took a pill. Always a bad sign. The next morning he blew up when Guadalupe came through the back door at eight A.M. He gestured Dana to follow him out of the kitchen and upstairs. He closed their bedroom door.

"What's she doing here again? If you don't work, you don't need help five days a week. Every time that woman comes up here from Mexico you have to pay her cash, cash that comes out of our checking account."

"What's got into you, David? I pay the bills. I know how much I'm spending on Guadalupe."

"Listen to what has to come out of that account." Dana watched his jaw grind as he spoke. "The gas and electric, water for your big garden, two cars, insurance and a special school, and—"

"Honey, your face is so flushed. I think you should check your blood pressure."

"I've got a resting pulse of fifty-two, God damn it! Don't make this about me."

She began stripping the bedsheets. "If it'll calm you down, I'll send her home."

"This isn't about making me calm. It's about fiscal responsibility."

"I said I will send her home." *Like hell.*

"You told her you'd pay her, and now she's counting on it."

"She won't make a fuss."

"Dana, that's not the point." He watched her unfold a clean sheet and fit it to the mattress. She knew he was getting ready to blow. "This is about you, about the way you spend money. How'm I supposed to pay for your housekeeper and babysitter and—" He seemed at a loss for words. "We're not bloody rich, Dana."

She had intended to tell him she suspected Jason of sending the hate mail to their home. Immediately after she called Lieutenant Gary, she had tried to reach David at the office, but he hadn't answered his phone. Before going to sleep she had written a note in lipstick on the bathroom mirror—*wake me when you get home important*—but either he had not seen it or had ignored it.

"What about the message?" he said.

Now he was a mind reader.

"What was so important?"

Just because he could shift moods in a minute did not mean she could. She did not want to talk to him about anything; she just wanted him out of the house.

"It can wait."

And it was only a suspicion she had. Nothing had been confirmed.

"Just go to work, will you? We'll talk tonight."

If you can manage to get home before midnight.

* * *

Later she went down to the kitchen, where Bailey and Guadalupe were washing dishes. Bailey stood on a stool at the sink with her hands in the water almost up to her shoulders. A Spanish-language station was playing on the radio while Guadalupe talked a streak, though Bailey had no clue what she was saying.

I'm not sending her home. I pay the bills.

Another hundred dollars or so wouldn't break them.

In the middle of the radio broadcaster's blast of jackhammer Spanish she heard Bailey's name and then David's and Jason's. She ran upstairs and turned on the television in the bedroom. While she clicked through the channels with her right hand, she turned the radio dial with her left.

Nothing.

She called Information for the local public radio station and eventually was connected to the news director, who told her there had been an arrest in the Bailey Cabot kidnapping. The police were holding an unidentified juvenile who apparently knew the family and was active on the committee to find Bailey.

"No," Dana said.

The juvenile was also in trouble for threatening the family, David Cabot in particular.

"I never said he took her. I absolutely did not say that."

"Ma'am?"

She hung up and was about to call Gary when the phone rang.

Lexy said, "The police have arrested Jason Gordon."

"I just heard."

"You knew?"

"Actually, Lexy, I was the one who called Gary yesterday. I wasn't sure, but I told him about the picture, the one of David with the noose around his neck, and I remembered Jason took it for the newsletter the week Bailey came back. Plus, his friend has a white van."

"He's confessed to the letter-writing, and now Gary's accused him of kidnapping Bailey. Beth just called me, half-crazy. They rousted him out of bed at seven A.M., slapped handcuffs—"

"I must tell Gary who really did it. At first I wasn't going to, Lexy, but then I realized I have to." The receiver was cold in Dana's hands. "I'm sure the charges'll be dropped. There's no evidence against Jason. I don't think he'll even be arraigned, but they might keep him overnight. He's only a boy, and he must be terrified."

What amazed Dana was that all around her, life thrived. Downstairs Bailey and Guadalupe amused and entertained each other. In the park the city workers were mowing the grass and yelling back and forth in Spanish. She could hear the cars speeding down the Washington Street grade. Busy people, busy lives. And in the midst of all the normal hubbub, Dana's life, her family, and friendships, were all afire; her life was a wildfire no one could extinguish except her. She could tell Gary everything, the whole truth, and the fire would be out. But what would remain of her life in the ashes?

She said, "And Beth . . . she was so good to me, Lexy. I can't let her suffer needlessly."

"I know. Jason's a jerk, but he's no kidnapper. But of course that's what I would have said about Micah, too." In the long pause Dana heard Lexy breathing. "Do what you have to. He's dead. I guess it doesn't matter what people say about him now."

"Lexy, I am so sorry it came to this." The phone was dead by the time she'd said it.

Dana walked down the hall to Bailey's bedroom, where everything she saw—the cubbies and the oval rag rug, the bunk beds she and David had put together—

glowed with a patina of emotional significance. It had taken them hours to sand the beds to a satin finish. For several days afterward Dana had awoken in the night with aching shoulders and the whir of the electric sander still ringing in her ears. She remembered the laughter and the grousing. When it came to the fifth layer of varnish and yet another sanding, she had complained loudly, and David had said he'd do it himself, and she said she wouldn't give him the satisfaction. Later they'd ordered Chinese and eaten it on the back deck with Moby between them, just a puppy, begging bites of orange chicken. How strong and pure and good they had been together in those days.

She sat on the edge of the bed, her arms folded across her midsection. She thought of what she was about to do and of the consequences. She thought of her guilt and prepared herself to take responsibility.

First she called David and asked him to come home.

"I'm due in court at one."

"There's time. It's not even ten yet."

"What's this about, Dana?" He was still angry with her.

"Just come home."

His voice was muffled as he spoke to someone in the office. He told her, "Sorry, it'll have to wait."

"It can't. Not this time."

"Is this about Bailey?"

"It's about all of us."

A windy sigh echoed down the telephone line.

"Give me thirty minutes. And Dana?"

"Yes."

"This better be good."

"It's not. It's not good at all."

* * *

After hanging up she stared at the phone for a long moment, then pressed a speed-dial button and eventually was connected to Gary. As she told her story he interrupted only to ask clarifying questions. Where was the sash now?

"I have it. And the note."

"Well, that's a surprise."

His voice sounded dry and pinched when he said he would have to come and take a statement from her.

"I need to tell my husband first, but he has a court date. He'll be gone by one. You can come here after that." She hung up, not waiting for him to agree.

From the bottom of her jewelry box she dug out her emergency money, two twenty-dollar bills and a five, and went down to the den where Guadalupe and Bailey were sorting a pile of plastic pieces by shape and color. Dana handed Guadalupe the money.

"Walk up to Big Bad Cat and have lunch, will you? I need the house to myself until about three." In a mix of Spanish and English it took a few moments to get the point across.

Guadalupe's dark eyes were full of sympathy.

For years Dana had not cried, but lately she could not stop. She tried to smile as tears rolled down her cheeks. "Bad times."

"*Ah, pobrecita.*"

Chapter 39

From the bedroom window Dana watched David cross the deck. She imagined the house shimmied with the force of his heels hitting the wood. Drawing a long breath, she looked around her at the bedroom where they had slept together for the last eight years. These might be the last moments of her marriage, and she wanted to pay attention to everything, because the room would never look the same after she and David talked.

He came through the bedroom door like a storm system, his brows drawn down and his jaw squared.

"This better be important," he said as he threw his keys on the bed.

"Can we sit down?" She realized how frightened she was and grabbed her hands together to steady them.

"Just talk, Dana. I'll sit if I want to."

Please don't be so angry. Not before you know anything. There won't be anywhere for you to go except over the top.

She perched on the windowsill and started with the easy words. "Jason Gordon is the person who's been sending hate mail to the house."

"You mean the kid on the Bailey Committee? Why would he do that?"

"I don't know, no one knows yet. But . . ." She told David how Beth had said Jason had a crush on her, and how she had heard Bender and Jason expressing their disapproval of David defending Frank Filmore.

"It was the picture of you with the noose drawn around your neck that gave it away."

"Dana—"

"I was going through the mail and looking at the latest bulletin, and I realized that the noose picture came from St. Tom's bulletin." His face bore a look of intense concentration, as it did when he was in court. "I called Gary, and I mentioned that Jason had been very helpful and that he worked at a copy shop."

"So is he the one who hit Moby?"

She nodded.

"What about the note in your car?"

"It was Jason."

"He's confessed?"

She nodded again.

"He's confessed to everything? The kidnapping too?"

"No, not the kidnapping."

He sat in the small easy chair near the window, visibly more relaxed than he had been a few minutes earlier. He tapped his index finger against his lips. "One thing's for sure. He couldn't pull off the kidnapping alone. Whoever else was in on it—"

"He didn't take her." She looked around their bedroom a final time.

"How can you be so sure?"

"Because I know who did."

He stared at her.

She rushed on. "It was my fault, David. I made it happen."

"That's ridiculous, Dana. How—"

"The kidnapping had nothing to do with Frank Filmore."

"How can you be so sure? Is this what Gary says?"

She was dry-eyed now, surprisingly calm.

There was a limit to the amount of deception a person could live with before her whole life was infected by dishonesty and there was nothing left that was good and pure and strong. If God was in the business of teaching lessons, then this must be what she was meant to learn. Perhaps she had learned too late, and nothing would be left of the life she had loved. Not a single coal burning anywhere.

"David, if I knew some way to spare you this, I would."

She watched something change in his face, a subtle shift and firming of the contours. He looked at his watch. "I don't have much time." He sat with his hands on his thighs.

"You know I love you . . ."

"That's established, Dana." In a court of law, love did not count for much. "Just say what you have to."

"I had—in Florence I had . . . an affair . . ."

His face was impassive.

"With Lexy's brother."

"You had sex with someone?"

"Lexy's brother," she repeated, unable to say his name. "It was a stupid thing to do, I don't know—"

"Wait a minute." He held up his hand. "You mean you fucked this Michael? Micah?"

"You make it sound—"

"What? Cheap? If it wasn't, what was it? Are you going to tell me he was the great love of your life?"

"Of course not. Don't put words in my mouth."

"Why not? I bet everything else has been in there."

She sucked in her breath and held it.

"You know, I should've figured it out when I never could get you on the phone. Jesus, what a klutz I was. It never occurred to me not to believe. I guess I never would have known." He shook his head, talking to himself. "I would have gone on assuming I could trust you, you loved me. . . ."

"I do. Love you."

"Did you tell him that, too?"

She no longer remembered what she had felt for Micah or said to him. This moment and the revelations that preceded it had burned out her memories of Florence.

"Do you know how many times I could've cheated on you?" He stood up. "Going way back, Dana, I could've fucked half the cheerleaders and paralegals—"

She covered her ears with her hands, and he pulled them away, holding her wrists so hard she thought the bones would snap.

"But I never did. I never even gave it serious thought. I guess I was a jerk, huh?"

She started to say that if he gave her another chance she would make it up to him. He told her to shut up.

"Dana, I always believed in you. I believed in us. We were a team."

"Yes," she cried. "Yes, and we still are."

He dropped her wrists, threw them down as if he couldn't stand to touch her. If he had looked angry or hurt, she could have taken that. Instead she saw something she had never seen in his expression, a terrible neutrality that told her that in his mind he had already begun to separate from her.

"David, don't shut me out. Please. It was a stupid, stupid mistake, but I learned something about myself . . ."

"I don't care what you learned."

"Yes, you do. You always cared about me. You can't just suddenly stop." She did not want to cry. Crying made her weak. She hated him for making her do it and herself for not being able to stop.

He shoved her away. She stumbled back, hitting her hip on the windowsill. In the fraction of a moment it took her to regain her balance and rub her hip she realized that she had still not told him the complete truth.

"I'll tell you why I did it. Do you want to know?" She saw that he was torn. "I wanted to be someone else for a while."

"Well, me too, Dana," he said, his voice metallic. "Who doesn't?"

"I got away from you and Bay and everything I knew, and a part of me came out that I didn't know was there. And I couldn't stop myself." *I didn't even try.* Her words hurtled on, and he seemed to be listening. If she said enough, perhaps, eventually, he would understand. "It wasn't about cheating on you or not loving you. It was about stepping out of my skin and being someone else for a week."

"You want me to forgive you because—"

"Because you know me, because you know in your deepest heart that I love you." Loving David marked and identified her as surely as the curve of her ears, her thumb- and voiceprints. "I've lived my whole life fighting not to be my mother and grandmother, compensating for their influence, beating off anything that looked like it might drag me down to their levels. I paid so much attention to what I wasn't that I never had a chance—"

"Stop blaming those two for everything. It doesn't

work anymore. You're an adult, and what you do, you do because you want to. You wanted to fuck a stranger, so you did. That's it."

"David, listen to me. Micah wanted me to stay, he begged me to stay with him, but I wanted to come home. *I chose you and Bay.*"

He sneered. "For some reason that doesn't make me feel any better."

"I realized that if I left you I'd be leaving myself, the best part of myself. In a way, what happened was a good thing, David. I'm not excusing it, but sometimes it takes a terrible experience to make you understand—"

"Congratulations," he said. "Insight is a wonderful thing."

"Stop being a lawyer. Listen to me with your heart."

"Shit, Dana, I'm tired of listening." The mauve circles around his eyes seemed to have darkened in the last half hour. "Just tell me the rest of it. He took Bailey. Where?"

"Mexico, I think."

"And his reason?"

"To hurt me."

"Nice guy."

"He didn't hurt her. That's something I know."

"Maybe."

"It didn't mean anything. It meant nothing."

"That is such a stupid thing to say." He looked at her with incredulous disgust. "Fucking is one thing, but stealing our child—"

"He was unbalanced, but the man I knew in Florence would never—"

"Stop trying to blame him. You started it. You couldn't keep your pants on. Just say it, Dana. It's your fault," David roared. "Bailey would not have been stolen, her future, her *world—our* world—would be a different place if you hadn't decided to experiment with the limits of your personality."

Panic spiked through her, and she fell against him, wrapping her arms about his neck, pressing her face into his chest.

"Forgive me, just forgive me. I admit everything, David. Say you'll forgive me." She searched his eyes for a star of hope.

Something to work toward.

The cosmos could have been created in the length of time it took him to answer.

Chapter 40

Work was the only cure for what sickened David. After the scene with Dana, he went back to the office, gathered his papers together, and went to court, where Gracie said he argued brilliantly on behalf of a seventeen-year-old boy being tried as an adult accused of assault and battery by an old man with faulty eyesight and a distrust of any non-white below the age of seventy-five. David barely remembered his words to the jury.

It was the kind of case he could put his heart into. The boy was not too smart, not too cunning, and not mean enough to be guilty. If the criminal justice system got him, he would be lost forever. This was why David had become a defense attorney, to make sure boys like this did not get railroaded into jail and have their lives ruined.

The jury was out just over an hour before returning a not-guilty verdict. On the walk back to the office, for about fifteen minutes, he felt right with the world. Then he thought of calling Dana to report his success, and the world caved in on him. He closed himself behind his office door and sorted through his messages. Three from Dana, which he threw away. Nothing from Peluso.

That night he bought an expensive dinner at Morton's Steak House and indulged in a one-hundred-and-twenty-dollar bottle of Merlot. If Dana could have Guadalupe eight days a week, he deserved a good meal when he wanted one. He sat in a booth alone, the day's copy of the *San Diego Transcript* propped in front of him as camouflage. While he ate and pretended to read the front page, he watched the women at the bar in their short skirts and fuck-me stiletto heels, the muscles of their calves outlined like diagrams in an anatomy textbook. He could have almost any one of them. The blonde in the red silk suit and diamond ear studs—he had only to stand at the bar, engage her in conversation, and let slip that he was David Cabot. It would be so easy, it wasn't worth doing. He did not want to wake up in a strange bed looking at someone whose name he could not remember. He wanted to be with Dana the way it was before and never would be again.

He couldn't digest his steak and left half of it on the plate. He left the restaurant and went into a sports bar. Watching the end of the Monday-night matchup, for the first time in many years he wished he were still a quarterback. Five seconds on the field and Dana would be out of his mind and the game would be everything. David walked through the Gaslamp, down Fourth as far as Island, then right, and left again to Seaport Village, where he sat on a bench with his back to the dark shops and watched the lights on the harbor and Coronado. Over and over he told himself he had to figure out what to do about Dana. And over and over again he asked himself what was the point of pretending there was anything to figure out. They were finished. Their marriage was over. He shifted his thoughts to Frank Filmore's defense. How could he do it if Peluso said no to the plea? And then he thought of Bailey, and he loved her and missed her and wanted to kill Micah Neuhaus. But he was already dead. His suicide denied David the only course of action that made sense to him. He thought of Dana again.

He slept restlessly on his office couch in his shorts and T-shirt, covered with the red, black, and white afghan his aunt had knitted for him when he went off to Miami. He was cold, and barely slept, and when he awoke he felt like an old man with rust in his joints. Before anyone came into the office he made coffee, brushed his teeth, and washed his face—but still he looked awful. Barely past forty, he saw his father's jowls and droopy eyes in the mirror, the result of days of stress and short sleep. He wondered what his father had been like before power and greed had corrupted him. If David had been able to get beyond the man's bluster and vulgarity, might he have learned something to help him through this time in his life?

Yesterday's shirt was too wrinkled for court. Barbara came in at eight-fifteen, and he sent her out to Target to buy him another one, apologizing profusely for asking her to run a personal errand, promising to make it up to her.

A little after eight-thirty Gracie entered his office and shut the door. She looked at the afghan and then at him.

"You slept here?"

"I don't really want to talk about this, Gracie."

"You didn't go home at all?"

"Did you come in for some special reason?"

"Yeah. To say you look like shit."

She left and came back a few minutes later with a liter bottle of water.

"Drink this."

"I don't want water." He'd already had three cups of coffee.

"You need it. Your cells are dehydrated." She looked around the office. "Where's your shirt? You can't go to court in your undershirt."

"I sent Barbara over to Target. Nowhere else is open at this hour."

Gracie shook her head. "You'll never learn."

"I apologized to her."

"So why didn't you sleep at home?"

It went against his nature to talk about his marriage with a third party, even Gracie. The sentences on his computer screen swam before his eyes. "Just let me get through this motion."

"Allison can do it."

"It's not easy."

"And she's not stupid. Isn't that a lucky break?" She called Allison into the office. To David she said, "Tell her what you need."

He explained the motion to Allison, and she said she'd have it done in no time and disappeared, closing the door behind her.

Gracie said, "The whole office knows something's up. You don't know how wasted you look."

He tilted his chair and stared up at the acoustic-tile ceiling. Automatically, he counted a line of dots across one tile and then a line down. He remembered lying on a couch in the hospital waiting room after Bailey was born, staring at the ceiling, counting and multiplying, getting confused and starting all over again.

Gracie sat in the wing chair. "What's up, Boss?"

"It's such a mess, I don't think I could explain."

"Try."

He managed a wan smile, but his face stiffened and

he looked away, out the window at the two immense cranes like Star Wars contraptions already at work on a building a block away. "I don't know what to do about Filmore."

"We can start with him."

From the other side of the door he heard the office at work, keyboards, telephones ringing and voices. He told her about the receipt from Owens Garage, his conversations with Marsha and Frank Filmore, and Peluso's apparent rejection of the plea offer.

"You met on the Madeleine Hill?" She grinned. "You're working the high wire there."

"He thinks he can beat us."

"Well, of course he does. He's a prosecutor, the Almighty Hammer of the Lord."

"I think about going into court and defending Frank and I get physically ill. Sick."

"What does Dana say?"

He stared at the crane until his tired eyes began to water.

"Do you believe in what we do, Gracie?"

"I couldn't do the job if I didn't. Of course there are times and there are clients. Like Filmore. . . ."

"Marsha says it's the whining that sets him off. The way she tells it, killing Lolly was a natural kind of mistake."

"Like taking a wrong turn?"

"Yeah, he only meant to scare her."

"She goes for that?"

"I don't know what Marsha Filmore goes for."

"And I doubt you want to."

A knock on the door and Allison stuck her head in. "Want to read this, Boss?"

David gestured her forward and quickly scanned the motion.

"You're a scholar and a saint," he said.

Allison blushed. "Anything else I can help you with?"

"Is Barbara back?"

"Sorry." She left the office, closing the door softly. *Treading on eggshells,* David thought.

"So what are you going to do?" Gracie asked, and for a second he thought she meant about Dana because even when he was thinking of Filmore, Dana was in his deeper thoughts.

"I'm stuck with him unless I could convince the judge to take me off the case. You could handle it, you and Larry?"

"Thing is, Boss, the judge'll never let you do it. He's a hard-ass about changes once a trial's on the docket."

"Yeah."

"You ask me? Personally? I think you should talk to Dana about this."

He felt the sadness in his expression and couldn't change it. "Well, that's not possible today." Or tomorrow, either.

"David, I know how it can be when you've been married awhile. Things happen. Problems that don't go away for a while. But you and Dana have a good marriage. You've been through some heavy shit together, and you held each other up when you had to. I don't know what's going on now, and you don't have to tell me. But if you're smart, you'll take my advice: go home and mend some bridges. I've known you a long time; you oughta listen to me."

She had been the most striking woman among the first-year law students. Tall and strong, with glistening black hair cut short as a man's, her skin the color of almonds. To class she wore tight Levi's, T-shirts, and exotic earrings, and none of the professors intimidated her. And she was smart. During orientation he'd asked to be in her study group. As a boy he'd had many friends. In college, and when he was a Charger, friendship had come easily to him. But there were only two people he had trusted completely. Gracie was one of them. The only one now.

"I guess we're splitting up," he said. "Shit." His eyes teared up. "I hate the way that sounds."

"Jesus, Boss, I'm so sorry. I had no idea things were so rough."

"Neither did I."

"Now I know you got to go home. Get someone to lock the two of you inside and don't let you out until you've made up."

"Some things . . . it's not always possible to make up."

"Boss, if you two can't make it, what hope is there for the rest of us?"

He could not answer that.

"What about Bailey?"

Or that, either.

A long silence followed, and eventually David began to speak about Dana and Micah and how their affair had led to Bailey's kidnapping.

When he finished they sat in silence for some moments.

"I suppose it would be different," she said, "if he hadn't taken Bailey. . . ."

His head snapped around. "You'd say it was okay then?"

"Not okay, but different. Not so bad."

He stared at her.

"David, sex happens."

"If Marshall did this—"

"Which he has."

David felt he'd started in one game and ended up in another.

"You forgave him?"

"I live in the real world, David. And just because Marshall put his dick in the wrong place, I'm not giving up on him. Or us."

"But what if he—"

She held up her hand. "Don't interrogate me. I'll answer your questions because you're my friend, not my judge, or Marshall's, either. It happened once. Marshall had an affair with a temp in his office, and I found out about six months after it was over. I was pissed, I was hurt, I wanted to toss him out." She leaned back in the wing chair. "But what he did couldn't change how I feel about him. I love him. What did change was my illusions. I don't have them anymore."

"It's a matter of trust, Gracie, of being able to count on someone's loyalty."

"Those are just words, they don't have feeling behind them. What do you feel?"

"Mad."

"Well, yeah, obviously. You've got a right to that. But what else?"

He doodled on the yellow legal pad in front of him.

She said, "Let me tell you a story. A few years ago my mom had this little dog that was just devoted to her. Trailed after her everywhere she went, slept on the bed. When I wasn't around I think she let the dog eat off her plate. It was kind of disgusting, actually."

David was grateful not to speak.

"So one day she calls me and she's crying because the dog has bitten her. Made her bleed. I drove over and took her to the doctor, got her stitches, and the doctor says she's got to take the dog to the vet, have it checked for rabies. Something like that. And that's what we did, and the dog's up-to-date on its shots, no problem; but the vet finds out it's got some kind of arthritis thing in its spine and it's in pain. The dog's in pain all the time, turns out, and that's why it bit my mom."

David rolled his eyes.

"You can be amused all you like," Gracie said, "but what you're feeling now, the mad part, it's a cover-up for something else. Maybe hurt, or even fear."

"I'm not afraid of anything."

Gracie looked at him, disgusted. "Of course you're afraid. You don't want your marriage to end, David. You wouldn't know what to do without Dana."

He would buy a townhouse, watch television at night, and maybe learn to cook for himself. He'd date blondes he met at Morton's.

It sounded like hell.

He said, "What makes you so smart?"

"Well, for one thing, I'm black, and everyone knows blacks are smarter than whites. For another, I'm female, and we're all of us just way smarter than you guys. Hands down."

His smile faded. "Some things can't be done, Gracie."

"Bullshit. I'm not saying it's easy. Believe me, I wanted to kill Marshall. And we've got guns in the house, so I could have done it."

"What changed your mind?"

"I didn't think you could get me off. And then I thought about all the guys I slept with before we got married and how none of them meant anything much—"

"Dana was a virgin."

Gracie threw up her hands. "Well, jeez, then you can't blame her, David. She had a fling. She wanted to know what it felt like to be with another guy."

He remembered Dana telling him that with Micah

she had discovered a part of herself she had denied all her life.

"Maybe it's different for a woman," he said.

"Are we talking the double standard now? You're smarter than that." Gracie looked at her watch. "What's your schedule?"

"I'm due before Smythe at ten."

"What case?"

"Joel Dexter. Motion to suppress the dope the cops found in his car."

"What else?"

"Desk work."

"Go home. I'll argue the motion."

"Wilson won't like it."

"Screw Wilson."

She came around behind his desk and motioned him to stand up. When he did, she took his hands. "Boss, let me tell you something I know as good as I know your name. It makes sense you're mad and hurt and scared now, but those feelings are like walking on wet cement. You gotta move fast through them. Get to the other side before you're stuck there. You get stuck, you guys split up, you'll regret it the rest of your life."

"You don't understand, Gracie. We were a team—"

"Enough with the football! You're husband and wife, lovers, parents. You're a couple, not a team, for God's sake."

If there was anyone in the world from whom he might take advice, it was Gracie. But in the end Marshall's peccadilloes paled beside Dana's. It crossed David's mind that his father would never have forgiven under the circumstances. So, he was a little like Claybourne Cabot after all.

Chapter 41

Lexy slumped in a choir stall behind the altar rail. The late-afternoon sun had dipped below the windows, leaving the interior of St. Tom's in deep shadow. In her hand she held the typed copy of her resignation directed to the bishop of the San Diego Diocese. The letter to the vestry was in her office and said the same thing. *It is with the deepest regret,* etc. She had read it through a dozen times, and there was not a word she wanted to change. *Due to personal reasons I find I am no longer able to perform my material and spiritual duties.* The next step was to get in her car and deliver the letter to the bishop's offices. But it was this she could not seem to do. She had come into the church to think, and had not stirred for more than an hour.

The letter to the bishop was formal and barely touched the truth. The letter in her head was very different.

I am no longer able to perform my material and spiritual duties because I have lost faith and no longer see the child of God in those to whom I minister. There is too much sadness in the world, too much anger in me, and I am inadequate to the task I have taken up.

I want to be free to mourn my brother and despise Dana Cabot and never forgive her.

From time to time a priest could have her doubts. It was to be expected. But this was not doubt. This was demolition. Of herself, not God.

Lexy heard the side door of the church slam shut and the clack of flip-flops crossing the tiles.

The tenth-grade volunteer who was earning school credit for answering phones and running errands said, "I just got another call? You're really needed. That's what the caller said. I don't know her name."

"Alana. Her name is Alana." Lexy sighed and stood up. "Call her back. Tell her I'm on my way."

Dorothy's bedroom was laced with bars of leafy green and white light that brought out the gold in the flecked wallpaper and turned the dark wood furniture coppery. Dorothy lay on her back with her small head sunk in the expanse of white pillow, her sparse hair fluffed out like a dandelion crown. Her hands outside the bedcovers were wizened and small except for knuckles the size of walnuts. She plucked anxiously at the tufts on the Queen Anne bedspread.

As Lexy drew up a padded lady's chair and sat down, she heard steps behind her, turned, and accepted the mug of tea Alana held out to her.

Lexy had brought her prayer book and a small bottle of consecrated oil. She made the sign of the cross in the air between them and said softly, "Dorothy, I lay my hands upon you in the Name of our Lord and Savior Jesus Christ, beseeching Him to uphold you and fill you with His Grace, that you may know the healing power of His love."

Dorothy's eyelids fluttered as if she were dreaming, and her fingers picked and pinched more rapidly.

"May Almighty God have mercy on you, forgive you all your sins through our Lord Jesus Christ, strengthen you in all goodness, and by the power of the Holy Spirit keep you in eternal life."

Lexy pulled the stopper from the bottle containing an ounce of holy oil. She dipped her thumb in the oil and made the sign of the cross on the old woman's forehead.

"Dorothy, I anoint you with oil in the Name of the Father, and of the Son, and of the Holy Spirit."

She had said the words, and she had done so mindfully, without letting her personal problems interfere with her duty. It was what Dorothy had wanted and expected her to do. Now there was only the waiting. It seemed unlikely she would wake again. The old lady's hands stilled and came to rest beside her; her breathing became shallow.

Lexy sat back. She had begun by not liking Dorothy Wilkerson, but the opinionated old woman had grown on her over the months of her slow dying. Now, at the end, Lexy felt a burden of sorrow descend upon her shoulders as she waited for death to come. She would miss Dorothy.

Lexy's eyes drooped. She had not slept well for many days and knew she would drift off if she did not try especially hard to stay awake.

Alana's tea was strong and sweet and invigorating.

Holding Dorothy's hands, she paraphrased a favorite prayer. "Lord, you have supported Dorothy, Your servant, all the days of her life. Now, as the shadows lengthen and the evening comes, and the busy world is hushed and the fever of life nears its end, and her work on earth is done, in Your mercy grant Dorothy a safe lodging with You and a holy rest and peace at the last. Amen."

The music of the old words lingered on the air like a sustained chord that resonates in the ear long after it is struck. A shudder went through Lexy, and she dropped back into the chair. Her hands were suddenly icy.

Dorothy opened her eyes. They were the color of the fog. "Hello, Ellen." Her voice was steady. "Thank you for coming."

Lexy began to say that she was not Ellen but stopped herself. She didn't know why, but at the last moment it seemed better to say nothing.

"Ellen, give me your hands," Dorothy said.

The air around Lexy grew soft, and a veil of dusty bronze silk dropped over her vision as she extended her hands.

"Child, forgive me. I judged you harshly, cruelly. Your father and I both. I have no way to say—" She closed her eyes. Lexy started to pull away, but Dorothy's grip tightened. "Don't go. Promise me you won't."

Lexy whispered without thinking, "I promise."

"Mommy. Say . . . Mommy."

"I promise." Lexy swallowed. "Mommy."

"The sixties . . . terrible times . . . but I never stopped . . ."

"I forgive you, Mommy. I was a difficult child." She did not think before she spoke. The words came from beyond her mind and were light and thin as wafers laid on her tongue by the priest. "I was as much to blame as you."

Dorothy sighed and released Lexy's hands with a pat. Lexy thought she would go quickly after that, but she lingered at life's edge. Lexy thought of a boat moving slowly toward the horizon. At any moment Dorothy would disappear over the curve of the earth.

Later Alana brought her another cup of tea; and when she had drunk it, Lexy began reciting in a whisper all the Psalms she had memorized. It would take the rest of her life to memorize the entire Psalter, but if she made a greater effort she could do it. As she spoke the words their harmony uplifted and opened her like an intricately folded kite; and though she was speaking, it sounded more like singing to Lexy. A whoosh of air fluttered and filled and billowed the bedroom curtains, and she felt a rush of love so strong it almost lifted her out of her seat.

Dorothy's pale eyes were open and watching her. "Thank you, Lexy, my dear. For everything."

Dorothy died three and a half hours later at eleven-seventeen.

Afterward Alana said, "Rest, Lexy. You deserve it. I'll take care of things now."

There was a midnight AA meeting in National City in the South Bay. Too wired to sleep, Lexy drove there. In the basement of a Catholic church half a dozen men sat on folding chairs; two middle-aged women and a teenage girl with gothic eyes were talking by the coffeepot. They stared at Lexy a moment before they smiled and asked her if she wanted coffee. She realized she was still wearing her clericals.

The meeting began in the usual way, and since fewer than a dozen people were present, all were expected to share.

Lexy told the room full of strangers, "I had the most extraordinary experience. I'd been full of doubt about my worth . . . as a priest . . . and I'd been planning to resign." She dug her letter from her purse and held it up. "I was going to take this to the bishop's office, but at the last minute I got called to sit with a woman who was dying. . . ."

She knew the people in the meeting would understand what happened at Dorothy's bedside, because like all recovering alcoholics they were accustomed to miracles. Their own lives were proof of God's astonishing reality. It didn't matter if they understood that she had lost her vision of God in the world. It did not matter if they were surprised by what she had done at Dorothy's—speaking prayers she did not think she had a right to say until she heard herself saying them, pretending to be Ellen Brownlee. And at the same time not pretending.

She told the alcoholics in the room that at Dorothy's bedside she had felt God's very touch. As she spoke through her tears the men and women nodded and smiled and murmured affirmations. When she finished speaking the meeting went on as if nothing extraordinary had happened.

Chapter 42

The van was again parked in Imogene's driveway, and Dana had to circle the block twice to find a spot big enough for her 4Runner. She got Bailey out of her seat and they walked back to the bungalow.

The violinist opened the door, smiling when he saw her, revealing big, square, yellow teeth. Imogene came up behind him.

"Well," she said with a snort of humor, "if it isn't Agent Double-O-Seven."

The man said, "I saw you sneakin' around the house the other day. Looked right at you, only I couldn't be sure. My eyes aren't so good."

Dana wanted to crawl off and hide.

"Come in if you're staying." Imogene looked down at Bailey. "Who's this big girl, anyhow? What happened to my granddaughter? You're way too big and strong to be her."

Bailey ducked her head and grabbed a handful of Dana's skirt.

"Don't tease her, Grandma."

"Oh boy, I don't recognize those feet," Imogene said.

"Those feet don't belong to Bailey-Bobble. You must be Miss Bailey-Bibble."

Bailey grinned and shook her head.

"My granddaughter, Miss Bailey-Bobble, likes to play the piano. Do you like to play the piano?"

Bailey nodded enthusiastically and let go of Dana's skirt.

"Maybe I'm wrong. I don't see so good these days." Imogene squinted horribly and bent over almost to Bailey's height. "Well, lordy, you are Miss Bailey-Bobble."

This affectionate playfulness was something new from Imogene, and it irritated Dana. She could not remember a single playful moment when she was growing up.

Imogene said, "Sit down, Danita, and stop looking so bad-tempered. Tobias'll get you some water. How 'bout you, Bailey-Bobble, you want some water? Some juice maybe? I got the grapey kind, wine for kids."

"Don't call it that, Grandma," said Dana.

"So what'll it be? Water or grape-juice wine? Say the word and you got it."

Bailey opened her mouth and silently formed the word *juice,* which was a better response than Dana had gotten from her for a long time. Part of her wanted to whoop with pleasure, but she would not give her grandmother the satisfaction.

Imogene said, "That the best you can do?"

Bailey nodded.

"Well, it's good enough for me," Tobias said. "Come on in the kitchen, Miss Bailey-Bird-Bobble."

Great. She's got him playing the stupid game.

"Stay here," Dana said. Bailey's mouth drew down into a scowl.

"Aw, let her go with him, for the Lord's sake. You came to talk to me, didn't you?"

As if Dana hadn't objected at all, the kitchen door swung closed behind Bailey and Tobias. Dana threw her purse onto the couch and dropped onto a cushion. "I don't know why I'm here."

Imogene harrumphed.

"Why do you do that?"

"What?"

"Make that . . . noise. It's so insulting."

"Well, I'm very sorry." Imogene looked amused.

"You do it just to get a rise out of me."

Imogene laughed aloud. "And that is so easy, my girl."

Dana stared at the carpet. "Is this new?"

"Ten years or so."

"It looks new."

"I take care of my stuff."

And I don't? Was this an oblique reference to Bailey's kidnapping? *Or am I just paranoid where she's concerned.* Dana wasn't sure of anything these days.

Imogene sat in her recliner and tipped it back so Dana could see the eraser-colored, corrugated soles of her shoes. Abruptly, Imogene levered the chair upright again and sat forward, pointing her finger at Dana.

"I know why you're here. You came over because of what I said about your mother. You've been chewing on it, right? That's why you were sneakin' around the side of the house like a creeping Tom." She shook her head. "You want to deny it, but for once in your life you should just go ahead and tell the truth. Surprise yourself."

"I'm not a liar."

"Your mother couldn't tell the truth if it was a snake with its fangs in her face."

Dana started to cry but stopped almost immediately. She wiped her eyes on the hem of her T-shirt and then started up again.

Imogene sighed. "It is a relief to see you cry. All your life I never saw you shed one tear. Even that time you fell off your bike and bled like a stuck pig. It's like there was something wrong with you."

"With me?" Dana tossed her head back. "If I'd cried, you'd just have used it against me. You'd have made me feel small and stupid and weak."

"Not me, honey." Imogene stuck out her lower lip and shook her head. "If you'd of broke down just one time, I might of had a chance to get near you. But you were dead sure I was the enemy. From day one."

Of course you were the enemy. My mother called you the old bitch, and the battle-ax. "I was afraid of you."

"Maybe. Some. But mostly you were pissed off because you had to stay with me and not with your mom. You wanted her and you got me instead, and that made me the bad guy. Only you never would come right out and say it. If you'd just got mad, Danita, you'd of felt a whole lot better."

"Why are you telling me this now? Why couldn't you have said it before?"

"You tell me."

"And why *did* you say that the other day? About her being in the kitchen?"

Imogene shrugged. "Pure orneriness."

Dana did not know how to respond.

"You never had time for me, Danita, but I did what I could for you. I tried to make a home. If it seemed like I wasn't too happy about it, well, you're damn right. I never wanted to be a mother myself. Your mom was a big accident, believe me. And then just when I thought

I was out of the woods, I had to go through the whole damn thing again with you."

"I never asked to be abandoned."

"You love that word, don't you?"

Dana stood up and grabbed her purse.

Imogene waved her hands. "Sit down, will you? Seems like you can't hear the truth any better'n you can speak it."

Dana sat, feeling angry and miserable, because for once she could not ignore Imogene's opinions. She had used up her defenses protecting herself against Lexy and David.

"Danita, I'm not saying it was so great for you being left with me. And I'm not saying I wanted you. But I did the best I could. That's what you never have got in your head. All you can think about is how rough you had it, but let me tell you, it would have been a whole lot harder if she'd of kept you."

"How do you know?"

"Just believe what I say."

"She loved me." Dana waited. "Didn't she?"

"She loved what she could shoot in her arm. That's that."

She had always known this.

"Maybe she quit." Lexy had told her it could happen even to hard-core addicts.

"Not that one."

"You've been in touch with her?"

Imogene's sigh fluttered in her throat. "Your mom's dead. She died less than a year after she left you here."

Dana waited for the world to end, but after years of hungering for and fearing the truth, it turned out to be just words.

"Why did you let me think she was alive?"

"I just never could talk to you, nor her, either. You're

as hardheaded as she was. You got your brains from your father, thank God."

"You knew him?"

"Met him once." Imogene chuckled. "'Bout as many times as she did. Good-looking except for that hair clear to the middle of his back and ratty as tumbleweed."

"Do you remember his name?"

Imogene shook her head.

Dana leaned into the couch and shut her eyes.

"Cops called me a few months after she left you here. They found my name and phone number in her pocket. She ran that big old Chrysler off the road somewhere in New Mexico. They said she was so high she probably thought she was flying."

Dana saw how it happened. The girl behind the wheel of the old car, maybe singing loud with the radio, moving her shoulders in time to the music, her eyes half closed and lost in the words—*a whiter shade of pale*—lost in the music, a curve on a mountain road, and then all of a sudden the road wasn't there anymore and she was sailing through the air, and probably it felt like fun, and maybe she was laughing when she hit the ground.

"I hope she was too stoned to know what happened."

"Me too."

Bailey rushed in from the kitchen with Tobias behind her. She threw herself at Dana's knees.

"You have a grape-juice moustache," Dana said.

Bailey spread her arms and began to twirl, making circles around the little living room until she fell on her back on the floor and laughed.

Dana watched in amazement.

Imogene said softly, "She's gonna be okay, Danita. Just give her the time she needs."

She did not know why she was crying. She had too

many reasons. "I never wanted to be like my mother, but I guess I am."

"Don't you believe it. Not for a minute." A heavy rose fragrance gushed from the warm places of Imogene's body as she stood and crossed to the big grand piano. She patted the bench and Bailey scrambled up beside her. To Dana she said, "You got all the self-discipline she never did, plus your own, and you got his brains. He told me he was studying to be a physicist or something like that. I remember it surprised me he wanted to spend time with my daughter. The only thing's the same as her is you're stubborn, and she never could stand to hear the truth any more'n you can."

Imogene played a few bars of "Heart and Soul." Tobias sat on the other side of Bailey and played the treble melody.

Maybe her grandmother was right. It was too noisy in the little room to think clearly.

The piano stopped, and Imogene said, "Tobias, how 'bout you go up to the ice cream store and get some Rocky Road? You like ice cream, Bailey Be-bop-a-lulu?"

Bailey bounced on the piano bench, nodding her head like a floppy-necked doll. A moment later, as she and Tobias were going out the front door, Dana felt an instant of alarm. She didn't know who this man was, and she was letting her daughter go walking away up the street with him. Imogene read her mind.

"Don't fret about Tobias. He's good as gold and my oldest friend."

"Back when I was here?"

"Oh yes. He was married then. His wife had MS and he tended her till she died. That was a couple years ago. He used up all his money, so I help him out from time to time."

"That's why you ask for extra?"

"I don't want to hear a lecture, Danita."

She was too wrung out to argue about anything.

"What's the matter with you all of a sudden?" Imogene went back to her recliner. "Talkin' about your mom. That why you come over here?"

"I don't know why I'm here. I just got in the car and this is where I ended up."

The recliner's tired cushions wheezed as Imogene sat down again. "You got trouble?"

It was pointless to pretend when she felt the misery on her face like a scar.

"You want my opinion?" Imogene said.

"How can you have an opinion when you don't even know what happened?"

"I know enough to know what I know."

Dana looked away.

"You do what you have to do to keep that little girl with her momma and daddy both. You hear me? If you have to crawl to that man, you do it, because if you give up you're as good as finishing Bailey off. If he did something bad, you just scrub it out of your mind. Your daughter needs the two of you together, and if you don't believe that, you just look to your own life."

"David won't even talk to me. I think he slept in his office last night."

"He got a girlfriend?"

"Of course not."

"Don't look so shocked." Imogene's mouth curled with amusement. "He's a nice guy, but think about it—he's no saint."

If Dana thought any more her brain would fry.

"So what'd you do, anyway? Have sex with the UPS guy?"

"Grandma!"

Imogene chuckled. "I just want you to lighten up a little, Danita. What you have to do is go down to his office, and if you're lucky he'll be there, and you can tell him you've been an asshole and he's too good for you and whatever you did wrong you'll make it up to him."

Dana stared at her grandmother. Imogene laughed.

"Guess you don't have to say 'asshole.' It's not quite your style. The important thing is to get him home, in the house with you and Bailey."

A gang of kids walked by on the sidewalk, their voices high and argumentative, then suddenly boisterously happy. She saw her life in this house like a book she'd written for herself, one long harangue of discontent and complaint. If it were a real book, she would toss it out and start a new one.

Imogene said, "Tell you what, I'll keep Bailey overnight, and soon as she and Tobias get back, you take your leave, go find your husband, and make it right with him."

Not once in seven years had Bailey spent the night with Imogene.

"Don't look at me like that, Danita. I'm not gonna harm the child. Lord, I've always thought she was a sweet thing."

"I thought you didn't like her. I thought she irritated you."

Imogene swiped at the air irritably. "Honest to Jesus, Danita, I could be the Virgin Mary with spurs on and you wouldn't give me the time of day."

Chapter 43

When Dana looked up four stories and saw the light on in David's office, she wasn't sure if she felt relieved or just frightened. She knew what she had to tell him but had no idea of how to be honest and persuasive at the same time. She had no fine feelings for herself or important-sounding excuses for anything she had done. She felt as if, with all the tears and talk, she had spilled herself upon the ground and become nothing but a body with needs. Maybe an infant newly born, if it had adult consciousness, would describe itself the same way.

The office was locked, but she had her own key and opened the door quietly. In the semidarkness the place looked a mess, crowded with cluttered desks and bookcases and untidy, disorganized desktops. Papers and file folders and boxes of documents were piled on the floor and on chairs. Cabot and Klinger could not keep an office manager for more than six months, and it showed. If David ever forgave her maybe she would sign on for the job. She no longer had any intention or desire to finish her Ph.D. She might win the lottery and buy Arts and Letters from Rochelle.

She knocked on David's office door and turned the knob. "May I come in?"

He looked terrible, bone-weary and worn to the nub of himself. Dana knew she looked the same. The remains of a pizza sat in its oil-saturated box on the edge of his desk.

"Don't tell me to go away, David."

"Peluso's not going for the deal. He just called."

"What deal?"

He told her.

"You're stuck then."

"Looks that way." His face sagged. "Gracie says I should ask you what to do next."

"If I hadn't come, would you have called?"

"No."

She realized how far out in the cold she was.

"He's a killer, and he'll kill again. I know it like I know you." He reddened as they realized together what a faulty analogy this was. "If I get him off, it's like I'm killing that baby Marsha's carrying, a little girl like Bailey."

In all their late-night conversations about The Law and Justice and the Rights of the Accused, David had never conceived of a defendant like Frank Filmore: rich, educated, and so obviously evil.

Dana said, "I think you have to go to the judge and ask him to take you off the case."

"You and Gracie."

"Even if he turns you down, if you do your best to convince him you have irreconcilable differences with your client, that you can't—"

"Wecker won't care. This judge, once you're on his docket he sets your name in concrete."

Dana heard the scratch of his whiskers as he raked his jaw with his nails.

"If I go to him he'll keep me on the case and make my life miserable."

"Couldn't you just go to court and do a halfhearted job?" She knew the answer already. It was not in David to do anything half-way, not his work or his marriage.

He said, "The bitch of it is Peluso's got no case. I could probably try the case by phone and get Filmore off."

The office was dark except for a circle of light from David's desk lamp. They sat in silence with only their thoughts between them. From the corner of her heart Dana heard a thin but hopeful melody. They had talked without arguing and tried to solve a problem together. This effort, though unproductive, might be a step toward reconciliation.

"About us . . ." David's face had a blank openness that revealed nothing but fatigue.

The music stopped, and her heart seized.

"I have to say, Dana, that compared to this thing with Filmore, the stuff between you and me doesn't seem like much. I can't think about both at the same time."

"Then don't think, David. Just give me another chance. You believe in second chances. I'm not Frank Filmore. What I did was wrong, and it had monstrous consequences, and I take responsibility for all of it, but I'm just an ordinary person. Not bad like he is." She paused a second, longing for a nod or an affirming word. He stared down at his desktop. "I'm a good mother, and I love you even if you can't see that now."

She wanted to touch him but didn't dare. She wouldn't survive the pain if he cast her off. "Go to the judge tomorrow. Lay out as much as you can. Maybe he'll surprise you, and if he doesn't, at least you'll know you did what you could."

It was a feeble solution and satisfied neither of them.

But couldn't he at least nod to let her know that he was listening?

"When it's all history," she said, "you have to be able to live with yourself."

He looked up. "What about you? Can you live with yourself?"

She twisted her hands together. "Barely."

"That baby's going to dic and it'll be my fault." It always came back to this.

Another time she would have put her arms around him and told him he was not alone. What happened to him, happened to her. She wanted to do it now but knew that he would interpret it as manipulation.

"Where's Bailey?" he asked suddenly.

"Imogene." She smiled. "And you know what? She was thrilled to stay over. She laughed, David. And twirled like she used to. When I left, Django was making her a hot dog and Grandma was teaching her the C scale." She added, "We have so much we need to talk about, David."

"I can't think about anything but the case now."

"Are you glad I came?"

"Go home."

She held out her hand. "You too. Come with me."

"I told you," he said, sounding for the first time more irritable than tired. "When the Filmore thing is finished we can talk."

As she pulled into the driveway she saw Marsha Filmore at the top of the stairs, wrapped in her mink, a cigarette glowing between her fingers. Dana had avoided the freeway and taken surface streets home, cruising up Fifth Avenue like a tourist with all the time in the world, thinking about what had to happen next.

"Care for a snort?" Marsha asked, holding up a bottle half full of red wine. "This is the last of Frank's cellar. When he gets out and sees I drank up several thousand dollars of wine I'll have to hire a bodyguard for protection." She giggled as she poured a glass for Dana. "I wish you smoked. I get so fucking sick of being the only smoker all the time."

"It's bad for the baby."

Marsha shrugged.

"You want me to think you don't care, but I know you do."

"In my experience, it doesn't pay to get too attached."

"I don't think you mean that."

"How the hell do you know what I mean?"

Dana said, "It's cold out here, and I'm famished. I didn't eat dinner. Come down to the kitchen. I'll make us both a BLT."

If Marsha preferred to stay on the stairs, Dana would stay with her; but it would be easier to accomplish her task in the comfort of the warm kitchen.

"I can't smoke in your house."

"Come on," Dana said, using a girlfriend voice. "You can do without nicotine for an hour."

In the kitchen Marsha moved around restlessly as Dana gathered the bacon and tomato for the sandwiches.

Marsha stood before the wall where Dana had arranged a dozen family photos. "Who are these people?"

"Friends, David's family."

"Where's yours?"

Dana sharpened a knife on the diamond steel. "I never knew my father, and my mother left me with my grandmother when I was little." Spoken aloud in a matter-of-fact voice, the truth sounded commonplace.

"I always wanted a big family," Marsha said. "Guess I married the wrong guy for that, huh?"

"I'd like to have another baby."

"The one you've got's enough."

"I think she'd like a sister or brother."

"You might get another one the same."

"No. I doubt that."

"Your funeral."

Dana held her breath to keep back the sharp retort that sprang instantly to mind.

Marsha sat at the counter and stretched her pale, thin legs out in front of her.

"Don't you want to take off that coat?"

"I like it." Marsha laid her palms on her stomach. "This one won't stop moving. She's always butting and kicking around like she's mad at me."

Dana took a breath. "She better calm down before she meets her father."

"What's that mean?"

Dana was so nervous she was afraid her voice would give her away. "I don't want to say it."

"I get it; you've been talking to your husband."

"I was the one who found the receipt from Owens Garage. I figured it out myself."

"And now you think you know what's best for everyone." Marsha's tone was insulting. She wrapped her coat around her as if she were cold.

"I don't know what's best for everyone. Just for that baby." Dana turned the bacon in the skillet. "Frank belongs behind bars where he can't hurt any more children, Marsha. You know that, but he's got you so tied up, you're afraid to say it."

Marsha took her cigarettes out of her coat pocket and turned the package end over end on the kitchen counter. "He's my husband."

"He's a man who kills children."

"He needs quiet to think."

Dana sat at the counter opposite her. "Maybe he does. But that doesn't change the fact he's killed at least two little girls, and when he has to, he'll do it again."

"You think you know, but you don't know anything. It's not his fault it happens. He never plans it. It's just he's so high-strung, and you know how it is with babies, the noise, and sometimes you can't—"

"Then he needs to be where there aren't any babies."

"Geniuses have special needs."

"Call the police. Tell them the truth."

Marsha stood up. "You think you can turn me against him."

"Think about Shawna."

Marsha's breathing broke into a short, sharp cry.

Dana reached across the counter and took a cigarette from her pack and lighted it.

"I haven't smoked since high school." Now was not the time to think about the surgeon general's report. She took a shallow puff, held the smoke in her mouth and exhaled it as Marsha lit up one of her own. She laid her cigarette across the saucer they were using for an ashtray and assembled the sandwiches.

"Did Shawna get on your nerves, too?"

Marsha's stubborn expression caved. Dana had never seen a more unhappy woman.

"You think you're better than me," Marsha said. "Frank says you're too middle class to understand someone like me . . . or him."

Dana chuckled. "I *am* middle class. He's got me there."

"He says your husband's a good lawyer, though. He says he'll get him off, and when it happens we can move up to Idaho and start all over."

"Use your head, Marsha. You know that's a daydream. In a few weeks you're going to have a baby daughter, and all babies whine and cry. Every one of them. There's no way you can train it out of them. It's normal. And when she does it, you'll be waiting, knowing what he might do. Even if he does nothing, you'll never know. You'll always be afraid." Dana picked a piece of bacon from between the slices of bread and fed it to Moby. "Frank's not the only smart person in your family. You're no dummy. You can figure out what'll happen. Maybe not right away, maybe you can protect your little girl for a while, but sooner or later . . ."

"If I tell the police, they'll put me in prison. Frank says I'm as guilty as he is because I knew, I covered up."

"The cops don't want you. Peluso'll grant you immunity." Maybe he would, maybe not. Dana didn't really care. The point was to get Marsha to tell her story to the authorities. "You'll be free. Free, and safe with your daughter."

"He'll get out and come after me."

"He's never getting out of prison."

"He'll send someone after me."

"Were you always so scared, Marsha? Can't you remember a time when you weren't?"

"Where would we go, my baby and me? How would we live?"

"You're an accountant, apparently a good one. People are always looking for someone to manage their money."

Marsha squinted at Dana through a blue haze. "I don't get this. If I go to the cops, there won't be a trial. Your husband loses his big chance to make a splash."

Dana nodded.

"But if I keep quiet, he can win. It'll be a big deal."

"Forget about David. And your husband. Do it for Shawna and the new baby."

Marsha stared at the ash end of her cigarette.

Dana stubbed out her own and went to the sink to wash her hands. "It wasn't your fault what happened to Shawna, or to Lolly, either. You didn't know he was going to kill them. But if something happens to this little girl, it *will* be your fault because you know now. You know, Marsha." This was the last of Dana's arguments. "You have the power to give this little one a happy life. And to give yourself another chance at the same time."

Marsha stared at her, eyes wide and her mouth slightly agape.

"Think about it."

"If Frank finds out—"

"It won't matter. He'll be behind bars. He won't be able to hurt you or anyone ever again." Dana waited a beat, then reached for her cell phone and laid it on the counter between them.

Chapter 44

After the AA meeting Lexy went to coffee with the two women who had introduced themselves at the coffee urn. She was surprised they asked her to join them. The collar intimidated most people. But they were both lapsed Catholics and curious. They wanted to know the differences between the Catholic and Episcopal churches. They'd each had more than enough to do with male priests and asked how it was for her. Did the men respect her? Did the congregation know she was an alcoholic?

"If you ask me, half the Catholic clergy needs AA," Marnie, a schoolteacher, said. "Drink and the cloth go together."

"'Specially if you're Irish," said Annie, and this started them talking about their Irish families, about their mothers and fathers, drunk uncles and maiden aunts who sipped sherry all day, and how eager they had been to leave home, get married, and start the cycle all over again.

Lexy listened with half her concentration turned inward. Where her fingertips had touched Dorothy, the whorls of Lexy's prints still buzzed electrically. Marnie was speaking of her parents and all the mistakes they had made. "In the end, though, you gotta forgive them. It's plain stupid not to."

"Once you've had kids yourself—"

Marnie groaned, and she and Annie laughed, sharing whatever it was they knew by virtue of having been mothers that Lexy never would.

When women had first been ordained in the Episcopal Church the problem of what to call them had seemed insurmountable. *Father* was out, of course; and even the standbys *Reverend* and *Pastor* had masculine associations in the minds of most people. Ultimately the women Lexy knew had accepted *Ma'am* or, more commonly, just their first names. Lexy was glad no one called her *Mother Neuhaus*. She had never wanted to be a mother, and the honorific was so inappropriate it would have embarrassed her with its connotations of, if not maternity, wisdom and sanctity.

For the first time in many years she thought about her aversion to motherhood and felt the smallest pinch of regret followed by an uncomfortable tightness in her stomach. Would she be more tolerant if she had children? Would she understand people better—Dana, her mother?

Lexy still had not told her mother that Micah was dead. His body remained in the funeral home waiting for her to decide whether to tell her mother a palatable lie or the truth and watch her suffer. Lexy felt meanness in her like nausea. She threw down money to cover the bitter coffee and sweet churro, said good-bye, and hurried out of the restaurant.

As if by leaving, she could escape herself. She had been touched by God beside Dorothy's bed, but that was only the beginning, the door opening. She had to take the steps, walk through into whatever waited beyond.

The air was cool and damp, and she raised her face to it, wanting to be washed clean. As she drove through the dark city, her mother's image sat beside her. The red and green lights at intersections blurred and doubled and tripled. She blinked, but her eyes filled again, and the tears rolled down her cheeks, unstoppable. She understood how hard most people tried to do the right thing, how often they were like her and made a mess of their lives despite the good intentions.

You've got to forgive them, Marnie had said. *It's plain stupid not to.*

Whatever Dorothy had done to earn her daughter's resentment, it had been, in the end, pointless. It wasn't necessary for Lexy to know what caused the rift between Dorothy and Ellen Brownlee; she knew it was as pointless as the anger Lexy had felt against her parents for so long that she could not remember a time when it was not a part of her. The lateness of the hour, the caffeine buzzing through her system, and the otherworldly experience at Dorothy's bedside combined. For the first time Lexy saw her mother as a child of God, one of the billions of souls struggling in billions of ways to reach the light.

Lexy had read the Gospels and tried to memorize the Psalms, she had preached and counseled, and ten thousand times she had asked God to forgive her trespasses as she forgave those who trespassed against her. But she had never really understood that the prayer meant she must not just say she forgave, not just say the words and then pretend. She had to forgive. If she wanted God to forgive her, this was the bargain, the deal, the demand.

* * *

Instead of driving home to Pacific Beach, she took the Washington Street exit off Interstate 5 and turned left on Goldfinch. It was after two A.M. now, and Bella Luna was shut down tight. There was no one on the Mission Hills streets. She could have walked there wearing a suit of gold and been unchallenged.

A safe neighborhood, Dana had called it. And then, as if to prove the point, Lexy saw her running down Fort Stockton, wearing her gray sweats and a hooded T-shirt. For years afterward, Lexy wondered if she would ever have gone to Dana's house to ask her forgiveness had she not seen her that night on the street. And if she had stayed away, would she have been able to move beyond her anger and self-loathing? Dana's sudden appearance seemed an indication that God meant to help her through the door and support her in the hard times beyond.

She turned her car into the curb, braked, and put it in Park. She got out and stood by the open door. Dana slowed to a stop. The night was cool enough that her breath condensed in the air between them.

Lexy said, "Sit with me, will you?" If Dana said no, she would ask again. She would beg if she had to.

When they were inside with the windows up, the space almost smothered Lexy. She quickly rolled down her window and rested her head on the back of the seat. She wished it could be like when she was with Dorothy and the right words had come to her without effort. Instead she had to struggle through her apology to Dana, muffing words, and sometimes the sentences barely made sense even to her.

When she finished Dana stared straight ahead. The silence had weight and texture and took up space.

Lexy tried again. "I wish I could say that I said what

I did because I was in shock and I didn't mean any of it. But I want to try to be honest here. I knew what I was saying, and I meant every word. That's what shames me the most. There's something in me, Dana, that can be so cruel and unforgiving. I wanted to hurt you. If I could've killed you with words, I would've."

She cut her eyes to the right, gauging Dana's reaction. Her friend's strong little chin was set hard.

"I have so much rage in me, Dana. It's why I see the therapist. It's been there a long time, it goes way back. Micah had his depression. I was the angry one."

"But a lot of what you said was true," said Dana. "I am a liar, and I did cheat on David. In a way, what happened to your brother, that was my fault."

"You know, Dana, if it hadn't been you it would have been something else. He was never stable. And even so there's no excuse for the things I said. I'm a priest." Anger was not a sin; it was part of the human condition. Except when it took pleasure in another's pain. Then it was a very dark thing. "You're the best friend I ever had."

"Me too."

They watched the empty street.

Lexy said, "I want you to know what's happening with me. I'm going to get Micah cremated, and then in a couple of days I'll take him up to Wyoming and tell my mom what happened. I think I'll spread his ashes over the Tetons. He loved those mountains." She paused until she could speak without tears. "But first, tomorrow, I'm going to ask the bishop to replace me at St. Tom's."

"No."

"I've got to get away, Dana, and we both know that if I'm gone for six months or a year Father Bartholomew can't handle the church. The bishop'll appoint an interim who can manage the job."

"I don't want you to go, Lexy. The last couple of days I haven't been able to stop thinking about what happened between us, and apart from everything else, I just hated to think we weren't friends anymore. You're like my sister."

"Yeah, me too."

"And I want you to know . . . about the kidnapping . . . I forgive Micah for that."

"How can you? It was a terrible thing. Nothing you did can excuse that."

"I don't excuse it. You're right, it was a terrible thing. But I do forgive him."

She and Dana moving along parallel but independent lines had reached the same destination. Lexy smiled, thinking of the people who said there was no God.

"I played my part, Lexy. I did wrong, and he did wrong in return. But he brought her back, and he never harmed her. I saw her laugh today, at Imogene's. Laugh and twirl and play games. She's going to be all right. But what I did. . . . You said I broke his heart. That can't ever be made right." Dana reached for Lexy's hand. "Don't leave St. Tom's."

Tears filled Lexy's eyes. "You don't know how much it means to me to hear you say that. But, there are things you don't know—shit, I barely know them myself. I have a lot of work to do before I'm fit to be a priest again."

"No, no, you're a wonderful—"

"In seminary there was stuff I never talked about, feelings I had about my family and myself and Micah. I thought I didn't have to, that the collar and being sober would make the bad stuff go away. . . . Well, I was wrong, and now I need to get myself straight with God."

"Will you stay in Wyoming?"

Lexy laughed. "I might need to do penance, but

that's asking a bit too much. I'm going back to the retreat house in Warrenton if they'll have me."

"For how long?"

"As long as it takes, I guess." Lexy yawned. "Then I hope the bishop'll let me go back to St. Tom's. He might not. You know he can be a real hard-nose sometimes."

"I'm going to miss you."

"You have Bailey and David."

"Maybe." Dana's head fell back against the headrest. "I don't know any more about anything than you do, Lexy. And I'm so tired I can't even begin to think about it. When I do it's like I'm on the bottom of one of those football pile-ons. There are four three-hundred-pound linemen on top of me."

"If there's anything I—"

"We've talked. It's up to him now."

In the shadows of the front seat they sat with too much to say and most of their energy gone.

"I'll drive you home."

"Let me make you coffee and French toast."

Lexy laughed and rubbed her eyes. "Dana Cabot's sinful French toast. I thought I'd never taste it again. And coffee. Yes, coffee. God, that sounds good. Do you have any half-and-half?"

Dana smiled. "A full quart."

"Bliss," said Lexy with a sigh as she turned the key in the ignition and shifted into Drive. "And after that I'm going up to your guest room and climb into bed and sleep until noon. Can I do that?"

"Of course you can."

Chapter 45

In early December on a clear, cool day in midweek, Dana and Bailey went shopping at the nursery opposite St. Tom's. The owner's big Rhodesian ridgeback was there, standing guard beside the seedling trays. Bailey put her hand out, knuckles first, as she had been taught, and the long pink tongue swiped it. She giggled and hid behind Dana.

She wasn't talking yet, but Dana believed it would happen soon.

David still slept in the spare room. Like his daughter, he was healing slowly. Lexy sent letters via e-mail, but she never called. She said she was through the door and halfway across the room, headed for the great outdoors. Dana had no idea what this meant, but it sounded hopeful.

Hope gave shape to Dana's days and kept her moving forward.

Shame and guilt and terrible regret still burned her insides, but the heat had diminished some. She was healing, too.

After going to Peluso and telling him about her role in the death of Lolly Calhoun, Marsha Filmore had stayed on in the room above the garage until her daughter was born. A black-haired little girl with jerky limbs who broke out in a lurid rash the first time she tasted formula. Dana heard her crying from the apartment, a pitiful sound like a small wounded animal. A sound Frank Filmore would never hear. And then one day mother and daughter were gone. Marsha left behind her clothes—except the mink—and dozens of empty wine bottles. According to David, Peluso knew where she was. She would return to San Diego and probably testify at the trial.

David said that if the Ethics Committee ever got wind of how Dana had persuaded Marsha to go to Peluso he would be in deep trouble. But she could tell he was glad for what she'd done. He would give Frank Filmore the best defense he could and make Peluso prove his case beyond a reasonable doubt. Marsha would testify, and Frank would be found guilty. David would argue hard against the death penalty.

At the nursery Dana intended to purchase a camellia. But when she saw the scrawny blood orange tree in a plastic tub, it called to her and said she must plant it in her garden and nurse it to health as a reminder of what had happened to them all that year. A reminder and a promise to survive and prosper.

When they got home she changed into her overalls, and Bailey had to wear hers too, which led to special shoes and a favorite straw hat. Everything was complicated with Bailey, but Dana rarely complained anymore, even to herself.

She thanked God every day for the miracle of Bailey and for giving her family a second chance.

She gathered an armload of tools from the shade house and carried them to a square of earth protected by the garage and the back wall, where the sun shone most of the day. Digging was a challenge because the soil was dry and crumbly late in the season before the slow, soaking rains that would come in the new year. She did not mind that her back and shoulders ached and sweat ran down from her hairline and stung her eyes. Beside her, Bailey dug away with the miniature shovel and hoe Santa had put under the tree the year before. She had outgrown them. She had outgrown almost everything, becoming a skinny, long-legged girl with soulful eyes. Every now and then she tugged on Dana's shirtsleeve and pointed to her work, and Dana praised her.

When the hole was three feet deep and almost as wide, Dana rested her tools against the wall and went around the far side of the house, where she had made compost in several large plastic bins. She filled the wheelbarrow full and mixed the compost with the dirt from the hole until she had a pile of nutritious soil.

She still thought of Micah and remembered him in her prayers. Sometimes she awakened after barely re-membered dreams, hot and yearning for what she had felt that week in Italy. Perhaps as a consequence, she had begun thinking of her mother in a different light, as not simply someone irresponsible and flaky, but as a woman seduced by pleasure as Dana had been.

Using the shovel, Dana whacked the plastic pot until it split. Rootbound. She imagined the tree sighing with relief as she poked a forked trowel into the dirt to gen-tly loosen the roots around the bottom and sides. She half-filled the hole with new soil and then tipped the tree in on top of it. On their hands and knees, she and Bailey scooped and tamped the remaining soil in the hole, then made a shallow watering ditch around it. She brought the hose from across the lawn and let it run slowly into the hollow, seeping down on the roots.

Dana sat against the wall and pulled Bailey onto her

lap. It was warm in the sun, and the gardening had worn them both out. She closed her eyes, holding Bailey more tightly. She wasn't happy, but for the most part, strangely, she was contented. Maybe next month she would want a job or another baby, but for now there was nothing particular to strive for, no mighty goal to aim at.

They were all broken inside. Sometimes she could feel it, like a joint that pops out of place and aches for hours after. Though there had been healing, nothing would ever be the same for any of them. It was not a matter of whether David would forgive her. She believed he would and maybe had already without quite realizing it. When David came back to their bed it would be because in the end love was the engine of forgiveness.

What she wanted for all of them was enough time for love to do its work.

In the far corner of her garden, protected on two sides, the blood orange tree had already begun to stretch its roots down into the soil. In a year or two, if all went well, it might bear fruit. By then Lexy would be back and David would call Dana Number One again. She prayed every day—to be honest and faithful and patient—and she believed God heard her. She asked for simple things. For Bailey's voice calling to her, for David's smile, and his hand on the small of her back, for absent friends and souls departed, for the raspberry sweetness of the blood red fruit.

ACKNOWLEDGMENTS

Thank you . . .

To Art, my first husband, for his wisdom and passion. Always.

To Susan Challen, Carole Fegley, Sharon Saunders, Peggy Lang, and Judy Reeves for their creative and spiritual advice.

To the ladies of the Arrowhead Association for always being there.

To Reverends Mary Moreno Richardson and Allison Thomas at St. Paul's Cathedral, who honored me with their candid answers to my prying questions.

To Professors Irwin Miller and Tom Barton of California Western School of Law and attorneys Nancy Rosenfeld and Chuck Sevilla for sharing their perspectives on David Cabot's ethical quandary. And to Wes Albers of the San Diego Police Department for his tactical suggestions. Any legal and procedural gaffs in *Blood Orange* are entirely mine.

To Andrea Johnson and Reverend Lee Teed for their inadvertent inspiration.

Thank you, finally, to the defense team of Steven Feldman, Rebecca Jones, Robert Boyce, and Laura Schaefer who inspired me to write *Blood Orange* as I did. To them and all the members of the defense bar who struggle daily to see that justice is done, I am immensely grateful.

October 2004